D1785149

E.R. PUNSHON
IT MIGHT LEAD ANYWHERE

ERNEST ROBERTSON PUNSHON was born in London in 1872.

At the age of fourteen he started life in an office. His employers soon informed him that he would never make a really satisfactory clerk, and he, agreeing, spent the next few years wandering about Canada and the United States, endeavouring without great success to earn a living in any occupation that offered. Returning home by way of working a passage on a cattle boat, he began to write. He contributed to many magazines and periodicals, wrote plays, and published nearly fifty novels, among which his detective stories proved the most popular and enduring.

He died in 1956.

The Bobby Owen Mysteries

E.R. PUNSHON

IT MIGHT LEAD ANYWHERE

With an introduction
by Curtis Evans

DEAN STREET PRESS

Published by Dean Street Press 2016

Copyright © 1946 E.R. Punshon

Introduction copyright © 2016 Curtis Evans

All Rights Reserved

Published by licence, issued under the
UK Orphan Works Licensing Scheme.

First published in 1946 by Victor Gollancz

Cover by DSP

ISBN 978 1 911413 43 1

www.deanstreetpress.co.uk

INTRODUCTION

SET IN THE WANING days of both the Second World War and the period of Deputy Chief Constable Bobby Owen's distinguished service in the police force of Wychshire, *It Might Lead Anywhere* (1946) is a mystery which comes straight from E.R. Punshon's top drawer, richly meriting the "Best British Brand" judgment afforded it in the *Saturday Review*; yet it also was the penultimate Punshon Bobby Owen detective novel to appear in the United States during the author's lifetime, the last, *So Many Doors* (1949), taking its American bow in 1950, after the appearance of three Punshon mysteries—*Helen Passes By* (1947), *Music Tells All* (1948) and *The House of Godwinsson* (1948)--that went unpublished in the US. During the remainder of Punshon's life--he passed away in 1956, at the age of 84--the author would never again see a publisher release one of his books in the United States.

How this dichotomous state of affairs, by which I mean Punshon's detective novels appearing annually on one side of the pond but not at all on the other, came about in the 1950s is a matter for speculation, with no definitive answer. Writing for the magazine *CADS* in 1995, the late Anglo-Canadian scholar and Punshon mystery fan William A.S. Sarjeant contended that "Punshon's plots and writing style appeal more directly to British audiences." Sarjeant noted that during the 1940s his own Yorkshire shopkeeper father "was among many readers waiting eagerly for the appearance of each new Punshon novel." Yet it was also during the 1940s that Punshon made his greatest and most sustained impact in the American mystery market, with the publication by Macmillan of five of the author's detective novels between 1944 and 1947, beginning with *The Conqueror Inn* and concluding with *It Might Lead Anywhere*. Prominent US print mystery critics, such as Anthony Boucher, Will Cuppy, Isaac Anderson and William C. Weber, highly praised Punshon's work. (Boucher still recalled Punshon favorably in the mid-1950s, five and six years after the author had last been published in the US.) My copy of *It Might Lead Anywhere*, which was cast off from an American lending library, contains stamps revealing that the book was checked out twenty-one times between 28 January 1947 and 19 January 1948, which suggests that Punshon's name attracted interest among US mystery fans.

Yet it is true that after the Second World War the classic British mystery that writers like E.R. Punshon so ably represented faced increasing competition in the US from new styles and forms in crime fiction, such as hard-boiled, noir and so-called "domestic suspense," or psychological mystery. In particular hard-boiled private eye tales began taking an increasingly large share of the American mystery market in the 1940s, especially in popular new paperback editions illustrated with titillating cover art depicting gun-waving men and bust-heaving women. Coincidentally, the same year that Punshon's *It Might Lead Anywhere* was published also saw the startling appearance of Mickey Spillane's *I, the Jury*, a kinetic tale of visceral violence and sex with a tough-as-nails, no-holds-barred shamus whose personal value system and, shall we say, extremely aggressive investigative technique seemingly could not have been more far removed from the gentle and gentlemanly Bobby Owen's. By 1953, the year a film version was made of *I, the Jury*, the novel had sold an astonishing 3.5 million copies. To be sure, the imperishable British Crime Queen Agatha Christie was well on her way at this time to becoming a household name in the United States (not to mention most of the rest of the world), but, as US publishers measured the totality of the dollar signs and shifted marketing priorities, many other distinguished Golden Age British mystery writers began vanishing from American libraries and bookstores, to be revived, after decades of neglect, only in recent years, much to the gratification of a growing audience of readers who have wholeheartedly reembraced classic mystery fiction.

With its teasingly clued puzzle, appealing rural setting and engaging cast of characters, *It Might Lead Anywhere* exemplifies the qualities which perennially draw fans of Golden Age British mystery. In the novel Bobby Owen is called on to investigate a perplexing problem in the "typical small country village" of Chipping Up ("Chipping" likely is derived from the Old English "ceapen," meaning market): the poker slaying of a nondescript individual named Alfred "Alf" Brown. As one of Bobby's police colleagues puts it, "Why should anyone want to murder a man like Brown? Quiet, inoffensive, harmless as possible, no woman in the case, why should anyone want to get rid of him?" Bobby makes a discovery at Alf Brown's cottage which casts a much different complexion on the matter, however. From this point it appears that the trail might indeed lead anywhere, even to, for example, the prim Reverend Alexander Childs, Anglo-Catholic vicar of St. Barnabas Church in the small neighboring town of Oldfordham; or to Duke Dell, former prizefighter turned religious exhorter; or to Denis Kayes, late of the royal Australian Air Force; or even to retired solicitor Maurice Goodman's pretty young secretary-housekeeper, Theresa Foote, who looks as "meek and demure as the heroine of a mid-Victorian novel come to life." In a way reminiscent of his uncouth fellow sleuth from across the pond, Mickey Spillane's Mike Hammer, Deputy Chief Constable Owen has marked suspicions about the oh-so modestly feminine Miss Foote, for he shares "the opinion of the London magistrate that 'housekeeper' was a word that covered many sinners." Readers likely will have their own particular suspicions too. Who can beat Bobby to the solution of a most complex and clever crime? Be advised to leave no stone unturned on this twisting trail, for Punshon's title is an exceedingly apt one.

Curtis Evans

CHAPTER I

RIOT AT CHIPPING UP

DEPUTY CHIEF CONSTABLE, Acting Chief Constable, Wychshire County Police, Robert Owen, too dignified now to be referred to as Bobby, except when he wasn't there or by a wife little impressed by high-sounding titles bestowed on one who to her still seemed most of the time a rather troublesome charge and responsibility, was on a tour of inspection, combining therewith some more or less official calls on various local dignitaries with whom he had matters to discuss or more simply with whom he wished to keep in touch for one reason or another. For a large part of a chief constable's duty lies not so much in maintaining law and order as in seeing that the wheels on which law and order run are kept suitably oiled.

The day was fine and he was enjoying his drive. He was alone, for man-power was still too scanty to allow the luxury of a chauffeur—incidentally he always preferred to drive himself—nor was he hurrying overmuch. Nothing of any great urgency needed attention. At the moment he had drawn up by the roadside, near a phone box. He wanted to ring up his headquarters in Midwych and also he had to decide on whom to call next. He consulted his notebook. There was Lord Martindale, recently appointed Lord Lieutenant of the county. But his lordship was a talkative old gentleman and Bobby knew that if he called there he would be lucky to escape having to stay to dinner. And that would not meet with the approval of Olive, busy with the dinner at home, for even a Mrs. Deputy Chief Constable is lucky if she can get hold of daily help and can hardly hope for a cook, now that these have grown as scarce and proud as duchesses. Then there was Mr. Maurice Goodman, retired Midwych solicitor, now a considerable landowner, keen on preserving game, though he hardly knew one end of a gun from another and was unlikely to see anything amusing in the famous remark of the lady novelist about the moors of Scotland resounding to the crack of rifles on the morning of every twelfth of August. But he had been complaining lately that the local police failed to keep a sufficiently sharp lookout for poachers. Bobby was uncomfortably aware that this complaint might not be entirely without foundation. After all, even a village policeman has to live with his neighbours; and though the habitual poacher is generally a lazy ne'er-do-well and a public nuisance, still an occasional rabbit or even pheasant is not unwelcome in a cottage kitchen. Besides, what are gamekeepers for, and why should police do their work for them? Every man to his own job; though of course Bobby would never believe that any policeman, certainly none of his own men, would ever be so lost to all sense of duty as to allow even the most wilful hare, rabbit or game bird to force its way into that policeman's very own kitchen. For such was the lamentable suspicion Mr. Goodman had hinted at in his last communication. It would have to be dealt with very firmly, very firmly indeed, with demands for concrete evidence, with counter hints about an action for defamation of character, with, in general, a shocked and grave surprise. But perhaps that had better wait for the present.

Then there was Mr. Young, a member of the watch committee and inclined to be fussy over small items of expenditure. It might be as well to consult him privately about the proposed new cottage for Constable Wiggins, stationed at Chipping Up, the nearest village to Four Oaks, the residence of Mr. Maurice Goodman. The cottage had been damaged by a stray bomb dropped at random by a German airman whose machine had been injured by ack-ack fire and who had thought it well to lighten his load as he strove to reach the warm hospitality and friendly welcome he knew awaited him in Eire. The damage to the cottage was serious and rebuilding was necessary. Would it be possible, Bobby wondered, to get a bathroom included or would Mr. Young be inclined to consider that came under the head of 'pampering the lower classes'? Better perhaps to talk about the new cottage in general terms and hope the bathroom would slip through unnoticed.

Bobby decided it would have to be Mr. Young for the first visit and, this settled, he alighted to put through his call to headquarters. His message was of no great importance, which was just as well, for he never got it delivered. As soon as it was realized at the other end of the wire who was talking he was asked to hold on, and then an agitated voice he recognized as belonging to the station sergeant informed him that a message had just been received by phone from Mr. Goodman, Four Oaks, near Chipping Up, to the effect that there was a riot in the village and that help was urgently required.

"A riot?" Bobby repeated, very much surprised; for though his police experience was wide and varied, a riot in a country village was something new. Besides, Chipping Up was a normal, quiet little place, rent through with internal feuds, of course, since human beings are never really happy unless they are quarrelling violently with one another, but with no cause for rioting that he knew of. Even the workers from the new factories in the neighbourhood seldom troubled the calm life of Chipping Up. The neighbouring small borough of Oldfordham saw more of them, and though Chipping Up had had its share of evacuees, most of them had now gone home again. "A riot?" Bobby repeated bewilderedly, as these thoughts flashed through his mind. "What riot?"

"Well, sir," the thin distant voice answered, though a little doubtfully, "Mr. Goodman, he did seem to think it was to do with religion like. I said as to-day wasn't Sunday but Mr. Goodman said as it was religion all the same."

"I'll go along and see what's up," Bobby said, uneasy now, for a riot about religion, even though not on a Sunday, might be serious, since the more serious the cause, the more serious the effect.

He left the road-box and drove off, turning soon by a signpost that showed the way to Chipping Up. But why religion? he asked himself, puzzled. People fought with passion in these days about systems of government, about material conditions, not about religious questions. He remembered now though that Mr. Childs, vicar of Oldfordham, the small neighbouring town, was an enthusiastic high churchman whose ritualistic practices had caused some criticism and given rise to one or two unseemly scenes in his church. But Oldfordham was some ten miles or so from Chipping Up and could it be supposed that Chipping Up was concerning itself with ritual in Oldfordham?

The road he had turned into would take him by Four Oaks, Mr. Goodman's residence, so it occurred to him it might be as well to stop there and ask for further information. He wondered, too, if it would have been wise to instruct the station sergeant to send a car with reinforcements in case of need. He decided he was glad he had not done so. An odd sort of riot, he told himself, that could not be checked by the simple presence and authority of a deputy chief constable, acting chief constable—especially when that same deputy, acting chief, was named and known as Bobby Owen.

Four Oaks came in sight. At the entrance to the drive leading to the house a man was standing, Mr. Goodman himself. He was a middle-aged man, of slight build but with a large, square red face in which a small squat nose and small, light-grey eyes seemed hopelessly lost. He had an unusually big mouth though, and a voice to match, for Bobby could hear it booming out already in what seemed a shout of welcome.

"Glad to see you," he thundered as Bobby drew up. "They rang me up to say you were on your way. Quick work."

In spite of its volume, it was a musical voice and of good pitch, and Bobby remembered having heard that Mr. Goodman was a liberal subscriber to the Midwych Philharmonic. Nearby, a little in the rear, was standing a young and attractive-looking girl, though rather of the china-doll type, with fluffy hair, a pink and white complexion, wide, innocent, china-blue eyes, her make-up not too obtrusive. She had a general air of fluttering apprehensively in the background; and now, as Mr. Goodman's voice ceased to reverberate around, Bobby heard her murmur:

"Oh, isn't it dreadful?"

"What's the trouble?" Bobby asked.

"Hot-gospeller fellow," Goodman roared back. "I was on the phone to Chipping Up post office and the woman there said they were fighting on the village green. Excited she seemed. There's a chap called Brown mixed up in it. I said I would ring the police. Better hurry. There may be a killing. Had I better come with you?"

"Oh, no," breathed the fluffy-haired girl. "Oh, don't." Evidently the word 'killing' had frightened her. Bobby, it had surprised slightly. He did not see why fighting on a village green should lead to 'killing'. A black eye or two or a bloody nose more likely.

"Might need help," said Mr. Goodman, but not too enthusiastically.

Bobby had no great desire for the help of a civilian who did not look as if good living and not much wartime austerity had left him in the best physical condition. But if by any chance there was truth in this suggestion of a possible 'killing', then the sooner he got to Chipping Up, the better. Not that the story was likely to be true. But it might be. Anyhow, as well to lose no time. Without answering directly Mr. Goodman's suggestion, he said:

"I had better get along. Thanks for phoning. Very sensible and helpful. Much obliged. Which is the nearest way? Straight on?"

"Turn sharp to the left," Mr. Goodman told him.

By Mrs. Cox s cottage, that thatched one, I mean, you see there. It cuts a corner off the Chipping Up road."

"Thanks," Bobby said, and trod on the accelerator as hard as he could, so vanishing in a great cloud of dust and in some small anxiety of mind.

CHAPTER II

THE PREACHER

HERE WAS NO built-up area and Bobby, turning sharp by Mrs. Cox's cottage as directed, was soon flying along at the best speed his car was capable of, though indeed the twists and turns of the narrow country road with its overhanging trees and high banks and hedges did impose a frequent slowing down.

Soon he came to Chipping Up, a typical small country village with its one long, straggling street, its church that was said to stand on the site of a Roman temple, its great house now empty, half ruinous, wholly desolate, because its last owner had died in the wars, and the Australian heir showed small eagerness to bother about an inheritance that was chiefly mortgage and debt.

Sweeping round by the churchyard wall bordered by tall elms, Bobby came in sight of the village green. Along one side ran a small stream, the Becker, now swollen by recent heavy rains. Here swayed to and fro an excited crowd and on the banks of the stream stood a huge giant of a man, roaring defiance.

"If any come against me," he was thundering, "I turn the other cheek, as it is written, and then will I smite them also, as it is written again—yea, and cast them in the water hereby for the betterment of body and soul."

No one in the general excitement had paid any attention to Bobby's arrival. He stopped his car and jumped out. Nearby, a little group was clustered round a burly fellow who was half sitting up, half lying down, and whose bleeding and bruised face a woman was busy bathing with cold water. Bobby wondered if this were the man, Brown by name, reported killed and certainly showing signs of having been pretty roughly handled. Bobby said:

"What's all this? What's going on here? Who's this man?"

"It's Big Bill Barton," a bystander answered and added admiringly: "Yon chap outed him proper, easy as picking apples."

The woman engaged in bathing the prostrate man's battered face looked up angrily and said:

"Pity it wasn't you, George Simpson, and all the pack of you scared like mice when the cat comes in and daren't say a word when that big bully scandalized us all and named my own girl a whore to her face. Duck him, why don't you? if you're men. No wonder the war goes on the way it does if all the men's like you."

"Hold your tongue," Bobby told her sternly, for her voice had been shrill and loud, addressed really to the milling crowd through whom it ran like fire through dry autumn leaves.

Now there followed her exhortation one of the most formidable of all sounds—the low muttering growl of a mob in the grip of a mass emotion, about to translate that mass emotion into mass action. It swayed forward, then backward for an instant, hesitating before the grim, undaunted figure on the bank of the stream.

"I forgive you," he was shouting. "I forgive you all freely. Now come on and feel the weight of an arm that the Lord upholds."

For just one moment more the crowd hesitated, not so much because of the other's formidable aspect but because of an uncomfortable feeling that it was best to proceed with caution against one who claimed to be upheld by the powers above. It might be true. But a voice from behind, a shrill girl's voice, cried:

"Give him something to forgive us for if you aren't to^ frightened."

Again from the crowd came the response of that low muttering, prelude to action. But this second or two of delay had given Bobby his chance. He dashed between the crowd and the grim, solitary figure waiting its onslaught. He shouted:

"What's all this about? Get back to your homes or your work, all of you. Who is responsible for this? I'll see he answers for it."

He paused. The crowd gaped, taken by surprise, unwillingly impressed by so confident a tone of authority. Bobby noticed one hulking fellow who had pushed to the front and who held half a brick in one hand. Bobby pointed a threatening finger at him.

"You," he ordered. "Drop that. Drop it at once. What's your name?"

The fellow he spoke to obeyed instinctively. He dropped the half brick, but then seemed inclined to pick it up again. There came a menacing forward surge among others in the crowd and someone yelled:

"Who are you, anyhow? Mind your own business."

And a boy shouted:

"Throw him in, too."

"Who said that?" demanded Bobby. "All right. I see him. I'll attend to him later. I'm a police officer and deputy chief constable of this county. In the name of the law I call upon every man here present to come to my assistance. I warn you, any who refuse are liable to prosecution, and, if found guilty, to fine or imprisonment at the discretion of the magistrates."

Probably only in this country could such an appeal by an officer of the law to a mob, already half out of hand, for assistance by itself against itself have been effective. Most of them, all of them perhaps, would have faced far more willingly a baton charge than this threat of fine or imprisonment, if found guilty. No glamour in appearing in a police court in peril of fine or imprisonment; no fun in that as there might be in testing yourself with a cudgel against a policeman with a baton. The man who had held the half brick put his hands in his pockets and began to stroll unconcernedly away. The one or two noisy youths at the back looked sheepish and grew silent. Bobby saw the day was won. His voice was milder as he said:

"Has anyone here been hurt? What about a man named Brown? Is he here or what's happened?"

The woman who had been looking after the man called Big Bill Barton had joined the others now. Bill himself was sitting up and taking notice in the intervals of feeling in turn each one of his separate bruises. Now it was this woman who called out:

"That's him what's dead and drownded and yon's who did it."

Bobby swung round on the grim defiant figure at whom had pointed the woman's accusing finger. Before Bobby could speak, however, the man said:

"It was my arm and hand, but guided by the Lord, for now Brother Alfred Brown will never deny the Vision, the Vision that I tell of, though these in their folly and their blindness willed not to listen or heed. Yet I forgive them; and for all that they have done or willed against me, I thank them. I thank you, dear friends, and I forgive you."

"Stop that sort of talk," Bobby ordered, for he knew, of course, that nothing is more likely to rouse angry passions than to be forgiven. It is an intolerable assumption of superiority. He said: "If you've been killing someone, you'll need, forgiveness yourself before you start forgiving other people. Where's this man's body?"

"They took it out of the water," someone told him. "They took it into Widow Adam's."

"Do you admit that?" Bobby asked the big man and went on when no denial came: "You had better say nothing now. You will have to come with me. You will be charged with manslaughter. The charge may be altered later on. That depends. You can make a statement presently if you wish to. But not now."

"Nay, friend, I'll make it now," answered the other, his voice rivalling or even excelling that of Mr. Goodman in volume though not in tone. "I am Duke Dell, man of Belial and winner of many fights, gaining much money thereby, till there came the Vision of which I am here to tell these poor brethren of mine, though they will not to listen."

"Vision be damned," interrupted one of the crowd. "Called himself a preacher and said our girls were bad girls and our lads worse; given over to the devil, he said, and suchlike. So we up and told him plain if he came again with talk like that he would get a ducking. But he came all the same and laid his tongue about worse nor ever, especial about our girls what's as good and decent as any ever you could wish for; you ask Vicar and Sam Wiggins, our policeman here, if you're the boss. Sam will tell you the same. So some of the lads tried to rush him, and a chap as had come along with him got between just as he lit out an almighty swing that caught his own chum and knocked him in there. He pointed to the little stream. "But no one didn't notice at first, what with all what was going on, and when they pulled the chap out he was a goner, they said, drownded as well as put out by the swing he took."

"I meant it not," said the big man who had given his name as Duke Dell, a name that was beginning to stir memories in Bobby's mind of former reports, in days gone by, in the sporting columns of the papers. "I aimed it not. It was the Lord guided my arm, for thus Alfred Brown is saved; and better far it is so, for now he can no longer doubt the Vision or say maybe it came with drink."

Bobby looked at him doubtfully, uncertain what to make of this. A huge, magnificently made man, past his prime now, no doubt, but still hung about as it were with all the splendour of his former strength and vigour. Nor did his features seem to show much sign of the prizefighting profession that had once apparently been his. It was his eyes that chiefly caught Bobby's attention. Sunken beneath great craggy brows, they seemed to change from moment to moment, now dull, half closed, indifferent, indeterminate in hue; then fixed and fierce and glaring, and of a burning angry blue; then again veiling themselves behind a kind of glassy film, remote and unseeing. To Bobby it seemed that sometimes they took in everything around down to the smallest detail, and sometimes that they saw nothing save what was invisible to others.

"Come with me," Bobby said to him. To the crowd Bobby said: "Which cottage is it? The one where the body was taken I mean?"

They pointed it out to him. He went towards it. Duke Dell went with him. The others followed. Duke Dell said:

"I meant it not, it was not my doing. Yet it is well. My arm was guided. It is very well."

"Say nothing now," Bobby ordered. "You can talk later."

The door of the indicated cottage opened as they drew near. Two men appeared. One was a tall, slim youth, fair-haired, with that far-off look in his eyes often to be noticed in the eyes of seamen and airmen used to watching for the wonders of the Lord in the great distances of air and sea. By his side was a little man, narrow-chested, stooping, with pale unhealthy complexion, a small straggling moustache, pale watery eyes, so lacking indeed in every marked feature that one might almost have believed nature had intended him for a kind of universal camouflage. Even his clothes, evidently made for a much larger man, seemed to aid this impression of general concealment, as if into the folds in which they draped him he could and might at any instant retire completely. Duke Dell said loudly:

"Why, it's him, he's not dead, no more than me."

"No thanks to you, Duke Dell," retorted the other, a little like an angry rabbit, "and my head ringing so I hardly know what I'm doing or where I am."

CHAPTER III

HIS MASTER'S VOICE

BOBBY, VERY MUCH surprised and rather doubtful, said, speaking half to Duke Dell, half to the bystanders:

"Is this the man you've been talking about?"

At first no one answered. They all seemed as surprised and puzzled as was Bobby himself. Getting no reply, Bobby repeated his question, this time more directly to Duke Dell. The moment before the big man's eyes had been on fire, fierce, overbearing and arrogant, their harsh gaze so formidable that Brown shrank visibly away, as from a threatened blow. But now they changed, their light faded, they became dull, withdrawn and strange beneath those great craggy brows which, to any professional boxer, are so valuable an asset. It was now as if they still saw, and saw intently, but with an interior, not an exterior vision, and therefore things not visible to others. Dell's voice, too, had changed from its former loud reverberating sound to the kind of harsh and toneless whisper in which now he muttered:

"It is not well. It is not well. No, it is very ill."

"What is?" demanded Bobby, but again got no answer. He turned to the tall, fair-haired youth who also was looking on with a very puzzled air. He said: "Can you tell me what's been happening?"

"Well, I don't know much," the young man answered. "There seemed to be a bit of a row on so I stopped to see what was up. Some of them seemed to be trying to rush this chap here." He nodded as he spoke at Duke Dell, still remote and distant in his own secret world, his own unseeing sight. "He stood them off all right," the young man continued, "and then this other bloke got in the way of one of his swipes and went flat into the brook there. I didn't notice at first but someone yelled out he would drown and I thought he had, too. He was lying face down in a good foot of water. We got him up here and he soon came round when we had emptied his tummy and he had been dried and had changed his things. I don't think he's much the worse except for a lump as big as your fist on the side of his head."

"I might be dead," said Brown himself, speaking in the same thin, resentful tone, "Easy as nothing I might be dead." He looked reproachfully at Duke Dell. "Through you," he said, timidly vicious.

"It had been better so," Duke Dell told him, his eyes still veiled and distant, his voice still the same harsh, unnatural whisper, as though a dead man spoke. "The Vision was given. You saw. You accepted. Then you doubted. 'Drink perhaps, drink or just dreaming,' you said, blaspheming. Had none meddled, now you would be in the presence of the Vision itself, for ever without end."

"Well, that's a thing to say," protested Brown. "Sorry about it, aren't you?" he snarled.

"For your sake, yes, for you it had been better so," Duke Dell repeated.

"If it had been like that," Bobby interposed, "you would soon be in the dock, answering a serious charge." But he had a feeling he might as well have said this to the wind, so little was it heard or heeded. To Brown, he said: "Do you wish to make a charge?"

"What? Me?" Brown asked and looked more like a frightened rabbit than ever. He even retreated a step or two inside the cottage as though to withdraw himself from so dangerous a proposition. "Oh no," he breathed, "it was only an accident. One of those things. It just happened. Accidental."

Bobby turned to Duke Dell.

"Apparently there has been an attempt at assault," he said. "Do you wish to make any complaint, any charge?" Duke Dell's expression changed abruptly. It was as though he were jerked back from the unseen world in which his spirit had wandered to the everyday world of material things. His gaze was no longer remote, withdrawn, strange. Nor was there in it now any trace of that fierce, dominating glare before which Brown had so shrunk away. Now, too, the big man no longer spoke in that dry and harsh whisper, unnatural, as though another power used his lips and tongue. In his earlier loud, reverberating tones, he replied:

"Charge? Complaint? Charge whom? What complaint? A little hearty horseplay. That's all. No harm meant, none done. Even otherwise, I should freely forgive, and you cannot both forgive and yet complain and charge." He spoke to Brown. "Come along," he said. "The sooner I get you home and into your own things, the better."

"Not so fast," Bobby ordered. He turned now to the little group of staring, curious bystanders. "Have any of you anything to say? I am an officer of police if anyone wishes to make any complaint of any sort."

At first there was no answer. Then someone shouted from behind:

"It's same as he said. There wasn't only a bit of fun."

"I think there wasn't," agreed Bobby. "I think more was meant."

He paused, hesitating. But there was nothing to be done. Plainly no one wanted any further trouble and without willing witnesses no charge could be sustained, even if one could be made. No harm had been done—unless Mr. Brown developed a cold. Still he could give them a lecture on the consequences of breaking the peace and of what a repetition of such a scene would involve. He proceeded to do so. They did not seem much impressed though they looked sulky and resentful. One man said:

"He didn't ought to come calling us the way he did and our girls bad names and him a stranger and all."

"It's a free country," Bobby retorted. "A man has a right to say what he likes. If he goes too far, a charge can be laid and he can be summoned. But don't try to take the law into your own hands. If you do, you put yourselves in the wrong at once."

They only looked sulkier still and began to shuffle away, muttering to each other. For the first time Bobby noticed a tall, ascetic-looking clergyman standing at the back of the rapidly dispersing crowd. To him Bobby said:

"Are you the clergyman here?"

"No, though I've taken duty here in Mr. Roberts's absence. He is away now, in hospital. My name is Childs, Alexander Childs. I am vicar of St. Barnabas, in Oldfordham. I was passing and there seemed something going on, so I stopped. Has Mr. Dell been making trouble again?"

"There's been a little horseplay from what I'm told," Bobby answered, as it vaguely crossed his mind that this was the second person who had happened to be passing and had stopped to see what was going on. "It looked more than that to me. Anyhow, it's all over now."

"Mr. Dell's activities are highly mischievous," Mr. Childs said loudly and severely. He turned, looking straight at Dell who had been standing quietly by, aloof, waiting for Brown to join him, taking no notice of Bobby's little speech or indeed of anything else. But now he responded to this direct challenge.

"Satan and his ministers find them so," he retorted, his voice thundering out with sudden and startling effect.

"That's enough," Bobby interposed, fearful a theological argument was about to develop, for Mr. Childs was evidently struggling to find words in which to express an indignation that for the moment had deprived him of the power of speech. "There's been too much talk already."

Bobby had taken care to speak directly to Duke Dell, but also loud enough for Mr. Childs to hear and take note, if he would. But the vicar's voice was still shaking with indignation as he said:

"I'll push on. I've an appointment with Mr. Goodman. I mustn't be late." In a lower voice, to Bobby alone, he said: "The man is a public danger. You must see what you can do. I'll have a talk with you later. Something must be done." Then he turned and called to Brown, now still farther withdrawn into the interior of the cottage. "Are you going my way, Mr. Brown? I'll walk along with you if you are."

"He comes with me," said Duke Dell, loudly and firmly. "Come along, Brother Brown, I'm waiting, and time presses."

Little Mr. Brown, answering to the call, came trotting out. Together he and his big companion went away, Brown keeping pace, with difficulty, with the big man's long strides.

"His master's voice," said the fair-haired youth, looking amused.

"Deplorable," said Mr. Childs. "Undisciplined and ignorant zeal can be most dangerous. Something must be done."

He was plainly a good deal disturbed but he said no more, except for a word of farewell as he mounted the bicycle on which he had arrived and rode off. Bobby was feeling a trifle disturbed himself.

The relationship between little Alfred Brown and Duke Dell seemed to him to resemble rather too closely that between the rabbit and the boa-constrictor. Uneasily he watched them till they were out of sight, hidden by the row of tall elms by the churchyard wall.

"What was that big chap talking about?" the fair-haired boy asked. "I mean all that about a vision or something."

"I don't know," Bobby answered. "Was his friend really in danger of drowning if you hadn't got him out in time?"

"Oh, rather. I told you, didn't I? He was dead out and lying face down in a foot of water." He paused and said more to himself than to Bobby: "Washed it all out if he had been."

"Washed what out?" Bobby asked and the other looked a little taken aback, as if he had not meant to speak aloud or had not wished what he said to be heard or noticed.

"Oh, nothing," he said and repeated: "Nothing."

But he spoke with a certain embarrassment or hesitation and Bobby looked at him.

"I thought you meant something," he said. "Didn't you?"

"I must be getting along," was all the answer the boy gave as he nodded a farewell and began to walk towards a motor cycle he had left standing against a garden fence near.

"You might let me have your name and address first," Bobby said, staying him with a gesture.

"What for?"

"Just in case," Bobby answered. "You never know. There may be more behind."

The young man looked more disconcerted than there seemed cause. He stood hesitating, doubtful and frowning.

"I don't see why you should say that," he muttered. "I don't see what makes you think that."

"You never know," Bobby repeated.

He had his note-book in his hand, waiting. The young man still hesitated. He said:

"I don't see why. I don't see what you're getting at. Suppose I refuse?"

"Oh, I'm sure you won't; why should you?" Bobby retorted smilingly. "But if people do refuse, we have to exercise our powers as police officers and ask to see their identity cards."

"Oh, well," the other grumbled, nor did he fail to notice that Bobby was already jotting down the number of the motor cycle. "Persistent sort of beggar, aren't you? Oh, all right. Flight-Lieutenant Kayes, Denis Kayes, Royal Australian Air Force. At present staying at Mrs. Jebb's. Aspect Cottage in Oldfordham. There's my card."

Bobby thanked him, accepted the card, said he didn't suppose for one moment that it would be necessary to trouble Mr. Kayes, but still, one never knew, one had to be prepared for everything, even the most unlikely. Flight-Lieutenant Kayes said, somewhat sulkily, that that was all right, and departed on his motor cycle. Bobby went towards his own car, meaning to resume his interrupted tour. By now the village green was deserted, except for two or three staring, curious children. In the door of one of the two or three shops the village boasted, a woman was standing. Bobby noticed that it was also the local post office. He went across to the woman and asked a few questions. She had not much to tell him beyond what he already knew. She did say that Duke Dell had visited the village two or three times before, and had annoyed everyone very much by a general and sweeping denunciation of them and all their ways. For one thing he had spoken very violently about what he had called 'popish and idolatrous' practices in the Church, and had been told with equal violence that it had nothing to do with him and he had better mind his own business for the future. Even greater and more serious anger had been roused by his use of the word 'whore' which had been taken as a direct imputation on the virtue of the village girls, though Bobby was inclined to guess Duke Dell had used the word more in the old sense of 'a-whoring after false gods.' The expression had been bitterly resented.

"They told him he would get a ducking if he came again," the woman said, "but he did, and it served him right what happened."

"People have no right to take the law into their own hands," said Bobby severely. "There was no need to listen to him or go near him for that matter. It was you who rang up about Mr. Brown, wasn't it?"

The woman looked puzzled.

"Mr. Brown? No. What about? Who is he?" she asked.

"Isn't that the name of the little man who got knocked into the stream there?" Bobby asked.

"Oh," she said, enlightened. "I didn't know. Mr. Goodman was on the phone and I was taking down his order and Betsy Green ran in and said a man had been killed dead and I told Mr. Goodman and he said he would ring up the police. It was you he rang, wasn't it?"

Bobby wondered why she hadn't rung up the police herself. She explained that Mr. Wiggins, the village constable, was out on his beat; and evidently considered that if Mr. Wiggins wasn't on the spot, only important and influential people like Mr. Goodman could do anything. Besides, he had offered his help and that freed her from all responsibility. Just as well, Bobby reflected, that he had been near at hand. It would have taken an hour or more for help to reach Chipping Up direct from Midwych, and by that time, with tempers roused to the pitch they had been at on his arrival, the trouble might have become really serious.

Fortunately he had arrived in time and he hoped the whole matter could be regarded as over and done with. He continued on his way, therefore; and, in the absorbing new task of steering Constable Wiggins's new bathroom past the eagle, economic eye of Mr. Young, he almost forgot the small excitement of the Chipping Up riot or near riot.

But it was recalled to his mind next morning when a paragraph in the *Midwych Courier*, in the stop-press column, announced briefly that a man named Alfred Brown had been found dead in his home at Oldfordham and that foul play was suspected.

CHAPTER IV
EXERCISE IN DIPLOMACY

TWICE OVER Bobby read the brief announcement and liked it less each time. He rubbed thoughtfully the end of his nose and across the breakfast table his wife saw the gesture and shook her head sadly. How she had tried to break him of that trick and how ill she had succeeded. Then she began to grow uneasy, there was a tense and eager look about him she did not like at all. She had seen it before. Bobby showed her the paragraph.

"Notice this, Olive?" he asked with an indifference she liked still less.

"It's Oldfordham," she pointed out. "You've no responsibility there, have you?"

"Oh no," said Bobby.

"If Oldfordham wants help, they'll call in the Yard," said Olive. "They won't ask you."

"Oh no," said Bobby.

"Nothing to do with you at all," Olive declared. "Is it?"

"Oh no," said Bobby.

"If there's one thing I do hate more than another," said Olive passionately, "it's when people go on saying 'Oh no' when all the time they mean 'Oh yes'."

"Well, you see," Bobby explained meekly, "it was a bit of queer business at Chipping Up and I suppose the Oldfordham force ought to know."

"Aren't there plenty of other people to tell them?" demanded Olive.

"Oh yes," said Bobby.

Olive made a gesture of extreme despair.

"And now," she complained as one appearing to High Heaven, "the man says 'Oh yes' when he means 'Oh no.' What can you do with people like that?" she asked sadly.

"Well, you see," repeated Bobby, and still more meekly, "they are sure to hear I was there because I did chuck about pretty freely 'in the name of the law' and all that sort of guff. And they are sure to want to know what I thought of it all—not that I know that myself yet."

"What you mean," said Olive, still severe, "is that you are simply aching and longing to try to find out all about it, and you think if you go there and make eyes at them, perhaps they'll ask you for help, instead of calling in the Yard."

Bobby was just about to say "Oh no" very indignantly when he realized suddenly that that was just exactly and precisely what was in his mind. So he gulped down what was left of his tea, glanced at the clock, remarked that it was time he was off, wondered if it would be any use trying to bluff Olive by saying something about having so much paper work to attend to, he didn't suppose he would be able to leave his desk all day, and knew very well she would not be deceived for one moment. So he said nothing and was glad he hadn't when Olive asked him if he had made sure he had enough petrol for the drive to Oldfordham.

More meekly than ever he replied that he thought so and anyhow he would have to call at headquarters first. It was quite true, though, that there was enough paper work waiting on his desk to keep him busy all morning and not till after lunch was he able to leave for his projected visit to Oldfordham.

Long years ago Oldfordham had been a place of high importance in days when bridges were scarce and the town's position on an almost always practicable ford had made it a centre of communication and the site of a yearly market to which people came from far and near.

Shrunken though was the pleasant little town, it was still a borough with a charter granted by one of the early Plantagenet kings. On its roll of citizens great names of the past were inscribed and here great events in the history of the land had taken place. The Church of St. Barnabas could have rivalled some cathedrals in size if not in beauty. The mayor's chain of office dated from Saxon times and could probably have been sold for enough to give the town the new water supply it badly needed, though of course no such act of vandalism had ever even occurred to anyone. Up to the time of the Reform Bill it had returned two members to Parliament and the loss of this privilege was still spoken of somewhat bitterly in local circles. In addition it could also boast of the smallest independent police force in the country—ten all told, including the chief constable, Mr. Spencer, whom Bobby was now upon his way to visit.

Mr. Spencer was a middle-aged, grey-haired man who believed in the quiet life and practised it to the best of his ability. Up to the present, he had found little to disturb it in the calm routine of Oldfordham days when even the war seemed far away—except when news arrived of some fresh local casualty or when on Saturday afternoons workers from nearby factories flooded the little town. At first Bobby found himself received with suspicion, even hostility. Some iconoclast, some reckless, would-be breaker of even the most treasured links with the past had once suggested that it might be a good idea to merge the gallant Oldfordham ten with the Wychshire county force. Naturally this had aroused a storm of indignation before which the rash proposer should have fled the district, though somehow he had managed to survive and even to stay on. Just at first, therefore, Mr. Spencer was inclined to suspect that

Bobby came with dark designs of using the Brown case as a lever for securing control. Bobby had some difficulty in dispelling this fear and soon saw the situation would have to be handled carefully. He began by explaining that he had thought it better, as an eye-witness of the odd little fracas at Chipping Up, to come to see Mr. Spencer rather than wait for Mr. Spencer to send for him. This at once relieved the situation. A deputy chief constable expecting to be sent for and hurrying to anticipate the summons, presented a picture very different from that of a deputy chief constable trying totalitarian tactics on a neighbour. Before long Mr. Spencer's long, thin, melancholy face was assuming an even more melancholy air as its owner admitted that he felt out of his depth. He had been chief constable of Oldfordham ever since his discharge from the army a few years after the first German war, but never before had he had to deal with any very serious crime. The worst offence known to Oldfordham until now had been an occasional larceny, a theft of washing from a cottager's back garden or something of the sort. Possibly, too, a little rowdiness on a Saturday night. He began to explain what had already been done. Bobby listened and approved. Unimaginative routine in fact, but Bobby didn't say so. Besides, unimaginative routine is necessary foundation. In his turn he told in full the tale of his experience at Chipping Up, mentioning but not emphasizing the two or three little points that had struck him as just a trifle odd. It was for Mr. Spencer to follow them up or not as he thought fit. Presently, in response to an innocent question or two that Bobby dropped in casually, there came the suggestion that possibly the Wychshire deputy chief might like to visit the scene of the crime. Bobby said it was indeed kind of Mr. Spencer but he feared he hardly had the time to spare. Besides, Mr. Spencer had evidently done all that so far was possible. Having said this, Bobby sat back and waited, in deadly fear lest Mr. Spencer should acquiesce. Fortunately, instead of acquiescence, there came reproachful protest. Of course, Mr. Spencer understood that the deputy chief of the Wychshire county police was enormously busy, but couldn't he spare just a few minutes? Mr. Spencer would be very grateful for any suggestions or advice Bobby could give from his greater experience. Bobby deprecated any such idea. Mr. Spencer was doing everything possible. That was evident. Certainly every member of every police force was bound to do his best to help every other member of every other police force. All had the duty of mutual aid. If Mr. Spencer really thought Bobby could be of any assistance, Bobby would, of course, willingly postpone his own pressing, but admittedly less grave, business and see if he could be of even the slightest assistance to him.

Friendly relations were now established and both men felt very pleased with themselves: Bobby, because, as Olive later on remarked with regrettable vulgarity, he had managed to poke his nose in; Mr. Spencer, because he was beginning to think that he might be able to avoid the odious necessity of calling in Scotland Yard who would come, if they did come, with overriding authority and a bill in prospect likely pretty nearly to double the Oldfordham police rate. And what would Oldfordham say then? Perhaps that it wanted a new chief constable?

By this time indeed Mr. Spencer was beginning to congratulate himself on the skill and cunning with which he had inveigled the deputy chief into offering assistance without there having been made any such formal request as would have involved promise of payment, not even of expenses. He dropped a hint about finger-prints. He admitted that just possibly in fingerprint technique Oldfordham might be a trifle behind Yard or Wakefield standards. In that one respect, perhaps not fully up-to-date, as was, no doubt, the Wychshire county force. In photography and in preparing plans and so on and so forth, Oldfordham, in Mr. Spencer's opinion, could hold its own. He himself had been training as an architect before joining the army in 1917, and one of his men was an enthusiastic amateur photographer, intending, indeed, to set up as a professional when peace came and he could retire from the force. But finger-prints were different; there, perhaps, Oldfordham was a trifle behind. Bobby at once offered to ring up his headquarters and ask his own specialist to come along. Mr. Spencer accepted with gratitude, and, the ice now thoroughly broken, Bobby felt in a position to ask a few more direct questions.

"Was Brown a native here?" he asked. "Anything known about him?"

Mr. Spencer looked at Bobby moodily and gave an answer that can only be described as succinct.

"Nothing," he said.

"Nothing?" repeated Bobby surprised. "Surely ... something?"

"Nothing at all," repeated Mr. Spencer firmly. "I thought I knew every living soul in the town. But not Brown. He came here several years ago. He bought a cottage in Market Row, near St. Barnabas. He has lived there ever since. Not one of my men knew anything about him. He just lived there. Every week he went to Midwych, where he did most of his shopping. He did his own cleaning, his own housework. Even his neighbours hardly knew him by sight. They say he was so quiet, so unobtrusive you never noticed him. One of them told me Brown could walk down an empty street in broad day without anyone seeing him. An exaggeration no doubt. But it gives you an idea. Until recently, until a few weeks ago."

Mr. Spencer paused dramatically. Bobby said "Yes?" Mr. Spencer continued:

"He got religion."

"Oh," said Bobby, puzzled.

"St. Barnabas is a high church," Mr. Spencer went on. "Very high it always was. The present vicar, Mr.

Childs, is even more ritualistic. Some of the practices he has introduced have been resented. Complaints have been made to the bishop. In general Mr. Childs has the support of his congregation. Some people may have left, but more have been attracted. I don't go myself but the church services are crowded, and the bishop has said publicly that he only wishes he had some more clergy like Mr. Childs. But then Brown came out of the sort of anonymous life he had been leading, took to attending the services and began to protest publicly against what he called popish practices. Mr. Childs consulted me. He was very upset, very distressed. It was hardly brawling in church, he thought, because Brown always walked out as soon as he had made what he called his protest. In any case, Mr. Childs seemed very unwilling to take any action. He didn't like the idea of forbidding one of his parishioners to attend church. Yet Brown was causing a great deal of unrest, interfering with the service of worship. In fact, creating an intolerable situation. He was even beginning to attract a following."

"I can understand that," Bobby said. "Many people are indifferent to religion and yet ready to get quite excited about any cry of popery."

"Mr. Childs," repeated Spencer, "was terribly disturbed. He felt the Church was being insulted, his own work gravely hindered, and yet he dreaded the effect of a public scandal and of sensational articles in the papers. Still, he told me he had made up his mind it had to be stopped somehow. One way or another. Well, now it has stopped—and for good." Mr. Spencer paused and looked slightly embarrassed. He said, somewhat hurriedly: "Mr. Childs is one of the most respected clergymen in the country. A man of the highest standards, a burning zeal. A burning zeal," he repeated. "Yes, I know," Bobby said gravely.

CHAPTER V
FULL CIRCLE

THE ATMOSPHERE HAD grown a little tense. Mr. Spencer looked embarrassed. He evidently felt he had been guilty of an indiscretion. How awkward if the deputy chief chose to imagine he had been hinting suspicion of the vicar of St. Barnabas, a man universally respected. He looked at Bobby almost pleadingly. But Bobby's thoughts were turning in another direction. He said:

"Why was Brown so interested in religion all at once? Was it Duke Dell? Has Dell himself taken any part in these disturbances at St. Barnabas?"

"None at all as far as I know. Dell came here a few months ago. No one took much notice of him at first. He seems to confine himself to preaching what he calls The Vision."

Bobby asked what that was, and Mr. Spencer shook his head and said he didn't know, but Mr. Childs called it rank antinomianism. From memories of his Oxford days when he had just managed to scrape through his finals and take his degree—pass, only—Bobby tried to remember what antinomianism was. Sympathizing with an ignorance he had shared until Mr. Childs's visit, Mr. Spencer said:

"It's a sort of idea that it doesn't matter what you do. You can do anything you jolly well like and it's all right, provided you have sufficient faith."

"Faith in what?" Bobby asked.

"Well, as far as Duke Dell is concerned, faith in what he calls The Vision. Mr. Childs says there was a German writer with much the same idea. 'Beyond Good and Evil,' he called it, and died in a lunatic asylum, and a wonder it wasn't gaol, if you ask me. Mr. Childs thought it was much the same thing in religion that the Nazis preach in politics. Good, according to them, is what suits Germany. Torture, murder, anything. Evil is what doesn't. Very handy sort of belief, too. Dell gets out of it by saying that when you've seen The Vision you only do the right thing. But you're the sole judge. Duke Dell had the insolence"—Mr. Spencer grew red in the face at the memory—"the insolence to tell me he didn't acknowledge my authority. Or that of anyone else, except the powers that sent him his precious Vision. I asked him if he thought himself above the law and he said: 'Certainly. No law can bind those whom The Vision has made free.' His very words. Dangerous, if you ask me."

"Has he ever said what he means by The Vision?" Bobby asked.

"I asked him that and he talked a lot in a very wild excited way. I couldn't make head or tail of it. I've asked Dr. Railes—he's our medical officer—if he could be certified. Railes didn't seem to think so. He said the man seemed perfectly sane otherwise. All the same— well, if Brown hadn't been a sort of follower of his, Duke Dell would have been the first man I thought of. But there it is—no motive. No evidence either for that matter. Only now there's this Chipping Up business you've told me about."

"It's certainly a fact," Bobby said thoughtfully, "that but for a young flying officer who was there Brown wouldn't have survived in the afternoon only to be murdered at night. You have to ask yourself: 'Did Duke Dell finish at night what he began in the afternoon?' Yet all I heard suggested that it was a pure accident."

"You wouldn't say there was enough to justify an arrest, would you?" Mr. Spencer asked wistfully.

"No, nothing like," Bobby answered at once. "They went off together apparently the best of friends. What about an alibi? Do you know anything about Duke Dell's movements last night?"

"It seems he was at his lodgings. He has a room with a Mrs. Soames on Running Water Farm. Soames is foreman there. It's about two miles out on the main Midwych road. We haven't seen Dell yet, he's out preaching somewhere. Mrs. Soames says he got home early and spent the evening as usual—reading the Bible and saying his prayers. He was still at it when they went to bed. Soames has to be up and out early so they're always in bed and asleep by nine o'clock. Probably they sleep hard, she says they never stir till the alarm goes. Plenty of time and opportunity for Dell to get here and back again if he wanted to. Nothing to show he did. Mrs. Soames says he seemed just the same this morning. He came down as usual at seven, but she thinks he is up much earlier, at his Bible reading and so on. After breakfast he goes out preaching and is often not back till late, after blackout. Apparently he only has two meals in the day—dry bread and hot water for breakfast, dry bread and cold water for supper. Nothing else.

Occasionally he may eat a cold potato." Mr. Spencer contemplated this diet with gloomy disfavour. "You know," he said, "feeding like that, enough to explain anything."

"I shouldn't like it myself," agreed Bobby, and could not repress a slight shudder, especially at the cold potato item.

"Though he seems to thrive on it," Mr. Spencer admitted. "Covers miles during the day—on foot always. But there it is—no motive, except for what you heard him say. Suggests disagreement or backsliding, even if they did go off together in a friendly sort of way."

"It certainly did sound rather a strong variant of the 'Better dead' theme," Bobby agreed. "'Better dead and here's a helping hand,' so to say. Not enough to take to a jury though, not enough by a long way. My advice would be: Remember it, keep an eye on him, but nothing more at present." He added thoughtfully: "Religion is a strong wine and goes to the head sometimes."

Mr. Spencer shook his own head.

"You can never tell," he said wisely. "There's nothing people aren't capable of, once they get religion on the brain. Very upsetting, religion."

"Most upsetting thing in the world," Bobby agreed. "Dangerous. Like electricity. It may give a blaze of light or it may kill, destroy. Power, and be jolly careful how you handle it or how you leave it alone. How religion began, I suppose. Seeing there was Power around and what had you better do about it? But does religion really come into this business? I don't see how; and as for Duke

Dell, nothing you can lay hold of. A long way from preaching a Vision to committing a murder."

Mr. Spencer looked very much as if he did not think it as far as all that.

"We must look for more evidence," he agreed, "but I think we've a good idea where to look."

But now it was Bobby's turn to shake a doubtful head.

"If you don't mind my saying so," he remarked, "the first and last necessity in our job is to beware of preconceived ideas. Get one idea fixed in your mind and you tend to overlook everything that doesn't seem to fit it, and exaggerate everything that does. My advice would be: Forget Duke Dell for the present, though keeping him on the list. Tops for that matter. When you get to know more other names may crop up and what one always looks for—the motive."

Mr. Spencer's expression suggested that he would be well content with one suspect and felt no need for more. However, he made polite noises of agreement with Bobby's little lecture, and, partly to avoid another, suggested that now the deputy chief might like to visit the scene of the crime and afterwards perhaps the mortuary? A very thorough and careful examination had been carried out, explained Mr. Spencer with a deprecatory smile, and here were the full reports. Probably the deputy chief, from his greater experience, would be able to suggest points that had been overlooked. Bobby said he could imagine nothing less probable, but he would regard it as a privilege to see things for himself. Then he would be able to understand the written reports so much better. The case was interesting, unusual. Impossible, for instance, at their present level of knowledge, to imagine any motive for the murder of so harmless, commonplace, and insignificant a man as Alfred Brown. What strange and hidden cause could there be why so anonymous a life should have blossomed suddenly into the dreadful notoriety of murder?

Their way took them past the ancient Mote House, dating from the twelfth century, into the High Street, where half a dozen chain store branches shouted their twentieth-century modernity. Turning by an 'Olde Curiosity Shoppe,' where a fragrant of a German bomb was offered for sale next to a Saxon sword dug from the bed of the Becker, they reached Market Row. Opposite the cottage, inconspicuous and retired in the south-east corner, that Brown had occupied was a small group of sightseers, gazing with vacant interest at shuttered windows and closed doors and paying small attention to the efforts of the constable stationed there for that purpose, to make them 'move on.' As Bobby and his companion approached, however, one young man detached himself from the group and came towards them. Bobby said with surprise:

"Oh, why it's—no, it isn't, though. I thought for a moment it was the young airman I told you about, the one who hauled Brown out of the water at Chipping Up."

The young man was passing them now. He nodded to Mr. Spencer and said a word of greeting. He did not seem to notice Bobby. Mr. Spencer responded, and, as soon as the young man had gone by, remarked:

"That was Mr. Langley Long. Young chap discharged from the army, medically unfit. I believe he is looking for a suitable place to start a guest house."

"I quite thought at first it was Denis Kayes again," Bobby said in a worried voice. "There's a strong likeness. I don't quite know where. He's dark and young Kayes is fair. Features different, too. I think it must be the facial bone structure. Or their way of walking, carrying themselves. I wonder if they are relations."

"I should hardly think so," Mr. Spencer said doubtfully. "I've never heard anything to suggest it. I've never heard that they seem to know each other at all."

"Do you know anything about Mr. Kayes? He said he was staying with a Mrs. Jebb. Aspect Cottage was the address."

"Oh yes," Spencer answered. "I knew Mrs. Jebb had a lodger, but I don't know anything about him. Nothing ever happens here— at least, not till now—so if anything does happen I generally hear about it, and I knew Mrs. Jebb was trying to get a lodger now Janet has come home. She didn't want Janet to have to do it all. Mrs. Jebb wasn't left too well off when her husband died but there was some cottage property in Midwych. It brought in enough for her to live on. But it was bombed in the big Midwych raid, so now there are no rents and no compensation either. Rebuilt after the war, but in the interval—nothing. Janet was on war work but got released on grounds of exceptional hardship. A nice girl, though too modern for some people."

"She stays at home now, does she? to help her mother?"

"Oh no, she's teaching at the St. Barnabas Church School. She has her degree so they were more than glad to get her. It was a sort of condition of her release, I think, that she took up teaching."

"Has Mr. Kayes any friends or relatives in the neighbourhood?" Bobby asked. "I was wondering why he came to a little place like this to spend his leave. Most men on leave make straight for London if they have no family claims—and sometimes if they have."

"I should guess," said Mr. Spencer, slightly offended by the implied slur on Oldfordham amenities and attractions, "he came precisely because it is quiet and peaceful here. Mr. Kayes wants a rest most likely, a chance to forget the war for a time. In peace-time we had many visitors, quite a tourist trade, indeed. Beautiful country. Wych Forest not so far away. Fine old buildings, too—the Mote House, for example, and St. Barnabas."

"Oh yes, I know, very ancient, most interesting," Bobby hastened to agree; without adding that the Mote House was of interest only by age, since in itself it was as dull and plain a four-square building as twelfth-century workmen ever put together, while St. Barnabas, after a disastrous fire, had been restored in the middle of the last century in the most self-conscious and pain-giving Neo-Gothic style of the period. He went on: "Mr. Kayes comes here to recuperate and Mr. Langley Long comes to look for a spot suitable for a guest house. Any difference between a guest house and a boarding house, do you know?"

Mr. Spencer explained that a guest house was of superior status; and Bobby said 'Oh, indeed,' he hadn't known that before. He supposed the hierarchy ran: lodging house, boarding house, guest house, private hotel, hotel de luxe, and, anyway, wasn't it just a trifle interesting that the arrival of these two young men in the town had been followed by the only murder there for very many years?

Mr. Spencer looked startled.

"But surely" he protested, "there's no reason to suspect any association ... any connection ... You don't think ... ?"

Bobby produced the special sigh he reserved for this type of question.

"At the start of any inquiry like this," he explained patiently, "I don't think. I only note facts—such as the arrival here of these two young men; the presence of one of them at Chipping Up; his remark, which very likely meant nothing much, that if Brown had been drowned something or another would have been washed out. Perhaps it's too much of a trifle to call it a fact that the other young man was having such a good look at this cottage. Just as a matter of routine I would keep an eye on both of them, if I were you."

"Oh, I will, certainly," agreed Mr. Spencer, looking quite shaken as there opened before him new and troubling vistas. More and more did he determine to grapple to him the deputy chief—or rather the deputy chiefs' experience and resources—as with hooks of steel. "There is one thing," he went on. "It can't matter. Not worth mentioning. But it might explain why Mr. Long chose Oldfordham for his guest house hunt. I hear he has been seen once or twice— mere gossip, you understand, and you know what gossip is in a small country town."

"Almost as bad as in a big city, and always most valuable," pronounced Bobby. "Give me gossip or Sherlock Holmes, and I take gossip every time. The detective's first aid and ever present help in time of doubt. What is this time?"

"Oh, it doesn't amount to much," Mr. Spencer answered, "only that he has been seen once or twice with Miss Foote."

"Who is she?" Bobby asked.

"Mr. Goodman's new secretary at Four Oaks. Gossip again— rather more than a new secretary, some people say. But first that kind of talk and then Mr. Langley Long being seen with her—well, it did make people wonder where he came in."

"So do I," Bobby murmured; and this time he was really startled, for it seemed as if a kind of circle were being established.

Mr. Goodman's phone call; Chipping Up; Mr. Kayes's presence there; his odd personal resemblance to Mr. Lanley Long; Long's friendship with Miss Foote, and so back to Mr. Goodman again. Full circle.

But if this circle enclosed the crime, what became of that sudden interest in religion the dead man seemed to have developed so shortly before his violent end?

CHAPTER VI

COTTAGE INTERIOR

WHILE THIS TALK was going on, and in more desultory fashion and more subject to various interruptions than it has been thought necessary to show in this record, Bobby had been giving close and careful scrutiny to the small, commonplace kitchen where the death that Alfred Brown had so narrowly escaped in the afternoon had found him in the evening.

Mr. Spencer showed the exact spot, marked by an outline in chalk, where the body had been lying, the head dreadfully shattered by a savage hail of blows that must have been delivered with maniacal violence. Yet the only sign of any struggle was that one of the kitchen chairs, now lying in a corner of the scullery, had a broken leg, the break evidently quite recent. But, if this broken chair was a sign and a result of a struggle between murderer and victim, why had it been put aside with such careful, odd precision? Still, murderers often do the strangest, most unaccountable things. Otherwise everything seemed to suggest, confirmation given by the very excellent and complete photographs taken immediately by one of the Oldfordham force, that the victim had been taken by surprise, stunned by a single, sudden blow, and that then the murderer, in a frenzy born of his own deed, had made sure.

One discovery Bobby did make. His very careful examination of the damaged chair in the scullery showed two or three tiny threads of black cloth caught in the splinter of the broken leg. He showed them to the slightly disconcerted Spencer. Bobby agreed that they were not likely to be of much value or importance. Certainly nothing to show they came from the clothing of the murderer. No bloodstain visible near or on them, or on the chair itself, for that matter. Still, anything might lead anywhere, as Bobby remarked, and was there in the cottage any material, clothing or curtain or anything, from which the threads might have come?

Mr. Spencer said he thought not, but the deputy chief could satisfy himself on that point when they went upstairs. All the dead man's scanty wardrobe, apart from what the body had actually been clothed in, was still upstairs. Bobby suggested that possibly it might be as well to send the threads to Wakefield for expert examination, and Spencer promised that that would be done. Not that he thought anything could be learned from such tiny threads, and Bobby didn't think so either, even though to-day miracles are three a penny in scientific laboratories. Spencer, still slightly on the defensive, went on to explain that Dr. Railes was certain that the murderer's clothing and person must both have been spattered with blood; and he detailed the precautions taken, such as instructions sent to all cleaners to be on the look out. Could the deputy chief suggest anything else that could have been done?

Bobby said no, indeed. Nothing more, he thought, was possible at this stage. Of course, if bloodstained clothing could be found, everything would be easy. But such good fortune was not likely. Clothing is easily disposed of. Soaked in petrol, for example, and burned. Even though ashes may be left, and ashes can tell tales. But it could be buried in some out-of-the-way spot. Or dropped inside a hollow tree in the depths of one of the lonely Wychwood glades. Or, even more completely, lost down one of the shafts of the various deserted and flooded mines in the neighbourhood, where a sheer descent of a hundred feet ended in a black, unplumbed depth of water.

Placated by Bobby's warm approval of everything done, and by the fact that he was showing no disposition to claim undue importance for the small discovery he had made—annoying, certainly, that those tiny little threads had been overlooked, though who could have thought that a broken chair in one room had anything to tell of a murder committed in another?—Spencer went on to explain that the discovery of the crime had been made about half-past one in the morning. The constable on the beat, passing by, had heard the wireless still playing. He had thought this odd, since, of course, the B.B.C. programme stops at midnight; and he had not realized at first that what was coming through was from America on a short wavelength. Then he had noticed that the cottage door was an inch or two open, though there seemed no light within. Thinking this more odd still, he knocked, and when he got no answer he pushed the door a little further open and flashed his torch within, discovering thus the first murder of which Oldfordham annals told for nearly a century.

Mr. Spencer further explained that the instrument used had been the heavy kitchen poker, found lying near the body.

Presumably the murderer had worn gloves, since neither on the poker nor anywhere else had any finger-prints been found, other than those of Brown himself.

For the rest, Bobby made no further discoveries, in spite of the very close, careful, and detailed examination he made of the cottage and its contents. It was a tiny place, four small rooms in all, a kitchen and a scullery below and two rooms above, one furnished as a bedroom, the other without furniture and evidently used as a receptacle for various odds and ends. Empty bottles figured largely among these; and Mr. Spencer mentioned that there was, for war-time, a remarkable stock of spirits, chiefly gin, in the kitchen cupboard. This had rather surprised the Oldfordham police, for Brown had never been known to enter any of the public houses in the town, nor had he ever been seen under the influence of drink. But apparently he had done a good deal of solitary drinking in his own home, in privacy.

The general aspect of the cottage was squalid enough. The furniture was cheap, old, and shabby. But if Mr. Brown had lived in no great comfort there was no sign of any pressure of poverty. There was in fact a curiously odd mixture of the cheap and the expensive. Cheap, deal chairs and tables, for instance, and coarse glass crockery, as against window curtains of highly expensive material. Cooking utensils varied from brand new aluminium pans, that in the war-time scarcity of aluminium must have cost a good deal, to cheap tin kettles showing signs of home-made repairs to keep them longer serviceable. There was, too, an elaborate pressure cooking gadget. It was priced, as Bobby knew, because Olive had been casting a somewhat hesitating eye on one of the same make, at a high figure, and yet apparently had never been used. Probably it had taken the solitary man's fancy and then he had never bothered to learn how to use it. But it was a purchase that showed no great need for economy. And there was a wireless set of the most elaborate make, a model no longer in production, and one that even before the war would have cost a considerable sum.

It seemed to Bobby that Mr. Brown had avoided spending money, had wished to live in the obscurity that poverty, gives, and yet could, when he wished, spend freely enough. Curious, Bobby thought, and since there must be an explanation, he wondered what it could be, and wondered if, when it was found, it would explain also the cause and reason of the crime. In every other respect this cottage interior showed as commonplace, inconspicuous, and non-committal as had apparently been the late tenant himself in life. Bobby made some remark of the sort to Mr. Spencer, who was, however, now bestowing all his interest on that expensive wireless set.

"Must have cost a pretty penny,' he remarked. "You can get America on it. Brown seems to have been listening in to America when he was murdered. The dial shows that. A concert over there. We checked up on that. Dr. Railes is quite definite death took place somewhere about half-past ten and two men passing about that time have come forward to say they heard sounds of what they call 'thumps' coming from the cottage through the music. They didn't pay much attention, but one of them remarked that 'old Alf Brown must be chopping up firewood ready for the morning.' Brown's watch stopped at twenty to eleven, too, though of course there's nothing to show it was right. Putting things together, though, there isn't much doubt but that the murder took place about half-past ten or a little later."

"Seems pretty conclusive," Bobby agreed. "Was the American concert something special, do you know? Did Brown often listen in to America?"

"We didn't go into that," Spencer answered. "Just made sure there was music on the air at the time the two witnesses say they heard music as well as the 'thumps' they talk about. Check up on everything, you know."

"Yes, indeed," agreed Bobby approvingly. "Never forget that. I was only wondering if the murderer had turned it on to drown any other noise. But that doesn't seem likely. No reason for tuning in to America if that was the idea, and everything points to a sudden unexpected violent attack with no precautions taken."

"That's right," said Mr. Spencer. He added rather enviously: "I wish we had a set like this. Expensive thing, though. We can't even get Paris." He had been twirling the knobs while he talked and now Paris came through, strong and clear. "There you are," said Mr. Spencer triumphantly; and continued, not unwilling to show his knowledge of French: "De Musset's 'On ne badine pas avec l'amour.' They never seem to get tired of it, do they?"

"You might keep it going for a bit, if you will," Bobby said. "I think there's someone trying to get in at the back."

CHAPTER VII
VISITING CARDS

HE MOVED CAUTIOUSLY into the scullery. The back door was both locked and bolted. No good trying to open it. Any intruder would be off and away at the first sound of turning key or drawn bolt. Quite possibly indeed the alarm had already been taken, though he had been careful to move quietly and had hoped that the French broadcast would cover any sound he made. But now the fumbling at the window, the cautious lifting of the back-door latch that he was sure he had heard, ceased entirely. He went back into the kitchen. Mr. Spencer said:

"No one there?"

"I'll slip round to the back and have a look," Bobby said. "Keep the set going, will you?"

He went out quickly. The constable on duty was still there, still patiently exhorting from time to time the ever-changing, ever-freshly recruited group of spectators to 'move on, please.' To them Bobby's sudden and hurried appearance was an ample reward for their long wait. Evidently something was happening and they thrilled to the knowledge. They were even more thrilled when Bobby disappeared at a run down a narrow alleyway that led to the back of the cottage. Some of them showed certain disposition to follow, till the constable on duty sternly waved them back.

At the point where the alley turned at a right angle to lead to the back of the cottages and beyond, Bobby almost collided with a woman hurrying away. He had only seen her once before, and only for a moment or two, but his memory for faces was naturally good and was highly trained and practised as well. He said:

"Miss Foote isn't it? Didn't I see you at Mr. Goodman's?"

"Yes," she answered, her round baby face, her wide, child-like, innocent blue eyes, candid and untroubled. She added, for she had recognized him, too: "You're the gentleman Mr. Goodman told about the fight at Chipping Up, aren't you?"

"What are you doing here?" he demanded.

"Oh, I'm not being naughty, am I?" she asked, lifting her eyes to his in troubled appeal. "There was such a crowd in front little me couldn't see anything, so I thought I would be awfully clever and get a peep from behind. Oughtn't I?"

She was still looking up at him, trustfully, pleadingly, quite plainly asking him not to be hard on a poor little silly girlie like herself. Bobby didn't much like either her or her manner, but the explanation was plausible. Curiosity explains much and the scene of a murder—the spot marked 'X' in the newspaper photographs—has a fascination for many. Less amiably than it may be Miss Foote had expected, for her own manner of sweet girlish innocence diminished notably at the sharpness of his tone, Bobby asked:

"Was that your only reason for trying to open the back door?"

"Oh, I didn't," she answered promptly. "That was Miss Jebb. I expect she was doing the same, trying to get a peep. She was just coming out of the back yard and going away, so I did, too. I should never have dared try to go inside. She must be awfully brave. I should be Frightened."

"Wait here, don't move," Bobby said; and went down the alley at a run. But there was no sign either of Miss Jebb or of anyone else. Plenty of time, of course, for any intruder to get away. A second narrow alley, further on, led in the other direction, straight into the busy main street of the little town, where the Mote House and the chain-store branches jostled each other incongruously. Escape that way was easy, pursuit obviously useless. Anyone—Miss Jebb or another—could be by now harmlessly making purchases in one or other of the main street shops. Bobby went back to Miss Foote, patiently powdering her nose as she patiently waited. She said winningly:

"It's an awfully big thrill to be ordered about and bullied by a real policeman. You are, aren't you? Mr. Goodman said so. It's almost like being suspected yourself. O-o-oo. Perhaps I am. Handcuffs?"

She held out to him two small gloved hands in the prettiest way imaginable and Bobby repressed a strong desire to box her ears. Flirtation could be jolly good fun in its time and place, but this was neither. He asked:

"Are you sure it was Miss Jebb you saw?"

"Oh yes," she answered. "At least I think so. I don't know her very well. I've never spoken to her. I shouldn't Dare. She looks so severe. I think teachers always do, don't you?"

"If you don't know her, why do you think it was her?" Bobby asked.

"I only mean not to speak to," Miss Foote explained. "The schoolchildren got up a concert and I went and it was Awfully Good. The children sang ever so well and Miss Jebb taught them. She made a little speech. I don't know how anyone dare—I think Miss Jebb must be awfully clever and efficient and managing, don't you?" and Miss Foote's eyes, wider than ever, invited comparison between such severe efficiency and her own appealing, clinging femininity.

"Mr. Spencer is here," Bobby said. "I think he would like you to tell him about this yourself. He is in the cottage if you'll come with me," and as he spoke he turned back along the alley, Miss Foote trotting confidingly by his side.

"I think Mr. Spencer is such a nice man, don't you?" she chattered, as they walked along. "I do hope he won't think I was silly and scold. I didn't think there was any harm trying to get a peep. But he's always ever so nice and kind."

A slight acidity in her tone as she said this suggested she didn't altogether consider her present companion had shown himself worthy of such praise. But Bobby was busy with his own thoughts and hardly listened. He and she emerged from the alley; and so was sensation greater still, for he had entered alone, as all had seen, and now he returned in company, as all could see. Whispers arose, stares were unashamed. Bobby glared. But it is difficult to rebuke a stare or answer a whisper you have been more conscious of than actually heard. Then it happened that he caught the gist of the murmured remark of a gaping youngster near.

"Lummy, he's got her, he has," the lad had said, and Bobby's hand shot out and grabbed him by the collar.

"What's that?" he demanded. "You be careful what you say or you'll find yourself in bad trouble. Remember that. You won't get another warning."

He released the lad; who fled as fast as shaking legs and knocking knees permitted, persuaded he had escaped instant prison by the narrowest of margins.

Bobby transferred his glare to the rest of the startled onlookers.

"Clear out, all of you," he ordered. Forgetting that his foot was no longer on his native heath, that here his warrant was null and of no effect, he warned them: "Some of you will be getting charged with obstruction if you don't mind. Hurry now," and as he spoke he lifted a hand towards the slightly astonished constable on duty at the cottage door, much as if inviting him to carry out various arrests on the spot.

That imperious gesture, that voice of command, air of authority, had their effect, and indeed Bobby could look formidable enough when he chose. The group of spectators dispersed, sulkily and slowly, but still melting away. To Miss Foote, Bobby said:

"This way. It's in here." To the constable on duty, he explained: "The young lady has some information to give Mr. Spencer."

They entered the cottage where Mr. Spencer was still absorbed with the beauties and delights of that super superb wireless set.

"You can get practically anything anywhere," he said enthusiastically as Bobby and Miss Foote came in. Then when he saw who it was he looked very surprised, turned off the set, and said: "Oh, Miss Foote, isn't it?"

"They all think it's me," Miss Foote told him, opening those big blue eyes of hers more widely than ever. "Isn't it a thrill? Little me doing murders and hitting men with pokers and things and killing them ever so dead. I expect," she went on complacently, "everybody will be most awfully frightened of me now, don't you?"

Mr. Spencer looked bewildered. Miss Foote giggled. Bobby said sourly:

"Miss Foote was in the alleyway at the back of the house. She tells me she saw Miss Jebb trying to open the back door. I thought she had better report direct to you. Some of those fools outside saw us and started staring and whispering. I gave them a bit of a talking-to—to shut them up."

"They won't," Miss Foote told him. "They'll go on gossiping. Of course they will. I like gossip myself," she added candidly.

"I don't quite follow," protested Mr. Spencer, still bewildered, and then, catching at the one fact he had really grasped, he said: "Miss Jebb? You saw her? What was she doing there?"

"Trying to open the back door apparently," Bobby said.

"But really," protested Mr. Spencer. "Well, why should she?"

"I expect she just wanted a peep, don't you?" suggested Miss Foote. "Like me. I did, too. It's so awfully fascinating, isn't it? A murder, I mean." She lowered her voice to a hoarse whisper. "Was it—here? Right in here?"

She looked pleadingly at Mr. Spencer. Mr. Spencer seemed not wholly unresponsive to the young lady's kittenish charm. The conversation between him and Miss Foote began to take on the semblance of a flirtation—heavily paternal on his side, respectful and admiring on hers. With some interest Bobby watched the staid, elderly Mr. Spencer blossoming into a kind of juvenile gaiety of spirit. Not for Bobby, though, to show any surprise or impatience. He had to keep on the right side of Mr. Spencer or he might find himself incontinently booted out and some meddlesome thruster from the Yard—for so, sad to say, did Bobby in this moment of feared frustration think of former colleagues of his—taking over a case that seemed already full of odd possibilities and strange dramatic twists of human character.

He turned to give his attention to a pile of papers, neatly arranged on the table. They had been examined by Mr. Spencer's sergeant and were now awaiting inspection from Mr. Spencer himself. They were few in number and none apparently had been considered to be of much importance. As always with this anonymous Mr. Brown, it was the negative, not the positive, that was suggestive. For there was nothing whatever to indicate his source of income. A few receipted bills, various circulars, but no letters, no personal documents, no bank book, no dividend warrants, nothing like that. There were two visiting cards. One was that of Mr. Childs and had on it a pencilled note: "Have called twice. May I suggest a talk? Can you come to the vicarage this evening?" The other was that of Flight-Lieutenant Denis Kayes.

Bobby regarded them both thoughtfully. Mr. Childs had wished to make an appointment. Had that appointment been for last night and had it been kept? And why had Denis Kayes called? Apparently

Brown had been out, but had Kayes called again; and if so, had his visit taken place the previous night?

CHAPTER VIII

MATERNAL INDIGNATION

THE FLIRTATION, or near flirtation, between Mr. Spencer and Miss Foote, so paternal on his side, so innocently kittenish on hers, was ending now. Miss Foote, with pretty little cries of horror at the lateness of the hour, hurried away. First though she bestowed upon Bobby, now apparently forgiven, her sweetest smile as she bade him farewell.

"Such a thrill," she assured him earnestly, "to meet a real live detective busy with a real dreadful murder."

Therewith she tripped gaily away and Mr. Spencer said:

"Pretty little thing." With a touch of envy in his voice he added: "You've made a conquest. All the time she was talking to me, it was you she was watching."

"Was it though?" said Bobby with considerable interest. "Are you sure?"

"Now, now, married man, aren't you?" said Mr. Spencer, arch and knowing. "Eyes in the boat, young fellow, eyes in the boat. Not that I blame you. If a pretty little girl gives you the glad eye, what can a poor devil do?"

He chuckled richly. Bobby gave a wan smile. His mind had been far too full of other things, of bewildering and ugly thoughts, for him to pay Miss Foote's charms the tribute they so plainly both deserved and desired. All the same, interesting to know that all the time of her flirtation, or near flirtation, with the paternal Mr. Spencer she had continued to give to Bobby himself her best attention. He said aloud:

"I wonder what she saw in me?"

Mr. Spencer laughed very much. He thought the remark naive in the extreme in its innocence and vanity.

"Youth," he said at last. "Six feet of youth and a bulging chest get the women every time. Women's rights are all the go, but the one right they all really want is a six footer of their own they feel can look after them, bless 'em. Primitive stuff, of course, but it goes deep."

"I suppose it does," agreed Bobby, "though I'm still wondering."

"Well, don't ask your wife," Mr. Spencer warned him. He looked a little melancholy. He said: "If I were only twenty years younger, I can tell you you wouldn't have it all your own way. No, indeed, not by a long chalk, you wouldn't."

"How old do you think she is?" Bobby asked.

"Oh, nineteen or twenty, not more," Mr. Spencer answered, a little surprised by the question. "Why?"

"Oh, I just wondered," Bobby answered vaguely. Her looks and manner were indeed those of that age, or even less, and yet once or twice Bobby had thought that there seemed about her a suggestion of an age, an experience, considerably greater. But then he supposed it sometimes was like that with quite young girls. They could in some strange way combine the freshness, the ingenuousness, of youth with what seemed an odd inherited maturity, as though there were innate in woman's soul the knowledge and the wisdom of past generations. But Mr. Spencer was thinking that really it wasn't at all dignified for two responsible officials engaged on the investigation of a brutal murder to be gossiping about the possible age of a girl acquaintance. Why, if they didn't mind, they would be talking about her eyes next or the fascinating gaiety of her manner. With a touch of austerity in his voice, he said:

"About Miss Jebb? Very nice girl but not very popular, too stand-offish. Intellectual. Been to the university. That sort of thing. Won't help her to cook the dinner, though. Makes some boys feel out of their depth and they don't like it." Mr. Spencer shook his head and Bobby was conscious of a faint and unworthy suspicion that at times Miss Jebb might have made even Mr. Spencer feel out of his depth, too. Mr. Spencer continued: "What do you think she can have been doing at the back here? Just curiosity?"

"It might be," agreed Bobby cautiously. "How about asking her? She lives somewhere near, doesn't she? I think we ought to know what she was up to, if it's the fact she was there."

"The fact?" repeated Mr. Spencer, surprised. "I thought you said Miss Foote saw her."

"I said Miss Foote said she saw her," Bobby answered. "You can't accept uncorroborated statements until confirmed. And pretty little blue-eyed girls can lie with the best of them at times."

"Oh well, yes," agreed Mr. Spencer, though slightly shocked all the same. "Of course, there are some girls who are born liars," and quite plainly in his own mind he excluded girls as charming, pleasant and smiling as Miss Foote—especially when so ready to display those qualities for the benefit of the middle-aged. Why, he could still hear her happy, innocent, girlish laughter. He continued: "Well, I suppose we had better see what Miss Jebb has to say for herself. Just a woman's curiosity, I suppose. Going a bit far though, trying to get in."

Bobby agreed that was going too far altogether. Miss Jebb should certainly be asked for an explanation. He thought Mr. Spencer was quite right in insisting upon that. Mr. Spencer nodded, looked determined, and said Aspect Cottage was only a few minutes' walk away, nestling as it did in the somewhat depressing Victorian shade of St. Barnabas. A very great age, the Victorian, but not at its best, one feels, in architecture. Bobby eyed the building with a faint distress. He found himself wondering if from Victorian neo-Gothic and from Georgian cubes and squares there might not emerge some day a new beauty. Wishful thinking, no doubt.

"Here we are," said Mr. Spencer.

Aspect Cottage showed itself a fair-sized house, formal and dignified, erected by a man who had never even thought of producing an architectural gem, but whose inborn sense of proportion had resulted in something at least pleasant and restful to the eye—the sort of thing at which, when you saw it first, you would hardly trouble to look again, but that nevertheless would always give you pleasure when you did see it another time.

Mr. Spencer knocked. The door was opened by Miss Jebb herself, still in her outdoor things. Evidently she had just returned home. She was a tall, dark girl, her low forehead, broad cheekbones and heavy-dark brows giving her a somewhat striking and unusual appearance. Far removed in looks and manner she seemed from Miss Foote's doll-like prettiness and sweet, beguiling ways. The other extreme, indeed, with an expression too withdrawn and serious for her youth, though the gravity of her expression would break at times into a slow, delightful smile. She greeted Mr. Spencer pleasantly, though with evident surprise, and at Bobby she looked somewhat questioningly and doubtfully. Mr. Spencer asked if they might have a few words with her and she looked still more surprised but invited them in.

She led them down the passage to the drawing-room. As she was opening the door Mrs. Jebb, a plump, pleasant-looking woman, appeared from the back regions where she had been busy with some household task. She, too, looked very surprised as she greeted Mr. Spencer and looked with even more surprise at the tall figure of Bobby in the background. She evidently assumed that Mr. Spencer's visit was to her, not to her daughter. He had to explain in a somewhat apologetic tone that there was reason to think Miss Jebb might be able to give some useful information about the murder that had taken place in the town the previous night. No doubt they had heard of it.

Miss Jebb said of course. Nobody could talk of anything else, the war for once forgotten, even a good supply of fish in the shops less thrilling than usual. Mrs. Jebb said tartly how could Janet know anything about it?

Mr. Spencer tried to suggest tactfully that he and his companion, whom he now introduced as the deputy chief constable of Wychshire, thought it might be better if they saw Miss Jebb alone. Mrs. Jebb bristled. She said with cold indignation that she thought Janet would prefer her mother to be present. She could not imagine what anyone could possibly suppose Janet knew, and she gave Bobby a very nasty look; evidently blaming him for this unmannerly intrusion, of which she was convinced Mr. Spencer, an old friend of her late husband, would never have been guilty.

So, as there was no way short of main force to prevent the determined lady from joining them, they followed her meekly into a small nearby room, originally, no doubt, intended for a breakfast-room, once used by the late Mr. Jebb as a study, and still bearing signs of former masculine occupation. They were evidently now considered unworthy of the drawing-room. In a distinctly hostile tone, Mrs. Jebb began the conversation.

"Perhaps,' she said coldly, "you will explain your reasons for supposing that Janet knows anything about this affair. I don't think you had ever even spoken to the poor man, had you, Janet?"

"I just knew him by sight and where he lived," the girl explained. "Everyone knows everybody in Oldfordham."

"Yes, of course, quite so," agreed Mr. Spencer.

"Well?" said Mrs. Jebb defiantly.

Mr. Spencer, feeling very uncomfortable, for he valued his popularity in the town, and saw it now exposed to the wrath of an offended mother—of which, beware —looked pleadingly at Bobby. Coming to his rescue, Bobby said:

"A statement has been made to us that Miss Jebb was seen a short time ago trying to enter Mr. Brown's cottage."

"What?" said Mrs. Jebb.

"Me?" said Miss Jebb.

"Fiddlesticks," said Mrs. Jebb in a voice like an exploding bomb.

"Oh, I never," said Miss Jebb. "Why should I?"

"You must please understand," Bobby said, "that we are merely inquiring into a statement made by a witness who claims actually to have seen Miss Jebb trying to open the back door of the cottage."

"Who told you such nonsense?" demanded Mrs. Jebb, all afire with the lust of battle.

"I am afraid we can't tell you at present," Bobby said. "Such a statement is confidential and privileged unless and until it's been tested. Miss Jebb, I understand, says there's no truth in it."

"Certainly not, it's silly," declared the girl.

"You have been out, I think, just returned? Do you mind saying where you've been?"

"In High Street. I had some shopping to do. Why <lo you ask?"

"Well, we shall have to try to clear it up," Bobby said. "At present we have a direct statement by a person claiming to have been an eye-witness, and we have your denial. That's where we've got to leave it for the time. Of course, it would have been more satisfactory if you could have told us you had been somewhere at the other end of the town or with a friend all the time you were out. We can only deal with facts. The story told us, your denial, and the further fact that you were in the neighbourhood at the time."

"Do you dare to suggest—" began Mrs. Jebb and choked. "Will you please leave my house immediately?"

"Mother, they had to ask, hadn't they?" interposed Miss Jebb mildly. "If somebody told them that about me, they had to say so."

"They ought," said Mrs. Jebb, unplacated, "to have known better. Someone's been making fools of them." She managed to indicate, very clearly, that this, in her opinion, was a matter of no great difficulty. "Utter fools," she repeated with relish.

Mr. Spencer started to stammer apologies—quite uselessly. Bobby interposed to ask if Mr. Kayes was in. Mr. Spencer, glad of the interruption, wiped a perspiring forehead. Mrs. Jebb said with infinite scorn in her voice:

"No, he isn't. Has someone seen him trying to get in at someone's back door?"

"Not that we know of," answered Bobby equably, "but there are one or two points on which he may be able to help us. Could you tell us when he is likely to be in?"

"No," snapped Mrs. Jebb and this time her voice indicated clearly that if she did know she wouldn't tell.

The two men took their leave then from a still fiercely indignant Mrs. Jebb, from a still extremely puzzled Miss Jebb, and the last thing they heard as the door was closing behind them was Mrs. Jebb's loud, clear voice, saying:

"Well, of all the impudence, of all the idiots—"

"She meant us to hear that," said Mr. Spencer unhappily.

"She did," agreed Bobby. "Very much so."

"I suppose you can't wonder she was annoyed," sighed Mr. Spencer, knowing well he had now a bitter and implacable enemy whose tongue would never cease till she had made life intolerable for him in Oldfordham's small and pleasant town.

"Was it only anger?" Bobby mused aloud. "Or was there fear as well?"

"Fear?" repeated Mr. Spencer, astonished. "Fear? What of?" He paused and stared, standing still. "You can't possibly mean," he gasped, "you suspect Janet Jebb of being mixed up in—in a murder?"

"I always suspect everybody," Bobby answered. "Why, I'm fully prepared to suspect you or the vicar of St. Barnabas or anyone else."

Mr. Spencer grunted. Privately he considered this remark in poor taste. He began to walk on. He said: "Personally I would as soon suspect Janet Jebb as—well, as the little Foote girl."

"So would I," agreed Bobby promptly, and Mr. Spencer gave him a startled glance.

"You don't mean—" he began.

"Only what I say," Bobby assured him. "I never mean more than that. It pays," he observed thoughtfully, "just to say what you mean, neither more nor less, it puzzles people. They keep trying to guess what they think you might mean, and sometimes it starts things moving. It's almost, but not quite, as good as saying nothing at all."

Mr. Spencer considered this. He wasn't sure he agreed. He was trying to formulate his objections when a small boy dashed up to them.

"Oh, please," he gasped excitedly. "Pop's upside down in a tree and he's stuck and he can't get down and please come quick."

CHAPTER IX
ILLUSION AND REALITY

BOBBY GRABBED the boy by the collar. Experience, even bitter experience, had taught him to beware of small boys. A deadly breed. He said:

"What's that? What do you mean? Trying to be funny?"

"It's Ted Allen," Mr. Spencer said. "Allen's on duty outside Brown's cottage."

"It's my dad," protested the boy, beginning to cry. "It ain't funny, upsides in a tree."

Bobby released the lad and began to run. Apparently something had happened. Mr. Spencer followed, the less swiftly as he was the more portly. The youthful Ted Allen had, however, taken a too pessimistic view of his unfortunate parent's predicament, for when Bobby arrived on the scene Constable Allen was once again right side up on terra firma, though his helmet, perched coquettishly on one of the branches of a nearby tree, offered circumstantial evidence of the truth of his son's story. Now, truncheon drawn, Constable Allen was advancing on the cottage, his expression firm, for he knew his duty, his knees unsteady, for his recent arboreal experience had not been reassuring. It was with a very considerable and very natural relief that he saw reinforcements arriving in the shape of Bobby at a run, Mr. Spencer in the distance, his own small son pounding along between them, the boy's short legs unable to keep pace with Bobby's long ones, but his lesser weight helping him to outdistance Mr. Spencer.

"He's in there," Allen said as Bobby joined him, his watchful eye upon the cottage door.

"Stand by," Bobby said and threw the door open.

Within, Duke Dell was standing, his hands clasped before him in an attitude Bobby later on grew to know as characteristic, his huge bulk even more noticeable in the small cottage kitchen it almost seemed he filled from floor to ceiling, from wall to wall. He gave Bobby's quick and violent entry an uninterested glance but did not move or speak, returning as it seemed to the rapt meditation in which he appeared to be sunk.

"What are you doing here?" Bobby demanded.

Duke Dell looked up mildly. He seemed a little puzzled at first, as if recalled so abruptly from his own thoughts he had not fully grasped Bobby's question. Then he said, speaking slowly and as gently as his naturally loud reverberating tones permitted:

"Is it true what I have heard? Is it true that our Brother Brown has been called hence by unlawful violence?"

"Unlawful violence," snorted Allen from behind. "What about throwing a bloke up in a tree?"

Mr. Spencer arrived, followed by small Ted Allen, who had till now been hesitating in the doorway.

"Now then, now then," panted Mr. Spencer, too much out of breath to say more.

"That's him, I saw him, I did," piped up Ted. "He put my dad upsides in a tree, so he did, I saw him."

"You cut off home," ordered his father, finding unprofitable this renewed insistence upon detail. "Off you go now. Quick."

Ted fled instanter before a large and threatening paternal hand. His father banged the door and turned a hostile but still wary eye upon Duke Dell. Even at odds of three to one—counting Mr. Spencer as one which only a strong sense of discipline allowed Allen to do— Duke Dell looked a formidable proposition. Allen said:

"He come up and I said: 'Move on, please,' and he said: 'I want to go in,' and I said: 'Well, you can't, no one can't,' and he up and took a hold of me before I knew it and there I was in that old beech tree out there, wrong way up, and my neck broken as like as not, only it wasn't, which I then got down and was proceeding to effect arrest when you gentlemen came along."

"Is it true," asked Duke Dell, ignoring this long complaint, "that Brother Brown has been called hence by another's violence? So I was told as I spoke on the green of Lainham village. I returned in haste to learn the truth."

"Is it the fact you assaulted my constable?" demanded Mr. Spencer.

"When that man would have hindered me, I dealt with him as I was guided," answered Duke Dell calmly.

"Oh, you did, did you?" snorted Mr. Spencer. "Do you realize that you have committed an offence for which you can be fined or imprisoned or both?"

"Those who have seen the Vision," Duke Dell answered as calmly as before, "can commit no offence."

"What do you mean?" demanded Spencer, impressed even against his will and reason by the simple certitude with which this was said.

"He's crazy," said Allen from behind. "That's where he gets his strength. There's no fairness in it, a lunatic madman against a sane man."

"You make a big claim there, Mr. Dell," Bobby said. "When the Vision has come, you claim nothing," Duke Dell answered. "Then all is yours."

"I don't know what you are talking about," Spencer said peevishly. "What vision? What's vision got to do with it?"

For the first time Duke Dell showed some signs of interest, even of animation.

"That is what I am here to tell those who have ears to listen," he answered. "Have you?" he demanded abruptly.

"The fellow's off his head," said Mr. Spencer despairingly.

"Mr. Dell," interposed Bobby, "will you please tell us what you know of Brown?"

"You have not told me yet if what I heard is true?" Dell countered.

"Mr. Brown was found late last night," Bobby answered, "or rather early this morning, lying dead with his head battered in. There was nothing to show who was the murderer. The poker had been used."

"It is well," Duke Dell said slowly, as if indeed musing aloud. "It is very well. For his call came after he had seen the Vision and now he knows the truth and now he can never deny it. To deny the Vision is the only sin that those who have seen it can ever sin and for it there can be no forgiveness. So now is Alfred Brown saved for evermore and it is well."

"Oh, is it?" snorted Allen in the background. "Been and done it himself as like as not and that's why he thinks it a bit of all right."

"Will you tell us," Bobby asked again, "anything, everything, you know about him? When did you first meet? Did you know him before you came here?"

"Till I came here I had never seen him. I spoke one evening in the old market place before his home. Many listened and scoffed as is the way of those who hear things they do not wish to believe or to understand. Many listened not, as is the way of those who care not neither do they heed. But after I had spoken Brother Brown came to me and we had much talk, and I wrestled greatly to expound to him the Vision. He was much troubled in his mind and he fought hard against me. There was that in his life that held him back."

"What was it?" Bobby asked quickly.

"He did not tell me nor did I ask," Duke Dell explained. "The past is nothing. It was and it is not. It is now that matters, for Now is the appointed time."

"Religious mania," said Mr. Spencer with an air of relief, for now he felt he knew it all.

"That ain't no reason for what he done to me," grumbled Allen.

"Was it because of what you said to him that Brown began to interfere with the services at St. Barnabas?" Bobby asked.

"It was rather a way by which he sought to escape the burden of the truth I laid upon him," Dell answered. "He sought to escape me in the Church. A poor escape, a weak refuge, poor and weak indeed."

"Blasphemy now," commented Allen, a choir member of long standing. "Assaulting an officer in the discharge of his duty and now it's blasphemy."

"The Church gave him nothing for it had nothing to give," Dell went on. "A blind alley, leading nowhere. But Brother Brown was greatly troubled, in great distress of mind, troubled again when he found practices in church which he called Romish or popish and he thought wrong. I warned him that none of all that, popish or Romish or anything else, mattered; nothing except the Vision that is high above all such little paltry matters, above all forms or laws or ceremony."

"Above the law?" asked Mr. Spencer. "You said above all laws?"

"The Vision is the only law for those to whom it is given," Dell answered tranquilly. "For them no other law exists or could exist."

"Well, we know where we are with you, anyhow," observed Mr. Spencer, eyeing him doubtfully. "But you may find the law does exist all the same, vision or none."

"What did Brown say that made you think there was something in his past that troubled him?" Bobby asked.

Duke Dell waved the question aside with some impatience.

"I forget, I paid no attention," he said. "I did not ask. It was of no interest or importance. Had he done murder or worse, what was that to him or me if I could lead him to the Vision? Yet it hindered and held him, whatever it was, this memory from the past. He was troubled too by thought of some sacrifice he would have to make, something he valued and that he possessed but seemed to fear he would have to give up. He feared the Vision. He feared it greatly. He feared it would compel him to remember, compel him to give up what he so much valued. That was well, for fear of the Vision is the first step. Fear of the Vision is the beginning of seeing it. So it came. Of all those to whom I have spoken, he was the first to whom it came." Duke Dell drew himself to the full of his great height so that his head just touched the low ceiling beam, he held out his arms as if in a huge embrace, he glowed with the fire of the intensity of his emotion and his belief. It was as though he had been rapt into another world. He lifted his hands. In the harsh, strained whisper Bobby had heard him use before, he said: "I think that it is coming now."

"Look out, sir," muttered Allen. "He'll be going for us next. Clean off his nut."

Slowly Dell lowered his hands, his tense muscles relaxed, he seemed to shrink as it were and he trembled slightly.

"It did not come," he said. "I thought—I hoped. But there was nothing. It faded, faded." He looked darkly at Mr. Spencer, without interest at Allen, more darkly still at Bobby. "It was your presence prevented it," he said. "But for you it would have come. Your mind is evil and worldly and unbelieving, and so how could it come?"

"Assaulting a police officer in the execution of his duty," commented Allen bitterly. "Blasphemy next and now it's using insulting language."

"You think I frightened away whatever it is you think you see?" Bobby asked. "Doesn't say much for it, does it? Looks as if I am the stronger. Is that it?"

Dell seemed a little puzzled by this, as if he had been presented with a new idea he did not quite know what to make of. He began to speak and then paused, uncertain how to continue. Finally he said:

"Nothing can be stronger than the Vision."

"Well, it seems T am," Bobby suggested, "since apparently it cleared off when it saw me. Of course, I haven't the least idea what you are talking about. If Brown had seen it, whatever it is, how could he deny it? Why should he, for that matter, if he had really seen it?"

"He doubted," Dell said. "Doubt is worse than denial. He told someone he knew about it and he was told in return that he had been drinking too much. That was true in a way."

"Who was it told him that?" Bobby asked; and asked eagerly, for he thought the answer might be useful.

But Dell shook his head.

"I never asked and he never said," he replied. "One he had known a long time and who had great influence over him. I know no more. All that was nothing to me, but when I found he doubted what he had seen, I wrestled greatly with him, for I was full of fear for him. I brought him at last to understand that never could any amount of drink have produced or created what he saw. Yet he was not wholly safe. Those who once begin to doubt never are safe. The grain of doubt is always there. There is always the danger that it may sprout again. So for his sake I rejoice—and greatly—that he has been called hence to where he will be for ever in its presence."

"If that's the way you look at it," Mr. Spencer said, "if you think it's such a good thing, what has happened, did you take care that it did happen?"

The question seemed to puzzle Duke Dell, as if he did not fully grasp its meaning.

"How do you mean? In what way?" he asked; and now his voice seemed more natural, more human, his tone less exalted. "How could I?"

"Was it you killed him?" demanded Spencer bluntly.

"Oh no," Dell answered. "Why should I? Did I kill him to make him safe, is that what you mean? I never thought of that."

"You might have done it if you had thought of it?" Spencer insisted.

"It would have needed much consideration," Duke Dell said seriously. "If guidance had come—but I don't think it likely. No. It is one thing to lead back the strayed, even to compel them; another thing altogether to use violence."

"You nearly killed him at Chipping Up, didn't you?" Mr. Spencer pressed.

"Not knowingly, not willingly," Duke Dell answered. "If it had happened so, then guidance would have been clear. But it didn't." He paused, looking more troubled, more disturbed than he had ever seemed before. "I must go now," he said. "You have troubled me. And I need rest and quiet. When the Vision nearly comes but not altogether, as just now, then you get the test, the trial, the exhaustion, but there is no revival of strength to follow. I must go," he repeated.

He moved towards the door, but there, his back to it, firm, courageous, determined, and badly scared, was Constable Allen. In a voice that shook a little but which all the same contrived to be resolute as well he said:

'No, you don't, not till Mr. Spencer says."

With unexpected meekness, Duke Dell turned.

"I must have rest and quiet; quiet, that's what I want. I will go upstairs to rest there if you like."

He went stumblingly and heavily up the stairs while the other three watched him with astonishment. Helplessly Mr. Spencer turned to Bobby.

"What do you make of that?" he asked. "Religious mania? Can we get him certified?"

"I don't think so," Bobby answered. "Not a chance. No doctor would call him irresponsible. All he says is quite coherent."

"Well, what is it?" Spencer asked. "Hypocrisy? Humbug?"

"Neither," Bobby said. "It's much too dangerous, too formidable, to be either one or the other."

"You don't think it's real, genuine? I mean all the talk about this Vision of his? You can't swallow that, can you? You don't believe it's real?"

"There's an old question," Bobby said. "As old as man. What is real? Don't they teach in India that all is illusion, Maya?"

"No illusion about Brown being murdered," retorted Spencer crossly; and in an undertone not meant to be heard but that Bobby's sharp ears picked up, Constable Allen said disgustedly:

"He's gone balmy, too. Catching, that's what it is." Bobby would have liked to agree to this last remark, but he gave no sign of having heard. Instead he said: "Oh yes, no delusion about the murder, but there's a difference between illusion and delusion. Duke Dell has certainly had some sort of mental experience. The question is: objective or subjective? I suppose in a sense both are equally real. Obviously, a dream is real in the sense that you have really had it. And it may really affect what you do, which may be real enough."

"Yes, but, hang it all," retorted Spencer. "Where does all that get us?"

"Isn't the question rather where did all that get Duke Dell, if anywhere?" Bobby suggested. "Even if Dell's Vision he talks about is mere imagination, mere imagination may have material results. Dell told us one or two things of interest though. What he says accounts in a very subtle and interesting way for Brown's outbursts at St. Barnabas, as an effort to escape from some old fear or memory Dell's preaching had started up again. Our next job is to get to know what it was and if it has anything to do with his murder. Then there's this old friend he visited. Important to get to know who. May be the key to everything. And apparently he talked about some possession of his he valued but might have to give up. What was that? None of his possessions seem specially valuable."

"Except that wireless set," Mr. Spencer said, looking at it longingly. "He seems to have got New York on it as easily as Home Service. Nothing else."

"Do you think there's any chance," Bobby suggested, "that there's something hidden somewhere here that hasn't been found yet? Something like the key of a deposit safe in Midwych? Or his bank book? Anything like that? There is nothing to show how he lived and he must have had something."

"Well, the whole place has been gone over pretty thoroughly," Mr. Spencer said.

"Yes, I know," agreed Bobby, "one can see that—very skilful, very careful search. Obviously. But did your men think of testing the floors or—or the water butt or anything like that, or under the roof? No reason why they should. I'm sure I wouldn't in their place. But that's the sort of thing I'm thinking about now."

CHAPTER X
TREASURE HUNT

MR. SPENCER LOOKED doubtful. In spite of all Bobby's tactful praise of the efficiency of the search conducted by his men, he felt slightly resentful of the suggestion that something of great value might have been overlooked. Besides, in these days of safe deposits, banks, and so on, why should anyone hide valuables in a cottage ill-secured itself and of necessity left unoccupied during its solitary tenant's frequent absences?

He hesitated still and Constable Allen remarked that the crowd outside was getting larger every minute. Some of the bolder spirits were even trying to peep through the windows. The tale of the policeman upside down in the old beech tree had spread already through half the town; and even those who could not believe such a story, too wild even for these so generally topsy-turvy days, were thronging hither to see for themselves. And there was at least a helmet poised high upon a lofty branch as circumstantial evidence that for once at any rate rumour did not wholly lie. The appearance of a still living Allen from the cottage was something of an anti-climax, since his death, or at the very least a broken back, had been widely assumed. A reasonable supposition, for what else but death is likely to separate a policeman from his helmet?

But the helmet retrieved and restored to its accustomed resting-place and thus Constable Allen once more, so to say, clothed with the majesty of the law, he reasserted himself to such good purpose, with such zeal and vigour in the exertion of the familiar 'move on' technique, that soon the situation outside the cottage became 'fluid,' as the war reports say. Only a small, decreasing and ever-changing body of spectators remained to stare and gape and gossip.

Within, the search continued with energy and keen scrutiny, though with no very great hope even on Bobby's part, and with none at all on Mr. Spencer's.

"You don't expect," he grumbled, "a murder case to turn into a treasure hunt."

"In my experience," Bobby told him, "a murder case may lead anywhere. Of course, there are the simple cases of murder from passion when some wretched man comes to tell us he has done in his girl because he couldn't stand it any longer, the way she was carrying on. But a deliberate and thought out, planned murder like this is in itself so unnatural and strange that there may be almost anything behind. Murder is a greater mystery in and by itself than any explanation for it; it's so alien, so unfamiliar. I suppose that is why it is also in its way—well, fascinating."

"It's unnatural and unfamiliar in Oldfordham anyhow," grumbled Spencer, "and I wish to God it had stayed so. What about the bedroom? Shall we try that next? Duke Dell's still there, isn't he?"

By now, as they had chatted, they had given the back room, crowded with all sorts of discarded rubbish, a thorough examination which had convinced them both that there was nothing there of any interest. They had tested the ceiling, the walls, the floor boards, equally without results. They went on to the bedroom, where Duke Dell lay motionless on the bed, his eyes wide open, his hands clasped before him, but as it seemed rapt away from all knowledge of his surroundings into some strange far off world of meditation. Only his wide, staring, unseeing eyes, an occasionally faint movement of his lips showed that he still lived, for indeed there was something not normal, unnatural, about the extreme rigidity of his body. Of their entrance he took no notice, even if he were aware of it. With some idea of testing this extreme abstraction from all things around, Spencer said loudly:

"He tells us he thinks it is a good thing it happened. In my view that suggests he made it happen."

"It's a possibility," Bobby agreed.

Duke Dell took no notice. He might not have heard. Perhaps he had not. Bobby turned his attention to the ceiling. Nothing to suggest that it had ever been touched since it had first been put up.

At any rate the accumulated grime of years provided satisfactory proof that it had not been disturbed recently. Bobby tested the walls, equally without result. They were far too thin and flimsy for any hiding place to have been found practicable there. The partition wall between this room and the other was of the thinnest lath and plaster. He gave his attention next to the chimney, equally without result. In order presumably to stop what some call ventilation and others a draught, the iron flap at the bottom of the chimney had been drawn down and had long since rusted into position. Quite impossible to raise it now without the use of tools. He turned his attention to the floor, covered only partially by an old and threadbare carpet, though by the side of the bed lay a good Persian rug that was certainly worth twenty or thirty pounds and that made an odd contrast with most of the rest of the furnishing. Threadbare carpet and Persian rug Bobby rolled up; and on his hands and knees, heedless of trousers and of how few clothing coupons he still possessed, proceeded to examine each floorboard in turn. Presently he said:

"Look at this."

He had found one board which showed signs of having been taken up and then replaced. There were a few tools in the kitchen below. Bobby went to fetch them, returning with hammer, screwdriver, and a very blunt chisel. With their aid he lifted the board. Beneath, there was a canvas bag, and then another and another in a long row. Bobby lifted the first one and opened it. The dim light from the curtained and grimy window showed a shining, glittering contents.

"Gold," Bobby said. "Sovereigns." He took out a handful. He repeated: "Sovereigns. I don't believe I've seen the things before. I may have when I was a child but I don't remember."

Mr. Spencer was staring, wide-eyed, open-mouthed, dumb with amazement. All he could do was to gasp and to stare and he was not far from pinching himself to make sure he was not dreaming. Bobby lifted out the other bags one by one. He opened each in turn, weighed it in his hands, put it with the others till there stood together, side by side, twenty and one. When he had made sure that all had been removed from their hiding place, he counted the contents of the first he had opened. It held two hundred of the shining, yellow counters that in the past, before the German curse had blasted the world, before the evil Teutonic fury had devastated man, had seemed the very symbol of the permanence of things.

"Two hundred," Bobby said. "Judging by their weight, all the bags hold the same. That means four thousand two hundred in all and a sovereign is worth nearly double to-day. Say, £8,000 at the present price of gold. Brown seems to have been spending somewhere about £200 or so a year. That means this little lot would have lasted him forty years."

"But ... I mean to say ... well, why did he? What was the idea?" demanded Spencer. He sounded really indignant. "I mean ... well, even in consols he could have got that much interest and kept his capital all the same."

"So he could," agreed Bobby, but thoughtfully, not indignantly. "Yes, so he could, couldn't he? But he didn't. Why?"

"Of course," said Mr. Spencer, thinking with melancholy resignation of his own salary, comfortable on paper, exiguous after the tax collector had passed that way, "he did save income tax."

On the bed, Duke Dell roused himself from his far-off abstracted mood. He lifted himself on one elbow. He said:

"That evil yellow stuff must be what troubled our brother's mind so greatly. It may well be the young man I saw here one night knew of it and that is why he came."

"Who was it?" Bobby asked.

"He told me he was in the air force. I don't think he was in uniform. I am not sure. I do not think I noticed. It was getting dark at the time. I had come because I wished to talk with Brother Brown. There wasn't any answer when I knocked, but I could hear someone in the kitchen. I tried the door. It wasn't locked and I went in. There was a young man there. He said he was waiting for Brown, but he couldn't stop any longer and he asked me to say he had been. He said his name was Kayes, I think. A name like that. When I told Brother Brown, he was troubled again, and I thought he knew who it was and why he had come. He said he was sure he had locked the door when he left, so how could anyone get in?"

"Not much difficulty about that," Bobby remarked, thinking of the flimsy window-fastenings, the cheap locks on both front and back doors.

They asked a few more questions but Duke Dell had nothing more to tell.

"When I saw all that gold," he said, "I knew what Brother Brown feared he must give up now that he had seen the Vision, and why he wished to believe that it was untrue, unreal, and he could deny it."

"Why should he give up his money because of something he thought he had seen?" Bobby asked.

"For those who have seen," Duke Dell answered, "nothing else ever matters—not that yellow stuff or anything."

"Well, I suppose you would still want something to live on, wouldn't you?" Bobby asked.

Duke Dell waved this consideration aside. He apparently did not even think it worth an answer.

"Anyhow, we know the motive now," Mr. Spencer said. "That was my difficulty. Why should anyone want to murder a man like Brown? Quiet, inoffensive, harmless as possible, no woman in the case, why should anyone want to get rid of him? Now we know."

"If it was that, why murder at all? Why not robbery?" Bobby asked. "The house seems to have been left empty for one day, at least, every week. Easy enough to break in. Put the stuff near the door ready for removal. Bring up a car, throw the stuff in, and be off at full speed before even the next-door neighbours have a chance to do anything. All as simple as pie. Only—if the murderer killed for the sake of the gold, why did he leave it all behind?"

"Most likely he didn't know where it was hidden, couldn't find it," Spencer suggested.

"Not much difficulty about that," Bobby retorted. "Anyone who knew it was somewhere here, couldn't help finding it. Twenty-one bags full of gold take some hiding. Not like a few bank notes or a safe deposit key. If you kill a man for the sake of a lot of gold sovereigns you know he has hidden, surely you look for them."

"Panic?" suggested Spencer. "When he saw what he had done, when he realized it, he lost his head and bolted."

"That is possible," agreed Bobby, "but I don't think it's very likely. If it was known about the gold, and the murder motive was to get hold of it, then that means the murder was planned and deliberate, and that rather seems to exclude panic, doesn't it? No signs to suggest panic, either."

As they talked they busied themselves securing the bags again and now they began to carry them downstairs, ready for removal to safe custody. Duke Dell for some time seemed to have lost all interest in these proceedings. Now he began to move towards the door, still completely ignoring the others. Spencer called him back, speaking sharply.

"What are you doing? Where are you going?" he demanded.

"I am going back home," Dell answered. "Here there is no more for me to do."

"I haven't made up my mind about you yet," Spencer said severely. "You've been guilty of assault. You are liable to prosecution—fine or prison."

"You can let me know about that," Duke Dell said indifferently. "I can tell of the Vision in prison as well as out."

With that, he went away. Spencer grunted discontentedly. He wanted badly to see Duke Dell prosecuted and fined for his outrageous behaviour, but had an uncomfortable feeling that Dell would get off very lightly. Possible even that his feat of strength in throwing a full-sized policeman over his head might arouse an unreasonable admiration, and, in any case, would add little to the prestige of the Oldfordham police. Others might be tempted to try. As for a murder charge, and that possibility was very much in his mind, so far he felt there was too little to take action on. It was a point of view Bobby strongly supported.

"We don't know anything like enough to act on yet," Bobby said. "It's a safe guess that when Brown went to Midwych on his weekly visits, he took a few sovereigns. Anyone would be glad to buy them. Gold still has prestige all right. A lump of gold is still what Macaulay would have called a 'semper eadem.' But that floorboard upstairs hasn't been lifted recently, so where did his weekly allowance come from? I don't suppose he ever sold more than a few at a time. He evidently wanted to avoid attention and too big a sale might have started someone wondering and asking questions."

"You think there may be more bags hidden?"

"One bag, I should say," Bobby answered. "My guess is he took out one bag and used it a little at a time till it was empty. What about another look round down here? What's a likely hiding place?"

Mr. Spencer directed a rather helpless glance round the kitchen.

"What about the oven?" he suggested. "You do hear of people keeping notes in an oven and getting them burnt up, but gold would be all right. Or there may be a tin box somewhere."

"There's the water-butt," Bobby remarked. "But that's outside. There's the cistern but that's outside, too. We'll have a look, though. Or the floor again. Or the hearth. But that doesn't look as if it had ever been moved."

He was prowling about the room as he talked, looking here, there, and everywhere. Opportunities for hiding-places seemed rare. He noticed a bag of artificial manure in one corner, a large bag. He remembered that the small strip of garden in front was both small and neglected. Behind the cottage was only a paved yard.

"Brown hadn't an allotment anywhere, had he?" Bobby asked.

"No. Not that I know of. Why?"

"Well, I was only wondering—why the artificial manure and so much of it?" Bobby explained.

He opened the bag and thrust his hand down in the fertilizer within. At once he felt something. He drew out yet another small canvas bag, this time one only, partly filled. He emptied it on the table. Some fifty or sixty sovereigns rolled out. But there was still something left within. Bobby took it out. It was a foolscap envelope endorsed, 'My last will and testament.' Bobby handed it to Mr. Spencer. "I think you might open it and have a look," he said. "Don't you? It may give us a pointer. Perhaps this young Kayes comes into it. It's odd the way he keeps turning up."

Mr. Spencer opened the envelope, and drew out a paper. Glancing at it, he said:

"Very short. Properly drawn up, I think." He read aloud: "Everything of which I may die possessed to Maurice Goodman, retired solicitor, of Four Oaks, near Chipping Up, Wychshire." He put the paper down and stared at Bobby. "What do you make of that?" he demanded.

CHAPTER XI
SURPRISE LEGACY

MR. SPENCER'S DESIRE to know what Bobby made of so unexpected a development, remained unsatisfied. For Bobby made nothing of it at all. So he said nothing and thus greatly impressed Mr. Spencer who thought that Bobby must be too busy thinking it all out, to have words to spare. Mr. Spencer suggested that perhaps there was some relationship between Goodman and Brown, though if so it was odd that as far as was known there had never been any intercourse between the two men. Bobby, always a believer in the direct approach, said he supposed the best thing to do would be to ask Mr. Goodman to explain.

First of all, however, the two of them conveyed the bags of gold to the Oldfordham police station for safe custody till morning when the money could be deposited in the care of one of the banks. That accomplished, they proceeded to Four Oaks, where, when they arrived, Miss Foote came tripping, bright-eyed and smiling, to open the door for them.

"How nice," she said, switching on the full battery of her charms, "but I don't suppose it's poor little me you've come to see. It's Mr. Goodman you want, isn't it?"

Mr. Spencer said gallantly that if they had come to please themselves, it would undoubtedly have been to see her. Unfortunately, business, even serious business, had brought them, and so it was in fact Mr. Goodman they had to interview.

Miss Foote dimpled and said he was a naughty man to talk like that; and of course they knew, didn't they, that Mr. Goodman had retired and now never undertook legal business or gave advice? But she would let him know of their arrival if they would wait a moment or two in the drawing-room into which she now ushered them. Then she gave another of her bewitching smiles and sidelong glances to Bobby, thereby subtly managing to convey to him that though a girl had to be nice to the middle-aged, it was those who combined comparative youth with a settled position who were really interesting.

"Charming little thing," said Mr. Spencer when she had left them, and he straightened his tie while wondering if he could spare enough coupons to buy a new one.

"Does she live here, do you know?" Bobby asked.

Mr. Spencer plainly thought the question indiscreet.

"Nasty-minded people," he said severely, "have been talking, I know. But surely a man of Mr. Goodman's age—sixty, if he's a day—" Mr. Spencer paused and looked complacent; for he was only forty-five, and the difference between forty-five and sixty seemed to him as the difference between noon-tide and the chill of falling night. He added: "Besides, Mrs. Fuller, the cook, is a most respectable woman. I believe Miss Foote acts as housekeeper as well as secretary."

Bobby made no comment, though privately he was of the opinion of the London magistrate who thought that housekeeper was a word that covered many sinners. No business of his though; and, following his usual custom, he began to look attentively round the room to see what indications he could gather of the character and habits of its inmates. Little enough. Probably everything had been supplied for a lump sum by one of the big Midwych furnishing firms. Conventional to a degree, and what better mask for secrecy than a strict and careful conventionality. That is, if there are secrets to hide, but then, there may be none. For, of course, convention can also very well hide nothing but itself. The door opened and Mr. Goodman came in. Bobby noticed at once that he looked pale and worried. He was evidently uneasy, there was a nervous twitching at the corner of his left eye Bobby did not think had been there before, he had developed a way of starting and listening to any unusual sound, to his two visitors he seemed to give but half his attention, as though their unexpected visit interested him little. Once he even rose in the midst of Mr. Spencer's apologies for troubling him, and went to the door and opened it abruptly, as if he suspected someone might be listening there.

"I thought I heard a knock at the front door," he explained, apologetically—and not very convincingly. "Miss Foote said she was going to Mrs. Cox's down the road and Mrs. Fuller is busy somewhere."

He offered them cigarettes, recommending them as being of a special and very excellent Balkan brand. Unobtainable now, he said, but he was able to get a few from time to time from an old friend and former client, who had been in the habit of importing them privately and still had a stock. Then he went off to the room he called his study at the back of the house to fetch drinks, he said. Returning with whisky and soda, he remarked that he took it their call was in connection with the information he had given the Wychshire deputy chief about the Chipping Up disturbance. But he didn't think there was anything else he could tell them. All he knew was the phone message from the Chipping Up post office he had thought it well to pass on. Was there any connection between Chipping Up and the Oldfordham tragedy that had taken place later?

"If it's a coincidence, it's a curious one," opined Mr. Goodman, shaking a doubtful head.

"There's precious little to go on so far," Mr. Spencer told him. "But in going through the house we found Brown's will."

"His will?" repeated Mr. Goodman as he asked them both to say 'when.' "His will? Had he property to leave? I understood he lived in a very poor way. It's not a will I drew up when I was in practice, is it?"

"Apparently the estate will amount to somewhere about eight thousand pounds," said Mr. Spencer.

Mr. Goodman turned and stared. Soda he was adding to the whisky he had poured out, splashed unheeded on the tray. He looked utterly bewildered, incredulous even.

"What?" he said. "What? Oh, that's impossible."

"It's quite true," Mr. Spencer assured him.

Mr. Goodman continued to stare. It seemed as if he still found it difficult to believe what he was told, and for the first time he seemed to forget those preoccupations—fears perhaps—which, till now, had appeared to prevent him from giving his two visitors his full attention.

"Impossible," he repeated. "He couldn't ... not Brown ... how could he? What makes you think ...? There must be some mistake. ..."

"Pretty solid mistake," said Mr. Spencer cheerfully. "The deputy chief and I had quite a job handling it. It's gold—sovereigns."

As if the weight of this information was altogether too much for him, Mr. Goodman collapsed into the nearest chair. His florid, flushed face, flushed even a deeper hue.

"Sovereigns," he repeated stammeringly. "Sovereigns—gold?"

"Twenty-one canvas bags," Mr. Spencer told him. "Each of them has about two hundred sovereigns in it. A sovereign is worth about double what it used to be, so that means £8,000 or thereabouts. A tidy little sum. It's all left to you. You are sole legatee and executor."

Mr. Goodman gaped, stared, and now the blood ebbed slowly away from his face, leaving it deathly pale.

"Me? Are you sure?" he stammered. "It can't be ... it's impossible."

"We were as surprised as you are, when we found it," Mr. Spencer said.

But to Bobby it seemed that something more than surprise was shown in Goodman's startled, staring eyes, his trembling hands, the alternate pallor and dark crimson flushes his features showed. Nor was there any trace of the pleased excitement most men would show at the news of an unexpected legacy of £8,000. Deep emotions, indeed, were evidently shaking Goodman through and through, but what they were it was hard to tell. Anger, Bobby thought, and fear, perhaps, or was that only his own imagination? Wild-eyed and staring, Goodman still sat there; and once or twice he put up his hand to his throat, as though he had difficulty in breathing. Then he saw how Bobby's keen eyes were on him, and by what seemed a supreme effort he tried to regain his self-control. He made a gesture towards the whisky and soda on the table near. Mr. Spencer interpreted it correctly and began to fill a glass.

"Bowled you over, eh?" he said smilingly. "I'll make it pretty stiff, shall I?"

The drink did Mr. Goodman good. He began to look less shaken, more normal. He sat for a moment or two with his head in his hands. He muttered:

"That explains ... only why?"

"Explains what?" Bobby asked.

Instead of answering, Goodman, still evidently struggling hard to regain and keep his composure, put out his hand towards the whisky tray. Mr. Spencer anticipated him, filling the glass once more.

"Stiff as you like," Goodman muttered. "You must excuse me—a shock, surprise."

"Explains what?" Bobby asked again, and Goodman gave him a sharp, upward, suspicious glance.

"Explains a lot," Goodman said. "It's restitution—that's what it means. The will I mean. Leaving it all to me. Restitution. It wasn't the name. Browns are common enough. Lots of them. It did just cross my mind it might be the same man when I heard there was a

Brown going about with some itinerant preacher and then all that about listening to a New York concert when he was killed. I didn't take it seriously, just a passing notion. It seemed too improbable. But this business of the legacy makes it clear."

It was now Mr. Spencer's turn to look very bewildered.

"How do you mean?" he asked. "Why restitution? I'm afraid I don't follow at all."

"No, no, of course not," agreed Goodman as he helped himself to yet a third drink, even stiffer than the others. Not that it seemed to have much effect. He drank very slowly, in sips. Between sips, he said: "You must excuse me. Brings back so much. Quite a shock. It must be the same man. A great shock. This money, I mean."

"I only wish," said Mr. Spencer feelingly, "I could have the same sort of shock."

"It's being gold, in sovereigns, that clinches it," Goodman said. He addressed all his remarks to Spencer, but it was Bobby he watched. He went on: "The cunning of it." He paused again, seeming to meditate on this with admiration. The other two waited patiently. "Untraceable. Untraceable. He left the whole lot to me, you say? His way of making restitution, I suppose. Threw me a bit off my balance. Well, what it comes to, is this. It must be the same Brown who was my managing clerk shortly before I gave up my practice in the thirties. I began to suspect he was gambling on the Stock Exchange with my money—I mean, my clients' money in the firm's care. I went into the accounts and I found a deficiency of about £4,000. Brown didn't wait to be questioned. He just disappeared. To the continent first; and afterwards anywhere in the world, or so I supposed. I knew he had a passport. I never thought of his doubling back and establishing himself almost on my doorstep. Cunning again. I told you, it had just crossed my mind lately that this Brown might be my old managing clerk. But not seriously. It seemed too unlikely. It was an old loss, long since written off as a bad debt. Serious, of course, but I was able to stand it."

"I suppose efforts were made to trace Brown?" Bobby asked. "Was a warrant issued?"

"Well, no," Goodman answered. "I preferred to say nothing and stand the loss myself. Severe enough, Lord knows, but not crippling. I had one or two strokes of real luck about the same time.

Compensation. It's often like that. Knock-downs and pick-ups. That's the way it goes. If you keep your head, that is. Frankly, I didn't want to make a fuss or prosecute. It doesn't do you any good if it gets round that your staff has been playing tricks with your clients' money. You're responsible. You're to blame. You ought to have been more careful; more wide awake. It might even be hinted that, perhaps, you had been standing in. At the best, it's your business and your duty to know what's happening to the money your clients have entrusted to you. If you don't, not much to your credit. I accepted the loss as my punishment for what I felt some people would be quick enough to call culpable carelessness—or worse. I had almost forgotten about it—not quite, the loss of a few odd thousand pounds does leave an impression—when I heard that a Mr. Brown, living in Oldfordham, had been talking about me. It did just cross my mind as a bare possibility that it might be my old managing clerk. There were one or two things I noticed. This Oldfordham Brown was said to be keen on music and my old head clerk had been that, too. Knew a lot about it. In a way that brought us together. I expect it made me trust him more completely than I might have done otherwise. I'm no musician but there's nothing I enjoy more than really good music. I got into the way of talking to Brown about it. When we had both been at the Philharmonic the same evening. He taught me a lot. It was he who told me about Sibelius. Made me a Sibelius fan like him. Not many in Midwych. Probably it was because of Sibelius that he was listening to that American concert the paper says he had tuned in to when he was killed. I expect I should have been listening, too, if I had known— and had a short-wave set. It made it all a much greater shock when I found out what he had been up to. Talking music to me and then going off to embezzle my money. Oh, well, you never know, do you? There was the preaching business, too. That sounded a bit like my man. He had religious fits from time to time—religion, music, and embezzlement, what can you make of that? Though his idea of religion seemed to be blaming the Jesuits for everything. Whether it was a railway accident or a war, he was always sure it was the Jesuits again. Exactly like Hitler and the Jews. Used to get very worked up about the Pope, too. He had a very poor opinion of the Pope. All the same, I never really thought it could be the same man.

Impossible, I thought. Incredible he should have the impudence to settle down almost on my doorstep, so to speak."

Bobby and Mr. Spencer had listened to all this with the greatest interest, the closest attention, and now Mr. Spencer shook a wondering head.

"Most interesting," he said. "Most remarkable. It seems we can take it then that Brown left you this money as a sort of making amends. Probably under the influence of this itinerant preacher. Well, well, a kind of 'Chickens coming home to roost,' in reverse. I congratulate you."

"Thank you," said Mr. Goodman. "Yes. Strange how religion can affect a man. I remember how it showed sometimes in the office. I used to try to stop it, all that talk about Jesuits and the rest of it. Really, one thought he would go off his head altogether some day. But I suppose it did help to make me trust him more. That and the music. My only excuse for the carelessness that allowed him to play tricks with my clients' money. Not that they ever knew; and now it all comes back."

"Very nice, too," said Mr. Spencer, still with a touch of envy in his voice as he thought how nice it would be if any such unexpected windfall came his way. "I congratulate you," he said again.

"I must think what to do about it," Mr. Goodman said. "Of course, there'll be heavy death duties. Fortunately, I'm not in need of it for myself. A loss long since written off. Perhaps some Oldfordham charity? You might be able to suggest something? Or some useful public object? A new wing to the cottage hospital? We must think about it. You'll be able to advise me?"

"I shall be delighted," declared Mr. Spencer beamingly, foreseeing all the kudos that would accrue to him as the chosen channel through which this welcome, fructifying stream of gold would be guided and directed.

"It's certainly a strange turn of events," agreed Bobby, "but it doesn't seem to help us very much to identify the murderer."

"No," agreed Spencer, recalled from happy dreams of civic ceremonies in which he would take a leading part; introducing Mr. Goodman, as the munificent donor, to such visiting bigwigs as the Lord Lieutenant of the County, the local M.P., and so on; making on them all a most favourable impression, through his super-efficient, smooth-running arrangements. "No, that's true." His tone suggested that it was also comparatively unimportant. "Still, if a man has a huge sum in gold hidden under his bedroom floor and it gets known—well, I ask you."

"Exactly," said Mr. Goodman. "Very well put. Very clear and convincing. Find out who knew about it and there you have your man."

CHAPTER XII

CONSULTATION

BY THE SKIN of his teeth, Bobby managed to get home before the dinner was entirely spoiled. Just as well, for Olive had succeeded in producing for to-night an unusually good wartime dinner in Britain—tinned soup, dried salt cod, dried egg omelette, dried milk pudding. But then Olive was used, as eels are said to be used to being skinned alive, to dinners that vainly awaited a diner still rushing about on some pressing errand or another that was really a sergeant's or inspector's job, but that in the prevalent shortage of man-power had to be attended to by a deputy chief constable. Gone were those happy days when an important executive simply picked up his phone and gave orders. Now he had to get out and do it himself. In fact, except on pay days, hardly worth while being an important executive at all. Fortunately, for in all things evil there is something good if we do but diligently distil it forth, there was no cook to lose her temper over a ruined dinner and give indignant notice, since not all the newly acquired dignity and prestige of a Mrs. Deputy Chief had availed to secure Olive a specimen of that almost legendary race. Indeed, she had to admit she was exceptionally fortunate in having the services of a resident maid of sixteen who knew nothing and of a daily woman who did nothing.

To Bobby's story of the gold hidden under the cottage bedroom floor, and of the will leaving it all to Mr. Goodman, Olive listened intently.

"If Mr. Goodman knew of the will," she remarked, "and knew everything was left to him, that would explain a good deal, wouldn't it? Because then he would have a reason for the murder and yet he needn't do anything about the gold. He could simply leave it where it was."

But Bobby shook his head.

"Goodman didn't know," he asserted positively. "That's as certain as can be. He was completely bowled over. A shock and not a pleasant one either. He didn't want it and he didn't like having it. Why?"

"Are you sure?" asked Olive doubtfully. "You can't imagine anyone not wanting all that gold. At least, I can't."

"There might be reasons," Bobby said. "He's very much the country gentleman now and perhaps he didn't like the idea of his name being mixed up with a murder case. Another thing. A curious thing. He was scared. I mean before we got there, before he knew about the will. He was badly scared of someone or something. Who? Why?"

"Was anyone there?"

"We saw no one except Miss Foote. There's a cook."

"Good gracious," said Olive, absolutely thunderstruck. "Are you sure? A cook? Well, anyhow, it can't be the cook, can it? Unless she's just given notice; and then he would have told you, and besides a man never minds about a cook till she isn't there. And I suppose it couldn't be Miss Foote?"

"Why not?" asked Bobby thoughtfully, as absent-mindedly he nearly gave himself a second helping of dried salt cod, only he remembered just in time. "I'm not too happy about that young woman," he said. "She had old Spencer where she wanted him all right. But all the time she was flirting her hardest with him, she was giving me the glad eye. Spencer wasn't too pleased. Well, why did she?"

"I simply can't imagine," said Olive, wrinkling her brow. "You wouldn't think any girl would want to, would you?"

Bobby looked at her suspiciously but decided it might be wiser to ask no explanation. Instead, he said:

"Either she lied about seeing the Jebb girl where she said she did, or else the Jebb girl lied in saying she wasn't there. Why?"

"Seems," observed Olive, "as if you can't simply say anything but 'why?'"

"Well, it's all one big interrogation mark at present," Bobby defended himself. "Of course, Miss Foote may have lied because she felt she had been nosey and was going to get told off and so invented a yarn about someone else being nosier still."

"It might be that," Olive agreed. "Only why did she say it was Miss Jebb?"

"That wants explaining," agreed Bobby in his turn. "Was Miss Foote trying to direct suspicion towards her? If it was that, well, then, obviously Miss Foote knows something."

"Do you mean that brings her in as a suspect herself?"

"Clearly. She turns up as a kind of combined secretary-housekeeper to Goodman who turns out to be the dead man's previous employer and now his heir. She has been seen in the company of one of two young men who also have turned up recently. She showed interest in the scene of the murder and then accused another girl of showing even more. Did her story that Miss Jebb was trying to get into the cottage mean that that was what was in her own mind? She flirted her hardest with old Spencer—my word, if he heard me say that, I would be out and the Yard would be in to-morrow, expense or none. But all the time she was flirting with him, she was giving me the glad eye. As if Spencer were just the stooge and I was the main objective. Of course," added Bobby, straightening his tie, pulling down his waistcoat, brushing away imaginary crumbs from his coat, "of course, she may be simply the sort of girl who just naturally falls for any fine, upstanding, good-looking young fellow she happens to see."

"What? What was that?" asked Olive, thunderstruck again. "What? Do you mind saying that last bit again?"

"Any fine, upstanding, good-looking young fellow she happens to see," repeated Bobby firmly. "Naming no names, of course, but there it is."

"If," said Olive, a little wildly, "you are trying to hint—"

"Hint nothing," interrupted Bobby. "I merely state facts." He added, more seriously: "Was it me, as me, she was aiming at, or me, as policeman? If the first: O.K. If the second: Why? Is Miss Foote simply an empty-headed frivolous little fool of a flirt or is she something very different?"

"Any woman," said Olive, and now she was beginning to look a little uneasy, "any woman who can pretend to be a frivolous little fool of a flirt when she isn't—needs watching."

"You're telling me," said Bobby, who had recently spent a few evenings at the cinema in order to study and learn the American language. "Then there's Miss Jebb. If it's true she was trying to get into the cottage —and someone certainly was, for I distinctly saw the back door latch lifted—then again: Why?"

"I'm beginning to think," Olive said, "I've married a gramophone which can only play one disc that says nothing but 'Why?'"

"It's how I feel," Bobby explained. "All one enormous 'Why?' Also it happens that Kayes, one of the two unexpected young men recently arriving in Oldfordham, lodges with Miss Jebb's mother. Rather a slender connecting thread but thin and slender threads may give strong leads."

"Only," Olive pointed out, "because you're assuming that there is something to be connected. Mr. Kayes may have nothing whatever to do with it."

"Why has he chosen a little country town like Oldfordham to spend his leave in? Is it only coincidence that he arrives shortly before the murder? He was at the Chipping Up disturbance and he gave me the idea even then that he knew something about Brown. We found his card in Brown's cottage, as well as Mr. Childs's. He said something about it being a complete washout if Brown was dead. Well, now he is. What's been washed out?"

"It's all pretty vague, isn't it?" Olive said doubtfully. "He is spending his leave at Oldfordham and he has to spend it somewhere. He happened to be at Chipping Up and so were other people—Mr. Childs, for instance, and you don't suspect him. He is lodging with Miss Jebb's mother, and another girl you don't much trust said something you don't much believe about Miss Jebb. And all that," said Olive with determination, "isn't a thread, isn't a bit of tacking even."

"Even a bit of tacking is better than nothing," Bobby told her, though with no great optimism. "There's one other thing to remember. There's something very like a family resemblance between these two young men—Mrs. Jebb's lodger and the one reported seen in Miss Foote's company."

"Wait a moment," Olive complained. "You go round and round in a circle. Whenever you say anything about anybody, you always go on to someone else till I don't know where I am."

"Exactly," Bobby agreed. "That's just it, and if it's all chance and nothing more, then all I can say is that chance has been working overtime and then some. The Miss Foote young man's explanation is that he means to start a guest house and he's looking for a suitable place. Quite plausible. Pretty country round here. Wychwood knocks out the New Forest any day. Only when two young men, with what seems a family likeness to each other, turn up in a small country town and immediately afterwards there's a murder, you have to—well, you start thinking, don t you?"

"If you can call it thinking," Olive said gloomily, "when all you're doing is going round and round in a fog, wondering where you are."

"Oh, I call it thinking all right," Bobby declared, "and one thing I can't help thinking—or noticing—is that religion seems mixed up in it as well as the gold Brown had tucked away. Duke Dell seemed to think it a pity Brown hadn't drowned in good earnest at Chipping Up, all for the safety of his soul as far as one can make out. Duke Dell has no alibi and when a man has seen what he calls a Vision, he passes out of the normal. Every living soul is unaccountable, unpredictable, unexpectable, if there is such a word. When you think you've see a Vision, a whole lot more so. The Visionary lives in another world than ours. People have often burnt each other alive for the good of each other's souls, so what's the matter with knocking you on the head for the same good reason? Duke Dell thought Brown a backslider, and that's one way of dealing with backsliders. Brown, according to Goodman, was always susceptible to religious emotion, even if only in the odd shape of believing Jesuits the cause and origin of all evil. And we know he had been making a nuisance of himself to Mr. Childs at St. Barnabas."

"Well, that can't have anything to do with it," declared Olive with conviction.

"Oh no," agreed Bobby, though with less conviction, and Olive looked at him sharply.

"What do you mean?" Olive asked. "Mr. Childs is the most unlikely person of all unlikely persons, isn't he?"

"So he is," Bobby agreed once more.

"You can't think your finding his card or his wanting to see Mr. Brown mean anything," declared Olive.

"Of course not," said Bobby, still agreeing.

"Well, then," said Olive.

"Quite so," said Bobby. "But I'll have to ask him when he saw Brown last and where. Only to check up on Brown's movements," Bobby explained; and Olive looked at him suspiciously and said no more, except to remark that it was time to go to bed.

Bobby agreed to that proposition, too, and as he was winding up the clock in preparation for departure upstairs, he said slowly:

"The two young men newcomers, Kayes and the other one. The two girls, Miss Foote and Miss Jebb. Miss Foote's employer, Mr. Goodman. The two preachers, Mr. Childs and Duke Dell. A sort of closed circle with Brown for centre, and all connected with each other in one way or another. The murderer's there all right, only which one—and why? And does the motive lie in Brown's gold or in Brown's religion—or both? Or neither?"

He found himself thinking how curiously gold and religion seemed to run together through it all; those two tangled, twisted, crimson threads that run side by side all through the strange and tragic history of man. Most strangely fascinating did it seem to him how in this way this case seemed like an epitome of all recorded history. But when Olive asked him what he had in his mind now, and why he had stopped in the middle of winding up the clock, all he said was that he was sleepy.

So Olive said she was, too, and they both proved the point by hardly stirring till morning when the tinkling phone informed them that Mr. Spencer was missing, and would the deputy chief please come at once and take over, as the speaker, the elderly Oldfordham sergeant and Mr. Spencer's chief assistant, simply hadn't the remotest idea what to do about it.

CHAPTER XIII
SEARCH AND FIND

A DEVELOPMENT as surprising as disturbing, Bobby thought, as he made hasty preparations for departure in obedience to a summons he felt to be urgent in the extreme. To him the Oldfordham chief constable had seemed solid, steady, workmanlike; the very last person likely to take risks or become involved in hasty or adventurous excursions.

"I hope," he said uneasily to Olive as he was starting off in his little Bayard Seven he still used for economy's sake, though, naturally, a deputy chief was entitled to a much larger and more dignified vehicle; "I hope nothing serious has happened. I can't imagine Spencer staying out all night if he could help it."

Bobby had already rung up his Midwych headquarters to warn them not to expect him that morning. Arriving at Oldfordham, he found a state of complete confusion, alarm, and even distress, for Spencer had been a well-liked chief. Nor was Sergeant Hicks, who had rung him up, able to give him any information beyond the bare fact that the Spencer family had retired for the night, leaving father and husband comfortably settled in an armchair and carpet slippers; for company, cigarettes, the evening paper, and a cup of cocoa, pale, ineffectual substitute for the pre-war glass of whisky and soda. When morning came, there were still the unread evening paper, neatly folded, the unsmoked cigarettes, the untasted cocoa, the unoccupied armchair and slippers, but no Mr. Spencer. His hat and a light overcoat had gone, his bed had not been slept in, the front door was unbolted, and that was all either a bewildered sergeant or a tearful and frightened family could say.

Bobby reassured them as best he could, and promised, more cheerfully than his inner feelings justified, to do his best to have news for them soon. He ascertained that the arrival of no visitor had been heard, no knocking or ringing at the door, no sound of voices, no phone ring. The unread evening paper, the untasted cocoa and so on, suggested clearly that whatever had happened had been immediately after the rest of the family had retired and before Spencer himself had had time to settle down. Somewhere about half-past ten, therefore. That, of course, made it still less likely that any sound of voices or any knocking or ringing, either of the phone or of the door bell, could have passed unnoticed by the other inmates of the house.

But any slight noises Spencer made in leaving, such as opening or closing a door, could very easily have escaped attention, or, if heard at the time, not remembered. Such sounds would have seemed merely preliminaries to settling down, probably caused by a glance outside to see if it was still raining or something like that.

Bobby, therefore, standing in this room that seemed to him a somewhat odd compromise between a prim feminine taste and Spencer's own hearty outdoor interests, felt the first problem he had to solve was what could possibly have induced a man who had made all preparations for a comfortable half hour before turning in, to abandon them and venture forth on a raw and inclement night.

Clear, apparently, that no message or messenger could have reached him. Clear, equally, that whatever it was, had been entirely unexpected and had seemed urgent. All those comfortable preparations had not been abandoned without good cause. A secret tapping at the window, perhaps, and some startling communication whispered through the lifted sash? But Bobby had already noticed that beneath the window was a wide flower bed that showed no trace of footmark or other disturbance. Moreover, the house was built on a slope so that the window was raised several feet above the ground.

Difficult to tell what had happened, Bobby told himself. He went to the window and stood there looking out. A fine view over the town, the river, the country beyond. 'A Room with a View,' Bobby reflected, remembering a celebrated novel he had once read with less appreciation than he knew it deserved. Could Spencer have seen anything out there that he had felt called for instant investigation? But it was dark. Nothing to be seen in darkness. Except, of course, a light. But why should a light have attracted any attention? In these last days of the European War the black-out regulations had been lifted, and a lighted window was no longer a hair-raising indiscretion. So, Bobby argued to himself, it must have been not the light itself, but something else about it, its degree, its locality, its growing or lessening intensity, that had seemed to require investigation. Growing or lessening intensity seemed unlikely. Degree of brightness was no longer of great importance. Locality, then? That seemed more probable. A light, then, seen where no light should be? But why not? And where? Bobby felt he might have narrowed down the problem but had, if anything, increased its difficulty. All the same, it did begin to seem as if Spencer had seen a light that for some reason had roused his suspicions. So he had slipped out quietly to discover what it meant, though, since probably it was nothing much, and he expected to be back before his cocoa had time to grow cold, he had not thought it worth while to disturb the rest of the family by telling them he was going out for a minute or two. Bobby turned to the Oldfordham sergeant with him.

"What church is that, right in line? Is it St. Barnabas?" he asked.

"That's right, sir," the sergeant answered.

Up to now he had been watching Bobby with much admiration for such, apparently, profound and certainly silent concentration on the problem; but now he began to think that, perhaps, the deputy chief wasn't so hot after all. Why, there wasn't a kid in all Oldfordham who didn't know St. Barnabas.

"Then those cottages that show up rather clearly to the left will be where Brown lived?" Bobby asked, all unconscious of the slump that had just taken place in his reputation.

"That's right, sir," said the sergeant again, less and less impressed, since that, too, was a thing everyone knew.

"Do you know who lives next door?" asked Bobby next, and this to the sergeant seemed not so much ignorance as irrelevance.

What had Brown's neighbours got to do with the guv'nor's very worrying disappearance?

"Well, sir, there ain't none just now in a manner of speaking," he explained. "Old Mrs. Harris lived one side but she's that scared after what's happened she's gone off to stay with her married daughter in Midwych, for fear it might be her next."

"On the other side?" Bobby asked.

"Been empty some time, sir," the sergeant told him. "It was Bill Edwardes lived there but he went off to London three months ago or more to help with the bomb damage they make such a tale about, as if nobody nowhere else hadn't had none, neither. Why, that bomb that as near as near did in Sam Wiggins and his home and missis, too, might as easy as not have been plump in the middle of Oldfordham and what about that?" asked the sergeant with a touch of gloomy triumph in his voice.

"Yes, indeed," agreed Bobby absently.

"Plump in the very middle of the town," repeated the sergeant, still more gloomily, still more proudly, for to him now it was much as though that was what had actually happened.

"Yes, indeed," agreed Bobby once more, on his side still more absently. More briskly now he said: "There was one of your men on duty in Brown's cottage last night; wasn't there?" for that had been a suggestion made by him and agreed to by Mr. Spencer as advisable.

"Yes, sir," the sergeant answered. "Alf Adams. Still there he is."

Was it possible, then, Bobby asked himself, a signal had been arranged by which Adams could summon his chief if that seemed desirable for any reason? But then surely, if it was like that, Adams would have said so, and have reported either Mr. Spencer's arrival in answer to the signal or else that he had never come at all. But Adams had said nothing.

Bobby gave it up. For the moment he could see no solution. Of all men he had ever known, he told himself again, Mr. Spencer had seemed one of the least likely to go out adventuring in the rain save at the plain and direct call of obvious duty. Yet it seemed impossible to suppose that any such plain, direct, imperative call had reached him. Nevertheless, Bobby felt certain that just such an urgent summons had somehow been given.

Only how, and through what channel?

He gave it up again. But it did seem as if it might be worth while to question Adams, still on duty in the Brown cottage, since, apparently, in the general confusion and disarray, he had not been relieved. Bobby said to the sergeant:

"I think I would like to have a chat with Adams. You might come along, too, will you?"

"Certainly, sir, very good, sir," answered the sergeant smartly, for that is the correct response the properly disciplined man always makes when a senior officer speaks.

All the same, Bobby's stock, if only he had known it, slumped to an even lower level. Just like the High-ups, the sergeant thought, always wanting to mess about, going over ground already well covered. Just as though, very first thing, Adams had not been asked if he knew anything; and as if Adams had not been emphatic that he had neither seen nor heard anything in the least suspicious or unusual all through the night.

They started off accordingly, but when they reached the cottage their knock brought no answer. Evidently there was no Adams there, and the sergeant looked very taken aback at first and then quickly recovered.

"I forgot for the moment, sir," he explained. "He'll have gone to get a bite of breakfast. A man's got to eat and I told him he could have from nine to half past and not a minute more."

"Oh yes, yes," Bobby said. Not for him to criticize another and an independent force. "A man must eat," he agreed, and glanced at his wrist watch. It was nearly the half hour. He asked carelessly as if not much interested: "How did he manage for supper last night?"

"From ten to eleven, a full hour Mr. Spencer said he could have when he asked, but to be sure and be back by eleven sharp," the sergeant answered. "Very conscientious man, Adams. You may depend on it he was back at eleven to the dot."

This last was said with a slightly defensive air, for the sergeant was beginning to be dimly aware of something in Bobby's tone or looks that was not wholly approving. For Bobby was thinking that between ten and eleven was almost certainly the time during which whatever had happened to Mr. Spencer, had, in fact, happened.

"I'm sure Adams would be back on time," he agreed heartily, even too heartily, so heartily indeed as to set the sergeant still more on the defensive. "I suppose," he said, "you are too short-handed to arrange for a relief while Adams is away, at breakfast or supper either?"

"Oh yes, sir, much too short," declared the sergeant, thinking this the most sensible remark the deputy chief had yet made. He was proceeding to expatiate on how the war had come home to Oldfordham with the reduction in its police force from the normal twelve to a bare and scanty nine, when he checked himself to say, not without pride: "Here's Adams now and St. Barnabas just going to strike the half hour."

Adams was, in fact, approaching at the usual regulation pace. Serene and dignified he drew near, a personification of the dignified, if at times a trifle slow, progress of British law. Bobby told Olive later that never, never had he come so near to bursting a blood vessel as when now he repressed his urge to yell to Adams to hurry, hurry, hurry. But he succeeded in so doing and if he went crimson in the effort that phenomenon passed unnoticed. Sooner or later, however, the weariest river winds to the sea, and presently

—a long, long presently, about a minute and a half really—Adams was there and producing the key to the cottage.

"Mr. Owen wants another look round," explained the sergeant, with good-humoured tolerance for the vagaries of one of the so often unaccountable, so often slightly absurd 'higher-ups.'

But Bobby, his patience exhausted just like that of any dictator, snatched the key from the safe but deliberate hands of startled Constable Adams, made one leap to the door, tore it open, and, without giving the lower rooms a glance since it was there the conscientious Adams would have spent the night, raced upstairs to the bedroom.

There, between door and bed, lay Spencer, badly injured about the head, unconscious, dead, Bobby thought at first, dying at the best.

To the horrified and amazed sergeant who had followed him up the stairs, he said:

"A doctor. Quick. Hurry."

The sergeant disappeared. He actually ran. A thing he had not done for years. Bobby felt the prostrate man's heart. He thought he detected a faint fluttering movement. He knelt there, waiting. Nothing he could do. If he tried to fan gently to help the injured man's breathing, or if he chafed those cold and stiffening hands, it was more for the sake of relieving his own feelings than with much hope of doing any good. He doubted, indeed, if a doctor could do much. All night long Spencer must have been lying there, while in the room below the conscientious Adams sat, comfortable and unknowing. Plain enough now what had happened. From his window Mr. Spencer must have seen a light in the cottage window. But he knew there should be no one there at that hour, since between ten and eleven Adams had permission to be at home, getting his supper. So Spencer had slipped out to see what was happening; and whoever had been there had taken him unawares and had left him for dead.

For the first time Spencer stirred, very slightly, so slightly Bobby thought at first it was his own imagination. But now Spencer's lips moved. He was trying to speak. Bobby bent nearer. He thought he could distinguish one word. It sounded like a name 'Kayes.' The faint murmuring ceased and once more Mr. Spencer sank into a coma perilously resembling death.

CHAPTER XIV
NO CLUE

SOON ARRIVED Dr. Railes, the Oldfordham police doctor, called even from his surgery by the hurrying sergeant's urgent tidings. Under his superintendence, Spencer was removed to the local cottage hospital. An operation would be necessary and would have to be performed with all possible speed. Little as the doctor said, it was evident he thought Spencer's condition very serious.

"Not hopeless," he told Bobby, and repeated: "By no means hopeless."

Great violence had been used, and by, once more, the traditional heavy, blunt instrument. Not the poker with which Brown had been attacked for that, of course, was in the safe care of the police, but something similar, of which, however, no trace was to be found. Bobby noticed one difference. Brown's injuries had been inflicted by a multitude of blows, delivered as in a frenzy, the kind of frenzy that does sometimes overtake the killer, as if his own dreadful action induced in him a kind of madness, a total loss of self-control, as if only so could he succeed in making tolerable to himself what he himself had done. Spencer's hurt, severe and possibly fatal though it was, had been inflicted by a single crushing blow, one delivered with great force.

"About twelve hours ago, or a little less," said the doctor; and nodded satisfaction when Bobby said there was reason to place the attack at about half past ten the previous night.

There was no other information the doctor could give; and to his added opinion, that the force with which the blow had been delivered showed that the assailant must have been a man of exceptional physical strength—'six foot heavy-weight,' said the doctor—Bobby was able to give but a doubtful assent. He knew that anyone, a woman, a man of slight physique, can at times display extraordinary strength. It was a strength, perhaps, not so much muscular as deriving from that reserve of nervous energy and power all can at times call upon; and that is most often released when the mental control goes, as in temporary madness, in hysteria, which is much the same, or even in some stages of drunkenness. Well, indeed, did Bobby remember how, at the beginning of his career in the police, in his uniform days, he and three or four other stalwart comrades had had all they could do to master a frail-looking elderly woman possessed by twin devils of drink and jealousy. More probable, no doubt, that Spencer's assailant had been what Dr. Railes called 'a six foot heavy-weight'; but Bobby did not mean to forget that that assailant might quite possibly be a man of ordinary, or less than ordinary, size and weight, or even a woman for that matter.

Nor did Dr. Railes think that much importance could be attached to anything Spencer had said in any momentary gleam of passing consciousness. It might certainly refer to what had happened. It might as easily, or more easily, be some mere, disconnected, floating memory that had drifted to the surface of a consciousness no longer capable of coherent functioning.

This time the doctor's verdict coincided with Bobby's own impression. He knew well that no jury, no court for that matter, would be in the least impressed by the report of a half-heard whisper of a so badly injured man. For that matter Bobby was not even certain that he had heard correctly. The word muttered by Spencer in that passing and momentary gleam of consciousness had sounded like the name Kayes. But then it might also have been in fact something about keys, or indeed, for that matter, something entirely different.

Close examination of the cottage revealed no clue. Whoever Spencer found lurking there had come and gone, leaving no trace behind. The Wychshire force finger-print expert, for whom Bobby had sent immediately, had no more luck this time than before. But as he said with weary resignation, for he was a man inured to disappointment, a man for whom frustration was as a familiar friend: "If a five-year-old starts in to-day to raid mummy's strawberry jam, he puts on gloves first." True, the general layout was plain enough. Spencer had seen a light where no light should have been. He had hurried out to investigate. The intruder, disturbed by Spencer's arrival, had waited, silent and hidden, till discovery became inevitable. Then he—'six foot heavy-weight,' or ordinary man or even woman for that matter—had delivered the fierce, sudden, unexpected attack which had left Spencer for dead. Not a deliberate, pre-determined murder by reason of some desperate, as yet unknown, unguessed motive, as in the case of the killing of Brown, but, though murder none the less, caused by sudden fear and need, the fear of arrest, the need for escape. The only hope, at least for the present, of learning the truth, seemed to lie in the chance of Spencer recovering sufficiently to be able to tell what had happened. And of that the doctor gave small hope, and none at all for some considerable time to come.

The customary steps Bobby had already taken, such as inquiry to learn if anyone had been seen near the cottage or indeed any stranger in the vicinity. He would also try again to get a talk with Kayes. There was always the incident of the visiting card to be explained. But he would make no reference as yet to that half-heard whisper uttered by the half-conscious Spencer. Too doubtful, too uncertain to be brought into the open at present, but nevertheless to be remembered.

To Aspect Cottage, therefore, Bobby took his way, and this time found Kayes there, smoking cigarettes over the morning paper but not, apparently, giving too much attention to what he was reading. He greeted Bobby pleasantly enough and without any undue signs of apprehension or uneasiness. He remembered Bobby very well, he said, from their previous meeting at Chipping Up, and added that Mrs. Jebb had told him of the previous call made together by Bobby and Mr. Spencer. He had wondered a good deal why they came; and he asked if anything had been heard of Mr. Spencer, of whose strange disappearance the whole neighbourhood was talking.

Bobby answered briefly that Mr. Spencer had been found in the same cottage in which Brown had been murdered; found so badly injured that his life was in grave danger, and Kayes looked very startled and disturbed, repeated more than once, 'in the same cottage,' and seemed as if he wished to ask questions that he also seemed either unable or reluctant to express in words.

Bobby waited patiently, hoping more would come.

Once or twice Kayes began vague, hesitant, disconnected sentences that he failed to complete. Finally he burst out:

"Does it mean Brown's murderer came back and Spencer caught him and got knocked out?"

"It might be like that," Bobby agreed. "Can you suggest any reason why the murderer should come back?"

Quite clearly Kayes did not much like this question. He had very plainly an air of wondering why it had been put to him in so direct a fashion. He had a distinctly wary look; in his voice was a note of caution, as, after a pause, he said:

"No. I can't. How could I? Don't they say a murderer always returns to the scene of his crime?"

"I haven't noticed it myself," Bobby remarked. "At any rate not so soon, I think. Do you think it could be because he thought something of value was still there? Hidden perhaps?"

Again Kayes did not answer immediately. He took out another cigarette and his lighter, but made a poor job of getting the lighter to act. Bobby noticed that his hands were not too steady. Bobby still waited. He had often found that to sit silently and wait was a very useful method of getting the other fellow to talk. There is something in silence that the uneasy conscience can seldom endure for long. Presently Kayes said:

"How should I know? Why do you ask me?"

"Well, for one thing," Bobby explained, "your card was found in Brown's cottage."

"What?" exclaimed Kayes. "What? Nonsense. It couldn't be. How could it? Why, I didn't even know where Brown lived until all this happened."

Bobby was a little puzzled. Long experience had taught him to put some faith in his capacity to tell when a man was lying, when he was telling the truth. A multitude of small signs he had learned or thought he had learned, to recognize, trusting not so much to any one of them as to all together. It is a faculty claimed by many barristers of experience, by many magistrates and judges. Bobby's impression now was very strongly that Kayes was telling the truth, and that this about his card came to him as a complete and baffling surprise. Kayes repeated, and now with anger and suspicion:

"It couldn't be. Is this one of your smart police bluffs?"

"If you care to call at the police station," Bobby answered quietly, "I daresay they will let you see it. Have you given your card to anyone here?"

"I showed it at the post office," Kayes answered. "I may have left it on the counter. I don't remember. And at the stationer's in the High Street, when I was asking about finding rooms. Oh, and I believe I gave one to Mr. Childs. And didn't I give you one, once? That's all as far as I remember. Oh, and I left one here when I took the rooms. What are you getting at in all this?"

"At anything," Bobby answered, his normally clear and pleasant voice taking on that stern and hard note it could show at times, "at anything whatever that can help to the arrest of the murderer of a man who seems to have been a quiet and inoffensive citizen. It is the duty of the police to protect every citizen. That's not always possible. When we've not been able to, it's all the more our duty to see it doesn't escape punishment. I am taking it for granted that I can depend on any help you can give me."

"What help do you mean? How can I?" Kayes asked, but all the same with a kind of sulky reservation in his voice. "I never saw Brown in my life before that time at Chipping Up. I told you before that until then I hadn't an idea even where he lived. And I haven't any idea either why anyone should want to kill him. So far as I'm concerned it doesn't make sense."

"Thank you, that seems very clear and definite," Bobby answered, though thinking to himself that this last sentence was a trifle odd. "If we knew the motive, it would be much easier. I think perhaps I ought to tell you that your name has been mentioned in connection with the attack on Mr. Spencer though not in a way we can take at all seriously—at present."

Once again Kayes looked very startled, though this time he seemed more indignant than alarmed.

"What do you mean?" he demanded. "What on earth ... who has?"

"I've said we don't take it seriously," Bobby repeated. "I'm afraid I can't tell you more."

"I've a right to know—" began Kayes stormily, but Bobby interrupted.

"No," he said. "We have to regard that sort of thing as confidential. At least, till we begin to think there might be something in it. At present, we don't. If we do, of course that will be different. But anything happening like this starts all sorts of gossip. If we repeated all we get told, we should make any amount of mischief. So we never say anything, unless and until there's good reason to do so."

Kayes didn't look as though this explanation went very far towards satisfying him.

"You're taking it seriously enough to tell me," he retorted. "I'm beginning to think I had better see my solicitors."

"Always very sensible," agreed Bobby.

"Even about something that isn't being taken seriously?" asked Kayes sourly. "Anyhow, I can guess who it is. That girl at Goodman's."

Now it was Bobby's turn to feel startled. Was this another instance of the revolving circle that seemed to bring first one and then another into prominence?

"Do you know her?" Bobby asked. When Kayes shook his head, Bobby said: "What made you think of her?"

"She was telling lies about Janet—about Miss Jebb," Kayes said moodily. "Who is she?"

"Mr. Goodman's secretary," Bobby answered.

"Is that all?"

"All we know."

"I don't see why she should pick on Janet or start talking about me," Kayes said. He got up and began to walk about the room. He was obviously disturbed and uneasy. Bobby watched him closely. Kayes said: "I don't understand all this. Why was Brown murdered?"

"I'm trying to find out," Bobby said quietly.

"I take it you've searched the cottage?"

"Oh yes, thoroughly," Bobby answered. No doubt the story of the hidden gold would have to be told sooner or later, but it might be as well to say nothing about it yet. He asked: "Do you know Mr. Goodman?"

"He was my uncle's lawyer," Kayes said. "He was one of the executors. The London and Midwych Bank was the other. I went to see him the other day about some of uncle's investments. By the way, I think I left my card there, too. He didn't know much. He's retired, apparently. He handed over all the papers to the man he sold out to. They've all been got rid of for salvage, apparently."

"When did your uncle die?" Bobby asked.

"Nine years ago. I was in Australia. I was born there. Father went there when he was a young man. This is the first time I've been in England. All my service has been in the Pacific zone, until now."

"I see" said Bobby thoughtfully. "You've given me some very interesting information." He paused and he did not fail to notice that Kayes shot at him a quick, searching, somewhat uneasy glance as if wondering what this 'interesting information' could be and what Bobby was likely to make of it. Bobby went on: "I must think it over: I expect when you called on Mr. Goodman you saw Miss Foote. Rather a flirtatious young woman, isn't she?"

Kayes evidently did not think so at all.

"Not by the way she looked at me," he said briefly.

"Oh, why?" asked Bobby.

"I don't know," retorted Kayes. "All I know is she looked at me as if I were poison and she wanted to give me some of the same. Lord knows why. I don't." And certainly he looked both puzzled and also a trifle annoyed, as if in his quality of good-looking young airman he was not much used to finding girls, flirtatious or not, looking at him as if he were poison.

Bobby thought it curious. Of course, Kayes might have mistaken a twinge from a too tight shoe or something of that sort for a glare of hatred. In any case he could not imagine in what way there came into it this young woman, so interested in the murder cottage, so ready to give the glad eye to one young man, and yet, apparently, regarding another as if he were poison. It might be significant. It might mean something. Or it might not. You could never tell. A detective's greatest difficulty is to pick out in all the criss-cross tangle of human relations, the significant threads, those that led to the heart of the labyrinth. When one did that, all became plain and easy. One simply went forward to the inevitable end. But how easy to make the wrong choice, to follow the wrong threads, and so wander hopelessly and helplessly in nightmare confusion till it became too late. For time is always against the detective, always on the side of the criminal, and unless the problem can be solved quickly, it can seldom be solved at all.

CHAPTER XV

TORN TROUSER

It was, then, in a thoughtful and worried mood that Bobby left Aspect Cottage. His instinct, his professional instinct he sometimes called it, told him Kayes had spoken the truth. But had he spoken all the truth? Yet if he were innocent, and surely he must be innocent if he had not even known where Brown lived, what was being held back and why?

A puzzle that would have to wait developments for solution, Bobby told himself. He turned into the steep, narrow, winding street that led uphill to St. Barnabas

Church and the adjacent vicarage, one of those enormous mansions that the Church of England loves to tie, like a millstone, round the necks of its clergy. Presumably, so that they may be cast into the deep sea of poverty and debt. The hour was still early, the vicar still at home, and Bobby was shown at once into Mr. Childs's study, where he was received with a friendly smile and handshake.

"I heard Mr. Spencer had been found," the vicar said. "I do hope it's not true that he's so badly injured he isn't likely to recover."

"I'm afraid the doctors seem to think his condition's pretty bad," Bobby answered.

"What did actually happen?" Mr. Childs asked.

"I'm trying to find out," Bobby answered. "All we know at present is that he was attacked, and left, probably for dead, in Brown's cottage."

"Is it connected with this extraordinary story of packing cases full of gold there?" Mr. Childs asked, and the question gave Bobby something of a shock.

Optimistic, he supposed, though, to expect that so sensational a tale could long remain a secret. All the same, he was looking rather glum as he said:

"Oh, you've heard about that? Who told you?"

"It's all over the town," Mr. Childs answered. "It is true, then? I could hardly believe it."

"It's true in a way," Bobby agreed cautiously. "There was a large sum in gold Brown had hidden. Hardly packing cases full, though."

"The motive of the poor fellow's murder?" Mr. Childs asked.

"Possibly. We don't know. It hadn't been touched, though it could easily have been taken by anyone who knew about it. I'm sorry the story's leaked out. You think most people know?"

"Oh, everyone, I should say," Mr. Childs answered. "The milkman told my housekeeper first thing this morning. I told her not to listen to such nonsense. I'm afraid I was a little sharp. I detest idle gossip and I thought that's all it was. So she's come to tell me every time she hears it afresh and that seems to be from everyone who has been near the house. I've had to apologize."

Bobby reflected, not too happily, that if 'everyone' knew, then almost certainly Kayes knew, too. But he had said nothing, asked no questions, showed no interest. It did look as if there were more to Flight Lieutenant Kayes than appeared at first. Only what? Something to do with the murder, or something private and personal and comparatively innocuous? If Kayes had been an 'O. R.'—an 'other rank'—then Bobby would have suspected a case of 'A. W. L.'—'absent without leave'—and how the army loves initials! But 'A. W. L.' isn't very likely in the case of a flight lieutenant. Or was it merely masquerade? A silly youngster trying to show off by pretending to be an officer in the R.A.F. It didn't seem likely, but a detective's motto must be 'Try all things,' and Bobby decided to ring up the Air Ministry as soon as possible. Or was it that for once his famous 'professional instinct' had failed him, and Kayes was simply a peculiarly good liar? He became aware that Mr. Childs was apologizing for the possession of knowledge he now gathered the authorities had wished to be regarded as confidential.

Bobby said it couldn't be helped. If everyone knew, then everyone knew, and that was all there was to it.

He went on to say that what he had really called for was to ask if Mr. Childs could give him any information about the dead man, about his habits, his way of life, anything that might be useful in solving the mystery of the fate that so strangely and so suddenly had fallen upon him.

Mr. Childs looked a little uncomfortable.

"I suppose you've heard," he said, "of the recent unfortunate brawling at our services and that I had been forced to consider taking serious steps to end it. Both my wardens advised legal action. We should have had the support of the church council. I was most unwilling. For many reasons. The scandal. The Church should be very reluctant to appeal to the State. Erastianism. Rather it should be the other way, the State appealing to the Church. The thing had flared up very suddenly and I did not wish to take precipitate action. I hoped it might end as suddenly as it began. After all, indifference is the real enemy. Neither hot nor cold. Not too much zeal. I hoped presently to bring Brown to a more reasonable frame of mind. I even hoped I might be able to harness his zeal to the true service of the Church. Especially as I associated his conduct with the appearance about here of a kind of itinerant preacher, a man named Dell. Duke Dell, I think. The man you saw that day at Chipping Up."

"Yes, I remember," Bobby said. "Brown hadn't been making himself a nuisance before?"

"No, no. He wasn't even a member of the congregation. I had talked to him once or twice. I try to visit every house in the parish once a year, though that's not always possible. Brown always gave me the impression of feeling uncomfortable, of trying to avoid me, in fact. He led a curiously solitary, retired life. I imagine misers often do. He did tell me once he didn't hold with Popery. I said I didn't either. My general impression was that that was merely an excuse. It did seem to me that his real reason was that he was afraid."

"Afraid?" Bobby repeated, somewhat puzzled.

"There are many like that," Mr. Childs explained. "I find it frequently. They fear the Church because they know they cannot obey the Church without entirely changing their way of life. And they don't want to. So they stay away, out of danger as they think. Easier to pretend religion isn't there than to accept religion. I suspected it was something like that with Brown. A miser wouldn't wish to be told to regard his gold as filthy lucre. Then there came this most unexpected development. Of course, I know there had always been an undercurrent of opposition in the parish. There are some who always seem to think that the more dead, dull, uninspired the worship offered, the more acceptable. But it was an extraordinary surprise to find it being worked up by Brown. Under," said Mr. Childs, frowning now, "under the influence of this man, Dell, who was very careful, though, to keep himself in the background."

"Thank you, that's very interesting," Bobby said, and indeed found it so, and perhaps even more than Mr. Childs suspected. "I gather Dell didn't take part, himself, in these disturbances?"

"No, indeed," Mr. Childs answered, and looked very much now the church militant. "I should have known how to deal with him." He paused and his flashing eye and grimly set mouth gave confirmation. "With my own hands, if necessary," he said. "I didn't take the unarmed combat course for nothing when I was chaplain to the forces." Then he explained as Bobby looked a little startled by this resurgence of the old Adam: "Dell was not a parishioner. He had no rights, none. Brown was a parishioner. He had rights. I had a responsibility for him. In my cure."

"Yes, I see that," Bobby agreed, though wondering if he did, wondering, too, how far this sense of responsibility might go. "We found a card of yours at the cottage with a message on it, asking Brown to call to see you."

"Oh yes, I remember," Mr. Childs agreed. "Some days ago. Either he wasn't at home when I called or he wouldn't come to the door. So I left a message."

"Did you get any answer?"

"No. No. It's one thing to create a disturbance during divine worship—" Mr. Childs paused and again Bobby had that impression of the Church very much militant; of strong, even passionate feelings held firmly in check. "It's quite another thing," Mr. Childs continued more calmly, "to face the priest—" He broke off again, as if unwilling to go on. "No, I got no answer," he repeated.

"Do you remember when was the last time you saw him?"

"Well, strictly speaking, I saw him, if one can call it so, on the night of the murder. I suppose I must make full confession. I expect it's bound to come out sooner or later."

He paused again. Bobby sat upright. He had no idea what was coming but the vicar's remark seemed startling. Mr. Childs went on:

"I do hope you'll believe it did not occur to me that I was doing wrong. I had stayed to dine with Mr. Goodman. I was on my way there when I saw you at Chipping Up. Mr. Goodman is not a parishioner—I only wish he were. But he has shown considerable interest in our work at St. Barnabas. If only we had more laymen like him. He made a most generous suggestion of financial help towards a very dear project of mine. He insisted on my staying to dinner and in spite of all I could say, he would send me home in his car. It was quite useless my telling him I had my bicycle and it was certainly a very dark night. I can't say I was altogether looking forward to the ride home in the dark. Some of the army lorry drivers seem to me to take undue risks. However, I do ask you to believe that it never once occurred to me that I was guilty of a criminal offence in the misuse of petrol."

"Oh yes, yes," agreed Bobby, blinking a little, for he was not much used to meeting consciences so sensitive. "Yes, I suppose so—strictly speaking. Still, more a technical offence than a criminal offence, I think."

"I am very relieved to hear you say so," said Mr. Childs gravely. "It seemed an unfortunate position. I was unable, as I should have done, to communicate with the authorities and explain my fault without compromising both Mr. Goodman and his chauffeur. I am perfectly certain it never occurred to Mr. Goodman cither that there was anything wrong in what he was suggesting. On his part it was pure kindness, great kindness. I do not like cycling in the dark— especially when you come to the main road where the army lorries are and the sometimes rather reckless young dispatch riders. I was, I fear, too relieved by Mr. Goodman's offer to realize the position. An unfortunate dilemma. No matter how much I tried to keep Mr. Goodman's name concealed, it would have been bound to come out."

"I don't think," Bobby said with a touch of impatience in his voice, for he really thought all this was making much too large a mountain out of a very small mole hill, "there's any need to bother. I can assure you we shan't prosecute. We shan't even ask Mr. Goodman where he got his petrol. As a rule we only take action if there seems to be deliberate, continued misuse. I imagine Mr. Goodman didn't come, too. He wasn't making his offer to you an excuse for a longer drive somewhere else?"

"Oh no," declared Mr. Childs, looking quite shocked. "I'm sure Mr. Goodman would never think of that. It was merely his kindness and hospitality made him forget war-time regulations."

"No doubt," agreed Bobby. "Well, it doesn't matter in the least. But how was it you happened to meet Brown, if you returned by car? Did you pass him on the road?"

"No. Nowadays, Mr. Goodman uses his small two-seater but, unfortunately, there was something wrong with it. I think Mr. Goodman was rather vexed; I think he was inclined to suspect that the chauffeur was trying to make excuses to avoid turning out. He spoke quite sharply. He said in that case the other car must be used. I tried to protest but he insisted he couldn't afford to let his man get away with a tale like that. So the big car it was. Enormous it looked in that darkness. It couldn't possibly have got up our narrow, winding streets. I made the chauffeur stop at the foot of the hill. I remembered the trouble there was once with Canon Wade's car, though that was nothing like the size. So I got out, retrieved my bicycle from the back, where Mr. Goodman had kindly placed it for me, and wheeled it up the hill. As I was passing Brown's cottage I saw him at the window. He was adjusting the blind. I waved to him. He may not have seen, though I was standing in the light from the window before he got the blind back in position. I was much inclined to stop and insist on a talk. But it was late. After ten, I think, and finally I went on home."

"Did you see or meet anyone else?"

"Oh no. No. We are early folk in Oldfordham."

"Do you remember if Brown had the wireless on?"

"Yes, it was one reason why I decided not to knock."

"Did you recognize the music? I mean, what piece was being played?"

"I'm afraid not," Mr. Childs admitted. "My ear for music is not of the best." He sighed, for this was a cross he had to bear. Even when he intoned a prayer during church service, he knew very well what silent—and not always silent—criticism he was being subjected to. Then he brightened a little. "At any rate," he said, "it was not one of the familiar hymn tunes. That, at least, I am sure of. I do know them."

"Could you tell me what make Mr. Goodman's car is?"

"Dear me, no," answered Mr. Childs, a trifle surprised and even amused at what seemed so irrelevant a question. "I fear I am totally uninstructed in motoring matters. Is it of any importance?"

"Any small detail may turn out to be all-important," Bobby explained smilingly. "One never knows. For instance, we found a thread of black cloth caught on a splinter of a broken chair at the cottage. That may mean nothing. Probably it doesn't. We have sent it for examination by the experts. They may be able to tell us something. Such small apparent trifles have, before now, led to the gallows."

Mr. Childs stared, gulped, went very pale. He rose to his feet from his chair behind the table where he had been sitting. He looked down and Bobby could see quite plainly where a small tear on the knee of one trouser-leg had been neatly and expertly darned.

CHAPTER XVI

UNDIGNIFIED AFFAIR

A SILENCE FOLLOWED. Mr. Childs kept his eyes fixed on that tiny, almost imperceptible, darn on his trouser-knee. So did Bobby. He waited. Silently. He had a great gift for silent waiting. Olive, in one of those moments of exasperation that occasionally add a touch of spice to normal married life, had told him once that there were times when it removed him from the category of the human. So he waited now, passive and watchful. An enemy might have said, like a cat watching a mouse, though Bobby's feelings would certainly have been much hurt by a comparison he would have felt to be so fundamentally unjust. It was the booming of the hour from the great clock of St. Barnabas that, at last, roused Mr. Childs. He said:

"The hidden things shall be made clear." After another pause he added pensively: "If there had been coupons to spare, I should probably have bought a new pair."

"Yes," said Bobby, and waited.

"It's not a thing I much care to remember," Mr. Childs went on. "It was—unfortunate. I knew Brown was avoiding me. He seemed determined to avoid a personal talk. I was equally determined to have one. I felt convinced that if we could talk, a great deal that he entirely misunderstood I could put in an entirely new light. And I felt that his careful avoidance of me showed that he was in a way uncertain of himself; showed a kind of inner knowledge he had that his position was unsound. I wished to make him examine it. I felt it a duty to make the attempt. He had zeal. He was not indifferent—oh, that awful indifference. Neither hot nor cold. If you only knew what it is to battle against it day after day. Better by far, even misdirected zeal. There is, at least, a chance of turning it into the right road. I confess I had my hopes of returning, bringing my sheaves with me. Of rejoicing more over one strayed sheep restored to St. Barnabas, than over the ninety and nine faithful who had never left us. I seemed to see him as possibly a most valuable fellow-labourer in the vineyard." He paused. "I'm afraid you may disapprove of what I did. Unconventional, I know. Illegal, even criminal, I suppose. And the result was—disastrous."

"Yes," said Bobby again, wondering what was coming next.

"As you may imagine," Mr. Childs continued, "I said nothing about it. There was no reason to. I hoped it would remain—well, a secret. So it would have done but for ... He paused once more and contemplated the tiny darn that told so much. "And I have no other pair," he said regretfully. He went on: "I knew Brown went to Midwych every week. Once or twice I have been on the same train. This time I came back early, on purpose. My idea was to be waiting for him when he got back—about five, generally, I knew."

"But surely," Bobby protested, "even if you were waiting, he could still dodge you. He could have gone off again or simply refused to talk—let himself in and banged the door behind him."

"Ah-h," said Mr. Childs, and for the first time he smiled with a kind of half-ashamed admiration for his own cunning, "you see, I meant to be already indoors, in the kitchen, waiting for him there."

"How were you going to manage that?" demanded Bobby, visions in his mind of a burglarious entry by one of the back windows. "Brown didn't leave his door open, did he?"

"I had the key of next door," explained Mr. Childs simply. "A member of the St. Barnabas choir lives there. He has been sent to London on bomb damage repair work. He took his wife with him and he left the key with me, asking me to keep an eye on his home. I think he was a little afraid it might be handed over to evacuees if more were sent here. I knew that all those cottages have much the same lock and that one key would probably do for them all. I found that was the case. I let myself in. In Midwych I had bought a few cakes and so on and so forth. And I had a large thermos flask with tea in it. I laid the table. I lighted the fire. I waited in the scullery behind." He paused and smiled again, half proud, half doubtful; like a child not quite certain whether it is going to be praised or punished.

Bobby guessed he was still inclined to think it had all been very clever, even though, apparently, it had not turned out very well. Mr. Childs resumed: "I hoped the tea I had prepared, not without pains, would, so to speak, break the ice. I meant to show myself while he was still too surprised to be actively resentful. I hoped it would show I only wanted a perfectly friendly chat. I trusted, I expected, I think I had a right to expect, it would be received as the friendly overture it was meant to be."

"Was it?" Bobby asked.

"Far from it," Mr. Childs answered sadly. "The teapot was instantly thrown at my head. The cakes followed. Fortunately the teapot missed. The cakes—er—did not. Especially the squashy, creamy ones. There was an attempt to use physical violence. Brown quite lost his head. He seemed to go mad. He was shouting something I couldn't make head or tail of at the time. I imagine now from what you have told me that he was thinking of his concealed store of gold and that he believed I knew about it and even had designs upon it. I had to defend myself. I learned how when I was chaplain to the forces, when I took some of their courses including the unarmed combat course. But his attack was so violent and fierce that a chair got knocked over and we both fell over it. That must have been when I tore my trousers. I managed to push Brown into the scullery and I retired—I suppose I must admit with more haste than dignity. I was afraid Brown might follow me. He contented himself with throwing a jelly. At the back of my neck—very cold, very slippery. I didn't notice what had happened to my trousers till my housekeeper pointed it out and mended it for me."

"Thank you," Bobby said, and he felt very worried indeed.

Was this odd story the truth or was it just an ingenious invention, a carefully prepared tale? Or was it true as regards the beginning but not as regards the ending? Had that ending been a grim and dreadful ending, very different from a hurried thrusting into the scullery, a hurried and undignified retreat? Admittedly, there had been a scene of violence. And when violence begins, who can tell when it will end? According to Mr. Childs's story Brown 'had seemed to go mad.' Was that true only of Brown? Had a kind of temporary madness overcome them both? No doubt it was the consciousness of his hidden gold that had excited Brown so much, and made him lose his self-control. Had his attack on Mr. Childs caused similar excitement, similar loss of self-control? In other words, had his frenzy, kindled by fear for his secret gold, called forth a corresponding, answering frenzy? The possibility was not one that could be forgotten or overlooked. Bobby did not like it at all. He said aloud:

"An unfortunate business."

"Most unfortunate," agreed Mr. Childs, "a most unfortunate ending. And I had such high hopes. They were very nice cakes," he added thoughtfully. "I got them in one of the best shops in Midwych." Still more thoughtfully, he added again: "Nice but squashy."

"Yes," said Bobby. "Yes. Very unlucky."

"Jam. Cream," said Mr. Childs, and lapsed into troubled reminiscence.

"I expect your housekeeper wondered what had happened," observed Bobby.

"I am afraid," said Mr. Childs, "I took some care she should not know. An undignified affair altogether. Fortunately she was out and I was able to tidy myself before she returned. Fortunately, too, managed to get home without anyone seeing me."

"Very fortunate," agreed Bobby and meant very unfortunate, since this meant no corroboration was available. If only someone had seen the vicar leaving Brown's cottage with visible traces on his person of what he had so feelingly described as 'Squashy' cakes—cream, jam—on his person, all would have been well. Then his story could have been accepted and forgotten as irrelevant. But apparently no such corroboration was to be obtained and so there was nothing to show his tale was true. If he had bought his cakes in Oldfordham the transaction might have been remembered and that would have been something. But apparently he had got them in a busy Midwych shop where no memory of any such casual sale was likely to remain. Bobby could not blind himself to the possibility that the whole story might simply be a cunning invention designed to hide the truth of what really happened. He supposed, not too happily, that so it would have to be left for the time in the hope that presently further evidence could be found at the best, to confirm, at the worst, to disprove, what he had been told.

He decided to change the subject.

"What I called for as much as anything," he said, "was to ask your opinion of Duke Dell. I understand you think it may have been through him that Brown began this brawling business?"

"Oh, undoubtedly," declared Mr. Childs. "Until Mr. Dell started what he calls his mission, Brown showed no interest in church matters. A typical Laodicean. Then Mr. Dell appeared and began making very ignorant, very foolish attacks on St. Barnabas. Soon afterwards, Brown also began his own disgraceful proceedings."

"What I am wondering," Bobby said; and felt that he was groping blindly for a clue that always evaded him, that indeed very likely was not there, "is this, can there have been—how shall I put it?—any special cause or reason or anything that made Brown specially sensitive to Dell's preaching? Brown seems to have been quite indifferent before—a Laodicean, as you say. What, so to say, provided the spark, fired the train, that led him to become suddenly excited about the St. Barnabas services?"

"There is always," Mr. Childs said quietly, "always and inevitably a spark in every man that only needs a breath of wind from the right quarter to become a flame. I cannot tell you why Dell's irresponsible, ill-informed preaching should have provided that breath of wind. I should like to think our work at St. Barnabas had so revived the spark in Brown's case that only the merest further suggestion was needed. Often he who gathers the harvest is not he who sowed the seed. That is as may be. I cannot tell. But my wish to know was one reason why I was so very anxious for a talk with him."

"Do you think Dell really believes he has had what he calls his Vision? He talked a lot about it when we saw him, but I couldn't make much sense of what he said."

"There are visions and visions," Mr. Childs said, still speaking very slowly and thoughtfully. "If they come from above, as we must believe, for they are recorded in Holy Writ, why not from below? If such visions need to be interpreted as again we must believe on the same authority, it seems to follow also that they can be misinterpreted, misunderstood."

"You know sir," Bobby said uneasily, "all this is very much beyond me. I've never known or heard of a case in which religious motives appeared. You don't expect religion to lead to murder."

"Religion may lead anywhere," Mr Childs told him. "People often try to think of it as an afternoon tea and hot-buttered-muffins affair. Rather is it strong wine that calls for strong heads. That is the value, the enormous value, of the historic background. The church has a history, a tradition, and therefore a discipline. Remember the Ethical Societies. They started off with a great flourish of trumpets, boasting of their higher standards, sneering at those who had to be kept in the right path by the bribe of heaven or the fear of hell. They needed neither bribes nor threats, they said; they rested securely, they boasted, on their simple humanity and sense of duty, on their self-respect. That was not so long ago. Now they think nothing of telling you that chastity and temperance are merely laughable taboos, or that the best teacher for children would be a woman of loose life because she would have more experience. That's where you get to without the historic background."

"Yes, I see," agreed Bobby, though not much interested in ethical societies or historic backgrounds. "What bothers me—of course, I'm speaking in strict confidence —is that Dell seems to have said more than once that Brown would be better dead. As far as I can make out, Brown said first that he had had a Vision like Dell, and then apparently began to hedge and to feel there might be more whisky than vision to it. We found plenty of empty bottles in his cottage. I suppose you can still get it if you are prepared to pay. Duke Dell seemed to think it would be better for Brown to be dead than for him to go back on his story. The question is: Did he think that strongly enough to—well, to see that it was so?"

"Oh, I can't believe that," declared Mr. Childs, and looked very surprised and startled. "A Vision misunderstood, misinterpreted, may lead astray but not like that, not to murder. Surely you can't suspect—?"

"It is my business to suspect," Bobby answered grimly, as Mr. Childs left his sentence uncompleted. Nor could Bobby help wondering if Mr. Childs, even though he seemed so odd a mixture of a child-like simplicity and of profound insight, could possibly be unaware that he himself was under suspicion. "The thing is—if you think a man better dead, what are you likely to do about it? Especially if you are under the influence of something you call a Vision. But I take it you are inclined to believe that Duke Dell isn't merely a humbug, that he may have had some sort of real experience, even if he can't or won't describe it?"

"The indescribable cannot be described," Mr. Childs answered. He was clearly both perplexed and troubled. "Such an experience may come to any, the wind bloweth where it listeth. It may be misunderstood, misinterpreted. But hardly in such a way as to lead to murder. And yet—and yet—and yet strange things have been done in the name of religion, under its over-powering urge."

"Then you do accept it as a possibility that Duke Dell may really have had whatever it is he means when he talks about his Vision?"

"Oh yes. Certainly. Why not? Glimpses of the unseen are not rare. Even in our days. The spiritualist mediums for example— those that are genuine at least. But what comes to them is evidently very often from undeveloped, even evil sources. When that happens outside the discipline and teaching of the church it is like a child playing with a high explosive bomb. Hitler, for example. Perhaps you know that Austria, especially the district Hitler came from, has produced some most remarkable mediums, though chiefly of a low physical type. Hitler's companions used to call him the medicine man. I don't doubt it. But he mis-used, misunderstood, misinterpreted. He heard of the kingdom and thought it meant the kingdom of this world for himself. He chose to believe as he wished to believe and so he was led deeper and deeper. There are depths in the unseen as well as in the heights. Man is always free to choose. Hitler chose. Possibly this man Dell, too, chose. I don't know. But this is all a question of belief, of possibilities. Have you any facts to base such a terrible suspicion on?"

"Oh, none," Bobby answered quickly. "I only wanted to know if from your experience you thought Duke Dell might be genuine or if you thought it more likely he was just a humbug? Or can he be both? Is that possible?"

"All possibilities exist in religion," Mr. Childs told him. "The Spanish Inquisition as well as the martyr Jesuit missionary. The witch hunter side by side with the good Samaritan."

"What it comes to," Bobby said, "is that the motive for Brown's murder may be something quite outside normal experience; and until I can get some idea of the motive, it's all very much groping in the dark. I do wish," he grumbled, "people would keep religion out of their murders."

Whereat Mr. Childs looked so shocked that Bobby had to try to explain away what he had said. He did not succeed very well.

CHAPTER XVII

MIRROR IMAGE

BOBBY LEFT the vicarage in a mood even more troubled, doubtful and uneasy. For now into the already tangled problem facing him had thrust themselves motives and impulses as profound and complicated and hard to understand as any known to humanity. For who can measure or guess the extent to which fanatical belief can drive the spirit of man? Possible, Bobby supposed, that Duke Dell, following what he called his Vision, had killed, believing he did so righteously. Was it not Pascal who said that men never did evil so willingly and completely as when urged by religious conviction?

Again, what had really passed between the dead man and Mr. Childs? Had 'odium theologicum' been the real cause of the quarrel and had the violence generated gone, as violence will, beyond all bounds? If that had happened, would Mr. Childs, certainly an honest man in grain, feel that he must deny it, preserve his secret, not so much for his own sake as to avoid resulting scandal and harm to the church? Some of the things he had said had certainly suggested that he was highly sensitive to public opinion.

But then, in that case, if that was what had really happened, the secret store of gold Brown had hidden away played no part in the tragedy. Bobby found that hard to believe. And what was the meaning of the will leaving it to Mr. Goodman, to whom certainly the bequest had been such a surprise? Again, who was it who had attacked and nearly killed Mr. Spencer and why? For what motive? Was it only a coincidence that Flight Lieutenant Denis Kayes had arrived in Oldfordham at this time? And who was the other young man who bore to Kayes a personal resemblance Bobby refused to believe was only a matter of chance? Bobby told himself moodily that everything he knew was contradicted by everything else. Of only one thing was he sure—that unless and until he could bring into the harmony of one completed whole all these diverse and contradictory elements, the murderer of Alfred Brown would go unidentified and unpunished.

Deep in the confusion of all these thronging thoughts, Bobby, who was intending to go to the police station, took a wrong turning. Not a difficult thing to do in this old part of the town where a labyrinth of steep and narrow streets climbed up and down the hill. He soon realized he had gone astray but he did not turn back— he never liked turning back. Presently he noticed without much interest that he was passing Mason's Temperance Hotel, the only hotel the town boasted, and 'Temperance,' so Sergeant Hicks had unkindly hinted, because Mr. Mason had been unable to obtain a license. Close by, on the same side, was a narrow opening with a sign saying 'To the Station, pedestrians only.' Bobby had nearly gone by before he noticed it. He turned abruptly as it occurred to him that this path would probably take him where he wanted to go, and in turning he came face to face with Miss Theresa Foote, who had apparently just left the Mason establishment.

A chance encounter, of no importance, the most trifling of incidents indeed. But what did startle Bobby was the look on the girl's plump and normally not displeasing features that he glimpsed for just the one passing, fleeting moment during which their eyes met as he turned so unexpectedly. Hate, rage, threat, in the extreme was what he seemed to read in her strangely contorted features, transformed as it were from those of pleasant smiling girlhood into those of a passionate and evil priestess of destruction. It was only a momentary impression, so momentary, so fleeting, in a way so incredible, that he wondered if he had not been deceived by some passing trick of light and shade, if he had not been letting his imagination run away with him. For now, as in the twinkling of an eye, she changed, she was once more the skittish, flirtatious self he had known before. Her voice was all honey and seduction, her innocent blue eyes soft with invitation, as she tripped towards him, holding out her small, daintily gloved hand.

"Oh dear, I'm always so dreadfully frightened when I see you," she twittered. "I always think you've got those awful things just waiting in your pocket, ready to put on anyone you see."

"What awful things are those?" Bobby asked smilingly.

Surely this innocent girlish chatter, those big, wondering, pleading eyes so trustfully upturned, could not be mere camouflage for the hard threat and deadly purpose he had seemed to see mirrored only the moment before in those same soft eyes. He told himself that this case with its mingled and opposed motives of gold and religion, was getting him down. What part in all that dark and evil tangle could this little flirting typist have to play?

"What awful things do you mean?" he asked again.

"Oh, you know," she said as she tripped along by his side, for it seemed she, too, was on her way to the centre of the town, whither this footpath led, "those things you make people put on when you take them away to prison so they can't do anything. Oo-oo." She gave a pretty little shudder. "I don't know how you can," she said. "I should—die," and again she looked up at him, her expression full of fear at the thought of what he could do and of complete confidence that he would never do it to her.

"You mean handcuffs?" Bobby suggested. "As a matter of fact, you know, we don't use them very often. We have to sometimes, of course, if people start giving trouble."

She seemed to lose her interest in handcuffs then, but Bobby was soon aware that she was trying hard to start a flirtation with him. Her little plump face of a china doll, her pouting mouth, her eyes all confidence and allure, were all called into play. Bobby did his best to respond. He was trying to decide whether Miss Foote was one of those girls to whom flirtation is as natural and automatic as breathing, or whether flirtation was being used to hide some deeper purpose—as, for instance, to make him forget what she might fear he had seen in that strange and passing moment when their eyes met.

He even dallied with the idea of suggesting a visit to the pictures—the classic step when relations have once been established. However, he contented himself when he got near his destination with a warm and lingering handshake, with putting on as soulful a look as he could manage, with telling her how much he hoped he would have the pleasure of meeting her again.

"I've such a lot to attend to at the moment," he lamented. "I expect you've heard Mr. Spencer met with an accident last night. He had a fall and hurt his head very badly."

Miss Foote said she had heard about that, and Mr. Spencer was such a nice man, wasn't he? And she did hope it wasn't serious.

Then they shook hands again and Miss Foote tripped away. Bobby had stopped to say goodbye a little further from the police station than was necessary and opposite a grocer's shop. Next to it, further on, was a hairdresser's with, in the window, as Bobby had noticed, a large mirror fixed at a convenient angle. After they had parted, after that handshake that had been just a fraction of a second or so longer than was quite necessary, Bobby moved quickly to get a clear view of what the mirror showed. Merely Miss Foote's back as she tripped away, fumbling in her handbag as she did so, and was it only his imagination again—or self-consciousness perhaps?—that made him think her shoulders were quivering with a sort of suppressed and sardonic mirth? And how did she manage to convey in her gesture, as she snapped to her handbag, a kind of defiant confidence, even threat? Or was that, too, merely fantasy and was he entirely losing his grip upon realities?

He walked on, angry and puzzled. Was it possible she also had noticed that so conveniently placed mirror in the next shop window, and knew very well why he had chosen to stop and say goodbye just where he had? Was she, he wondered, merely an empty-headed little fool to whom one pair of trousers was as good as another? Or was she something very different indeed? Nor was Bobby's temper in any way improved when he entered the police station to find Sergeant Hicks turning away from the window and looking almost as if he were about to venture on an understanding and sympathetic wink, had not a sudden, fierce glare from Bobby nipped any such intention somewhat more than frostily.

Unfortunate, of course, that a long, lingering hand-shake can be so easily misunderstood—especially when it seemed likely that that same long lingering handshake had not been in the least misunderstood by the recipient thereof. Anyhow, Sergeant Hicks had not misunderstood that frosty glare he had received for he was looking quite pale now. Bobby indeed never himself fully realized the formidable and devastating anger and resolve he could at times almost unconsciously put into a single glance.

There was a good deal of routine work to be attended to, paper stuff that Bobby had come here to supervise, work that is not in itself in the least dramatic or interesting, but that is the base all the same of all successful detective work—for that matter of all work everywhere. There were reports to be read and considered, other reports to be written, including one to the Home Office explaining the situation caused by the temporary disablement of Mr. Spencer. In all this Bobby directed and advised, taking great care that as little as possible was said about himself and his activities. Sergeant Hicks was deeply gratified to find that while formal and polite reference was made to the assistance rendered by the Wychshire county police he himself appeared as the fount and the origin of all activities. At first, the good sergeant was a little surprised by this, but very soon he began to think that after all it really was like that.

But the truthful chronicler, when drawing a portrait, must not omit the warts, and the fact is that Bobby was scared to death lest the Home Office should realize the exact position and he in consequence get a rap over the knuckles and instructions to attend to his own Wychshire duties. Enough, he would be told, to keep him fully occupied. All of which would probably mean a Home Office Inspector of Constabulary turning up with Scotland Yard not far behind and all ready to take over. Bobby had a great respect, both human and official, for all the Constabulary Inspectors he had so far come in contact with, but the further away they kept from Wychshire the more he liked them. His ideal Inspector of Constabulary would have been one seconded for duty in one of the more remote provinces of China. In all of which Bobby did less than justice to the perspicacity of the aforesaid inspectors who, as a matter of fact, were saying to each other that if young Bobby Owen, unable to resist the fascination and the challenge of the Oldfordham mystery, as the papers were beginning to call it, had managed to muscle in on the job, so much the better, and very likely the affair was being handled almost as well as it could have been by one of themselves. Anyhow, now it was his pigeon and he could carry on.

By now it was nearly lunch time—long past indeed in Sergeant Hicks's opinion—and he and Bobby had come to the end of their labours. Bobby, consulting his notes to make sure that nothing had been overlooked, said:

"Oh yes. Langley Long. I had almost forgotten about him. You said you would make inquiries. Any information?"

"Well, sir, nothing to speak of," Hicks answered. "Quiet sort of gentleman. Looking out for property to buy. Staying at Mason's."

"Is that the Temperance Hotel?" Bobby asked.

"That's right, sir," agreed Hicks.

"Do they serve lunches?" Bobby asked. "I mean to non-residents?"

"Oh yes, sir, very good lunches indeed," declared the treacherous and ungrateful Hicks, who knew very well that the Mason lunches were a byword in the town, but simply didn't care as long as he got Bobby off somewhere and a chance to adjourn to his own tasty rabbit pie he knew was waiting for him. "You have to send out for your drink," he admitted, "but it's only round the corner."

"I think I'll try them," Bobby said, and Hicks beamed approval.

Thither accordingly Bobby took his way, for he remembered that thence he had seen emerge Miss Theresa Foote, and Miss Theresa Foote was a young woman in whom he was beginning to take a real interest. He remembered having heard something about Langley Long having been seen in her company, and so it seemed likely that her visit to Mason's had been to meet Mr. Langley Long. And Mr. Langley Long bore an odd family resemblance to Denis Kayes. Further the two of them had turned up in this small country town at about the same time and only shortly before these events began. To Bobby, all this, apparent family resemblance, a nearly simultaneous arrival, suggested strongly something more than mere coincidence. Anyhow, it seemed to him plainly desirable to get to know more about Mr. Langley Long, and, in especial, to investigate his connection with a flirtatious young lady who nevertheless could look like a young goddess of death. The possibilities seemed vague, doubtful, uncertain in the extreme, but then this was a case in which it might be said of anything that it might lead anywhere.

CHAPTER XVIII
LUNCHEON AT MASON'S

BUT IN THE MASON dining-room, no Mr. Langley Long was visible. Bobby was disappointed. He had calculated that Miss Foote's call indicated Long's presence in the hotel during the morning and that therefore he was likely to be lunching there. Apparently not, however, so Bobby turned his attention to the menu of 'Mason's famous three-course luncheon for one and eight.' Nothing wrong with the price anyhow, and soup, main dish, and sweet were provided—coffee extra. Bobby, catching sight of the soup on the neighbouring table, shuddered slightly. He decided to give it a miss and proceed direct to the main dish. Here there was a choice of spam jardinière, egg and fish cake, omelette au spam, fish cake hors d'oeuvre, spam pie, fish cake varié, and finally, nobly alone— Spam. The vegetables were boiled potatoes and boiled cabbage. And boiled here means boiled. But Bobby was never one to flinch where the path of duty led and it was still possible that Mr. Langley Long might yet appear. He made his choice, though not without a secret hope that what he ordered would be 'off,' as generally happens to-day in a London restaurant. However, it duly arrived, and at the same time there bustled in Mr. Langley Long himself, apparently fearing, and not as might more reasonably have been expected, hoping, that luncheon was over. Bobby had only seen him once before and then only for a moment, but he knew him again at once. To Bobby's trained eye the resemblance to Denis Kayes was marked, though not so much in feature or colouring, as in a certain trick of carriage, in the distinctive shape of the facial bone structure and also in the unusually small lobe of the unusually flat ear. And Bobby always maintained that the ear was the most characteristic of all features and the one most difficult to disguise.

Langley Long did not seem to notice Bobby, sitting unobtrusively in a corner behind one of the enormous aspidistras that adorned several of the tables. Bobby dallied over his sweet if that can be called a sweet which has never known sugar, and then ordered a cup of coffee—unexpectedly good—and when it arrived took it over to Mr. Long's table, that gentleman, too, having by now arrived at the coffee stage. He greeted Bobby's appearance with that stare of outraged bewilderment and almost incredulous indignation with which any Britisher naturally resents such an intrusion. Bobby produced his most ingratiating smile.

"Mr. Langley Long, I believe?" he said.

Mr. Langley Long remained unappeased. He found relief in the classical retort:

"You have the advantage of me."

"Oh yes, I expect so," agreed Bobby and brought out his card.

He handed it across the table. Mr. Long was still being dignified, distant, resentful, when he took it, but then abruptly his expression changed. There was a startled fear in his eyes now, dismay in his dropped jaw. He became a little pale and even made a slight movement as if to rise and hurry away. Perhaps another glance at Bobby made him realize that that would not be allowed. Instead he muttered sulkily:

"Well, now then. Well, what do you want?"

"Well, you see, if you don't mind," Bobby answered, "there are just one or two things I would like to ask about. Routine inquiries, you understand. One has to do it. I say, this coffee's not so bad, is it? Didn't think much of their lunch, even for a war time lunch, but I've tasted worse coffee. Most people make it like tea—one teaspoon for each person and one for the pot, pour boiling water on and there you are but the coffee isn't. They seem to think it's like logic and mustn't be separated from its grounds. Have a cigarette?"

This chatter, the offer of the cigarette, were intended to put Langley Long more at his ease. The effort was not very successful. The cigarette was accepted, but with more suspicion than gratitude. Nor did it long remain lighted. It was quickly put down and forgotten, and something was mumbled about an appointment, an important appointment.

"I shan't keep you long," Bobby assured him. "If you prefer it, we could walk along together, if your appointment's not too far, and have our chat as we go."

The offer was not accepted. Bobby had not expected that it would be. He felt sure that the appointment was 'ad hoc'—invented for the occasion. Langley Long muttered again, nor had his obvious agitation in any way diminished:

"What's it all about?"

"Routine. Routine," Bobby repeated airily. "Red tape in fact. Police are great devotees of red tape. Have to be. By the way, may I see your identity card?"

"What for?"

"Part of the general check up," Bobby explained. "You'll have heard about the murder here? Poor fellow called Brown killed rather brutally and not a thing to show who did it or why. So all we can do is to make a general check up."

"I've an alibi," Langley Long said eagerly, a little too eagerly. "Some of us were playing cards that night. Solo. You can ask Mason. He'll remember. He ought to. He had nearly ten bob off me. We were at it till close on three." He turned to look for the waitress. Naturally she had her back to him, as is the habit and custom of all her tribe. He began to tap on the table with his spoon. "I'll ask the girl to get Mason—" he began, but Bobby interrupted.

"No, no, quite unnecessary," he declared. "I'm perfectly ready to take your word for it and anyhow I never thought of asking you for an alibi. Why should I? I merely want to know if you can help in any way. Don't forget your identity card, will you?" He added when Langley Long still hesitated: "I expect you know a police officer has the right to ask to see identity cards. I'm not in uniform, I know, but we could go along to the police station if you like."

Again the suggestion was not welcomed. Again Bobby had not expected it would be. Sulkily the thing was produced. Bobby took a note of the particulars. Not that he thought identity cards were of much value. They are easily forged, easily bought—or sold for that matter—in any large city. True, they can be checked to some extent. But not to any very useful extent. The officials concerned can say that such and such a card was duly issued, but there is no way of knowing that the person holding the card is the person to whom it was originally issued. The addition of finger-prints would of course make them more, so to say, realistic. As a policeman Bobby's considered opinion was that that would be a most useful and admirable development. As an ordinary Britisher he knew he would fight any such proposal to the death. He handed back the card.

"Thank you so much," he said. "I understand you are looking out for property to purchase?"

"Well, what about it? Nothing wrong in that, is there?"

"Dear me, no," said Bobby innocently. "You don't think then you can help us in any way?"

"I don't know anything about it," declared Langley Long, "only what I've read in the papers. I don't see why you should think I did."

"Then I suppose I needn't bother you any more," said Bobby, and Langley Long looked extreme relief. "Sorry to have troubled you, but in a case like this we have to worry a lot of people for nothing. Grab at any straw, so to speak. I do hope you'll forgive us.

I always say if there's anything at all unusual, any trifle even, even the mere arrival of a new comer in a town—check it up. It might lead anywhere. Oh, by the bye, do you know Mr. Denis Kayes?"

This remark produced immediate effect, even startling effect. Until now Langley Long, before Bobby's meek, almost deferential attitude, had been gradually regaining confidence. But this new simple question shattered it again. He stared, gobbled, jumped to his feet.

"I won't be badgered any more," he stammered. "I won't. You've no right." He put his hand to his throat and for a moment Bobby almost thought he was going to collapse. His agitation was so marked that one or two of those still lingering over their lunches looked up and stared. Bobby said sharply:

"Pull yourself together."

Without answering, Langley Long began to walk towards the door. This time Bobby made no attempt to stop him. Enough had been said for the present. The train had been laid and fired, so to say, and now it would be better to wait the result—explosion or fizzle. All Bobby's experience told him that developments were very apt to follow when suspects began to realize that the authorities were taking an interest in them. Either they were innocent, and decided they had better tell all they knew, even if that all included matters they would have preferred not to mention. Or they were guilty, and then almost inevitably they made some defensive or precautionary move that again almost inevitably provided fresh indications to follow, fresh clues to follow up. As in chess—or war— when one side has been manoeuvred into a position where he is obliged to move but can only move to his disadvantage. So now he let Long go, hoping that time allowed him for reflection would produce results of one sort or another. He contented himself with calling after Long's retreating figure in tones he tried to make as genial as possible:

"Well, come along and have a chat whenever you feel like it. Always glad to see you."

He hoped that not only would Long remember this invitation and act upon it if he decided to tell what he knew—if, that is, he did know anything relevant—but that also the friendly tone adopted would quench the suspicions and curiosity of those present who had begun to look up and stare and suspect trouble between their fellow guest and his visitor. Bobby hoped very much none of them knew who he was. He knew the little town was full of newspapermen and he had no wish to put any of them on Langley Long's track. Sometimes newspapermen brought in useful information, but there were some of them who had a tendency to put headlines above the claims of justice.

Langley Long, walking on towards the door, made no response, might not have heard. But when he reached the door and thought perhaps that in the shadows there he was well hidden, he turned to throw a farewell glance at Bobby. He had failed to notice, though, that from a small window without a beam of light crossed where he was standing and showed plainly his features twisted with hate and fear and rage till they were almost unrecognizable. There was indeed a look in his staring eyes that made Bobby think of a similar look he had received before that day—from Miss Theresa Foote.

"Caught it from her perhaps," Bobby said to himself. "Have to watch my step with those two."

He paid his bill then and as he was leaving the hotel noticed in the hat stand in the hall, near the entrance, several umbrellas and walking sticks. One of these caught his eye. It was of some heavy wood Bobby could not identify, it had a heavy silver head, and there was some unusual carving on it by way of decoration. He took it out to look at it. A suspicious voice behind said:

"That's Mr. Long's."

"Yes, I know," Bobby answered and of course now he did know. "I was looking at it. Quite unusual. Interesting."

The suspicious voice belonged to Mr. Mason, the proprietor of the hotel. He came forward and took it from Bobby's hand. Evidently he had no intention of letting Bobby walk away with it.

"Australian wood," he said. "Made by the black fellows out there."

He put the stick back firmly in its place. Just as firmly Bobby took it out again. Mr. Mason looked very indignant. Bobby made sure that his first impression was correct. Beyond doubt, it had recently been well and carefully cleaned—scrubbed and polished indeed. Traces of burning and scraping, too. No precaution neglected. Bobby made no comment. Suspects who felt that too much attention was being given to them, were apt to vanish silently away, leaving no trace behind. It made things much more difficult. Much better to keep them on tap, if possible. Bobby put back the stick, said 'goodbye' to the still suspicious and indignant Mr. Mason, and went on to the police station, nobly resisting on the way the temptation to get another lunch. At the police station a fresh report had come in. It was of some interest. It was from the Air Force people and confirmed that Flight Lieutenant Denis Kayes, R.A.A.F., was due to report for duty at the end of the month. It was understood he had already arrived in the country, but no one had seen him yet. He had been appointed on strong recommendation received from Australia but personally he was unknown in London and so no personal description could be given.

Bobby did not find this very helpful or illuminating. Most likely this Denis Kayes was the real Denis Kayes, but he would have liked to be sure. One had to check everything. Even if you were told that two and two made four, it was better to get the statement confirmed by a competent authority. He gave a few more instructions to Sergeant Hicks—a slightly sleepy Sergeant Hicks for that rabbit pie had been excellent—and then he got out his car and drove back to Midwych, to see to things there. Not but that his very competent subordinates were fully capable of dealing with anything likely to turn up. Then he drove home and asked pathetically if he could have something nice for dinner because he had not so much had a lunch as endured a nightmare. Olive told him sternly that there was a war on. She knew, because all the shopkeepers told her that every day if she ever dared ask for anything off the ration, but did he? Bobby said he had heard rumours and anyhow couldn't she muck in his breakfast with dinner, because he thought he had better spend the night in Oldfordham where Mrs. Spencer had promised to give him a bed.

Olive said she had never heard such a vulgar expression as muck in, disgusting when used in reference to food, and he had better muck out and let her get on with her work. Also, with considerable suspicion, in her voice, she asked why Oldfordham that night and what had he got in his head now? So Bobby said he didn't know, he only wished he did. Things were going round and round in his head till he felt quite dizzy. Now and then he seemed to get a glimpse of a pattern beginning to form and then it would dissolve again, leaving not a trace behind. The worst of it was that he had not been able to find a single material clue—except, of course, the scraps of black thread on the broken kitchen chair. And that didn't amount to much. Not much of an 'Exhibit A.' All the rest of it was psychological stuff and what was the good of psychological stuff for a show down before a British jury? Yet he felt somehow it was all there. If only he could see where it all belonged, and how to put together what he knew to make a reasonable and coherent whole, then at last the truth would emerge. Only he had no idea how to do that or even where to begin—whether with Mr. Child's torn trouser-knee; or Langley Long's cleaned and polished walking stick; or Duke Dell's Vision and his belief that it would be better that Brown should die rather than that he should live, denying it; or Mr. Goodman's legacy; or Theresa Foote's murderous eyes; or Janet Jebbs' reported interest in back doors; or the injured Spencer's murmur of Denis Kayes's name; or the dead man's hidden store of gold; or indeed any other of the oddly disconnected events that yet all without exception seemed somehow or another continually to act and react upon each other.

He was still in much the same worried and unhappy mood—'frustrated' is the fashionable word of the moment—when later on he sat in Mr. Spencer's room, reading and re-reading the various memoranda and reports of one kind and another that had already accumulated to make a formidable and ever growing pile.

Time and again he put down on paper what seemed to him the salient points of the case and time and again he tore the paper up and threw it in the waste paper basket. It was all very quiet. Everyone else in the house had gone to bed. He got up and went to the window to look out over the sleeping town. So Mr. Spencer must have stood and looked when he saw the light where none should have been that had sent him forth on the errand ending so unfortunately.

A light in Brown's cottage. That was what he had seen, Bobby felt certain, but whose light? And now Bobby saw it too—a light in a window of what should have been an empty cottage, since Sergeant Hicks had suggested and Bobby had agreed, that, especially as no one could be conveniently spared, it was no longer necessary to keep a constable constantly there on duty.

Quickly and quietly Bobby slipped out into the hall, closed silently the front door behind him and went out into the night.

CHAPTER XIX

NOCTURNAL TALKS

THE NIGHT WAS clear and starlit. Oldfordham had not yet been able to do much in the way of street lighting, not even within the limits now officially allowed; but here and there the lighted windows permitted in the 'dim out' helped to give a degree of illumination. Bobby was able to make good progress as he hurried along; and when he reached Market Row he could make out, standing there in the open space before the cottages, a figure of a size and bulk not easily mistaken. Bobby said:

"Mr. Dell, what are you doing here?"

Dell must have heard Bobby coming, for the sound of footsteps had been loud in the stillness of that quiet night, but he had not moved. Even now he did not stir or so much as turn his head. Presently he said and almost with a groan:

"I am troubled in my mind."

"Why?" Bobby asked.

But Dell made no answer. He seemed to have sunk again into deep and uneasy meditation. Not till Bobby had repeated his question twice over did he seem to hear it and then he said:

"Things come to me in my sleep or even when I am about my work. I think there is a meaning and a message, but I do not know what."

"What do you mean?" Bobby asked impatiently, for this was the sort of thing that his plain matter of fact mind, avid of facts only, did not much appreciate. "Do you mean dreams?"

"I do not know. I never remember," Dell answered. "When I wake I only know that I am troubled. All I know at other times is that there is something in my mind I cannot get at."

"But surely you must know what about?" Bobby persisted. "You must know what you've been dreaming about, or what's the connection if anything's worrying you?"

Duke Dell raised his great arm in an unconsciously dramatic gesture. It was his great gift as a preacher that his gestures were often dramatic but always spontaneous. Now his slow sweeping gesture rested on the cottage where Brown had died. He said:

"About our brother who is dead."

"Well, then," Bobby said. "Well?"

"I think there is something he greatly wishes but I am not sure."

"Perhaps what he wants is that his murderer should be caught and punished," Bobby suggested, somewhat tartly.

"No, no," Dell answered. "That's not likely. I don't feel that. Why should he? He's not likely to think that matters now."

"Oh, isn't he?" grunted Bobby. "Why not? It would interest me, I think. And you haven't told me yet why all that should bring you here at this time of night."

"I told you," Dell retorted. "I could not sleep because when I did I dreamed and then I woke and I could not remember anything except that it troubled me. So I dressed and came out here."

"Mrs. Soames would wonder what you were up to," Bobby remarked.

"I don't think I disturbed her or Soames either," Dell answered. "I made as little noise as I could and they sleep soundly."

At any rate, Bobby reflected, this question and answer demonstrated the worthlessness of the alibi suggested by Mrs. Soames's testimony that on the night of the murder Duke Dell had slept at her house as usual. Bobby did not quite know what to say next. A profession of ignorance is difficult to counter. If a witness says he doesn't know, it is generally impossible to prove that he does. On his thoughts broke the voice of Dell, speaking again. He said:

"Has any human being the right to punish any other human being?"

"You might as well ask," retorted Bobby impatiently, "if you have a right to keep a watchdog or a farmer a sheep dog."

"Dogs and sheep are not human beings," Dell answered and went on slowly: "There is a right of self-defence. We are bidden to sell what we have that we may buy a sword. There may be a duty to protest against wrong doing and punishment is a way of protest."

"Punishment has nothing to do with me, one way or another," Bobby told him. "My duty is to get at the truth. That's all. Then the law can carry on. The law's responsibility, not mine. My job is to find out who killed Alfred Brown and why? Do you know?"

"Oh yes," Dell answered.

The reply was so unexpected that it was a moment or two before Bobby, recovering slightly, said:

"Well, who?"

But Dell only shook his head.

"I shall not tell you that," he answered.

"Why not?" demanded Bobby, a little bewildered now. "Do you mean you want to help Brown's murderer to go unpunished?"

"Nothing ever goes unpunished," Dell replied. "The punishment lies in the act—in the thought."

"You were saying just now," Bobby reminded him, "that there is both a right and a duty to punish."

"Not my right nor my duty," Dell retorted. "Do your duty as you see it, but it is not mine."

"How do you know who is the murderer?" Bobby insisted.

"I must not answer questions," Dell answered. "I've never had any education. It is easy to get confused in question and answer, to say too much. If I answered your question I should soon be telling you what I saw and that I will not. I think that also is in what has come to me—the message or the warning that I can't get clearly enough to be sure of."

Bobby stared at him, baffled and annoyed. He had never come across anything like this before. The man might simply be a colossal humbug or possibly an example of self-delusion on a gigantic scale. Yet somehow he impressed. Perhaps by the mere force of the enormity of his deception—conscious or unconscious. Bobby asked:

"Is all this what you are told by your Vision you are so fond of talking about?"

"The Vision is not like that," Dell explained. "It shows you plainly where lies your home. But the way there is for you to find. If you seek it is shown, but for you alone. Others must first see the Vision themselves and then they too will be shown if they search."

A note of exaltation had crept into his voice. Huge as was his form it seemed to grow, to dilate, to grow till in that dim light it seemed to tower towards the sky. Bobby had to struggle against the impression that was being made on him. It was a feeling that he did not understand, that he resented because he felt that it was the intrusion of another personality upon his own, nor did he know whether it was good or bad. The feeling passed, but it left him better able to understand how enormous could be the influence Duke Dell might be able to exercise upon others. Bobby felt he could see him as the leader of some vast crusade. Then he told himself crossly that he had not come out here at this time of night to indulge in abstract metaphysical discussion. He said a little loudly:

"If you do know who the murderer is, it's your plain duty to tell."

But Dell only shook his head.

"No," he said.

"How do you know?" Bobby persisted, and this time Dell did answer for he said simply:

"I saw and heard."

"What?" Bobby asked, but Dell once again shook his head.

"It's no good asking me to say what I will not," he said quietly.

"Was it you yourself?" Bobby asked.

"Me myself what?"

"Was it you killed Brown?"

"No. Why should you think that?"

The voice was quiet and untroubled, not much surprised, not even much interested. Somehow it managed to convey an impression that the question was trivial, silly in fact, childish. Bobby said, and with a touch of self-defence in his voice:

"Well, you know, I heard you say at Chipping Up it would have been better if Brown had drowned in the stream where he fell when you knocked him down. If he hadn't been hauled out of the water in time he would have been dead. You would have been responsible."

"Should I?" Dell asked meditatively. "I remember that I wondered if my arm had been guided. But I did not know at the time what I had done. Truly, it would have been better had he died then, for he gained only a few hours of life and much, much would have been saved."

"If it would have been better then, did you help it to happen later?" Bobby asked.

"No. It is always far better to go hence. It is always better for little children to go home and what else is death? But we must wait till we and it are ready. The uninvited guest may not be well received. You must not run a risk like that, either for yourself or for others. Receive your summons with joy but you must wait for it."

"Oh, well," Bobby muttered. With an effort he added: "I'm not at all satisfied. I tell you that plainly. Do you want me to understand that there is nothing you will tell me except that your mind is troubled? I don't see why that should make you come wandering round here late at night when there's no one about. Have you heard people saying Brown had a store of hidden gold?"

"I expect everyone has heard that now," Dell answered. "At least I suppose so. He told me some time ago."

"Told you?" Bobby exclaimed. "Did you tell anyone else?" he asked suspiciously.

"Oh no. It was his affair, his business if he wanted to keep it secret. I told no one."

Bobby reflected gloomily that even if Dell believed himself to be speaking the truth, it did not go for much. Dell might very easily have said something that now he had entirely forgotten and that yet might have put someone else on the scent. The whole scope of the investigation seemed suddenly to have widened. Bobby said:

"It's probably why he's dead, that hidden gold of his. Were you looking to see if any of it was left when you were in there?"

"In where?"

"In the cottage," Bobby said impatiently, jerking a hand towards it. "I saw your light. That's what brought me out."

Dell shook his head.

"That wasn't me," he said. "I've not been in. If you saw a light it wasn't mine." Then he said: "There's someone coming out now."

Bobby turned sharply. The door of the cottage was opening. A man came out. Even in that dim half light, Bobby could recognize him. Bobby flashed a light from his torch to make sure. He said:

"Mr. Kayes. What's this mean?"

"The Deputy Chief, isn't it?" Kayes asked, coming towards them. "Always on the spot, aren't you?" he said in a rather rueful tone. "I wasn't doing anything."

"Why were you there at all?" Bobby demanded. "I should be justified in charging you—found on enclosed premises for a presumed unlawful purpose."

"Nothing unlawful in looking round an empty house, is there?" retorted Kayes.

"How did you get in?" demanded Bobby, prudently leaving this question unanswered.

"The door wasn't locked. That's why. I mean I only meant to have a look and then I tried the door and it wasn't locked so I went in."

Dell interposed.

"I'll be getting back to bed," he said. "I think I shall be able to sleep now."

Bobby swung round on him. He said with energy:

"Mr. Dell. I want to give you a very serious warning. If you really know anything and keep it back, you become an accessory after the fact. That means you make yourself liable to a heavy term of imprisonment."

"It wouldn't be the first time," Dell answered tranquilly. "There is much work to be done in prisons if you are there as one of themselves. It may be I am to be guided there. Good-night and God be with you. I think that you mean well, though blind and ignorant and much deceived."

He turned and strode away, leaving Bobby and Kayes staring after him. Kayes said:

"Queer sort of bloke. Don't know what to make of him, do you?"

"Just at present," Bobby retorted, recovering slightly from the shock of Duke Dell's parting address, "I want to know what to make of you, Mr. Kayes. You haven't given me a very satisfactory explanation of what you've been doing."

"I told you," Kayes answered sulkily. "I had to walk part of the way back. I've been in Midwych and I got the wrong 'bus coming back so I've had to walk from where they put me down. When I was passing the cottage I thought I would have a look and I tried the door and it wasn't locked so I went in."

"You went upstairs?"

"I told you I had a look round."

After a moment he added: "There's a rummy yarn going the rounds about a pile of gold sovereigns you've found."

"Who told you?" Bobby demanded.

"Everyone's talking about it," Kayes answered. "Is it true? The milkman had the story first thing this morning. He told them at the house. Now it's in the evening paper."

"Oh, Lord," said Bobby, with resignation, not with surprise. He had known that was to be expected. "You had heard this morning," he added sharply. "You didn't say anything when I saw you."

"Well, why should I? Nothing to do with me, is it? Only start you off bully-ragging again."

"People who keep things back and are found late at night in places where they have no right to be, invite bully-ragging, as you call it," Bobby retorted. "We think we are entitled to expect that anyone holding the King's commission should be more helpful than you seem inclined to be."

"You've no right to talk like that," Kayes retorted hotly. "I still don't see what harm there is in my having a look round the place. There's nothing 'helpful' as you call it that I know and I'm not keeping anything back. I mean anything about Brown's murder. I haven't told you the full history of my life, if that's what you mean."

"It isn't," Bobby snapped. "I mean I've found you where you had no right to be and I don't like it. Do you know Mr. Langley Long?"

"Langley Long?" repeated Kayes, slightly taken aback by this sudden change in the conversation. "Who is he? Never heard of him that I know of."

"He arrived in Oldfordham just about the same time that you did."

"Well, what about it? Why shouldn't he? Are you trying to make but we came together?"

"No, but he seems to know you so I wondered if you knew him."

"Know me? Well, I haven't the foggiest ... is he an Aussie?"

"I don't think so. Southern English, I should think."

"Well, then," Kayes said.

"I think you know Miss Foote, don't you?"

"No, and I don't want to. I told you so before. This morning she gave me the glad eye in the High Street. I think I'm getting nervy. Glad eye all right and meant to be, but it sent shivers all up and down my back. Last time she looked at me like poison and now the sweet come hither, and I didn't like it. So I pretended I didn't see her and she knew I did, and then she had the killer look and that's God's truth."

"What do you mean? The 'killer' look?"

"I've seen it before," Kayes answered slowly. "When it's you or the Jap—one or the other and you both know it. If you've seen it once, you know it all right when you see it again and that girl had it. Now go on and tell me I'm lying or drunk or something."

Bobby made no reply. He knew no more what to make of this, or of Theresa Foote herself, than he knew what to make of Duke Dell. Nor was he much inclined to think that Kayes was talking at random. There was an odd accent of nervous intensity in his voice that carried conviction. Yet how to reconcile a 'killer' look with the lip stick, the carefully powdered nose, the tiny artfully deranged curl, all the other small feminine tricks in which the flirtatious Miss Foote was so evidently, almost ingenuously, expert. It was as though you went to gather roses and from among them there hissed at you a deadly snake, it was as though sweet music changed all at once to the shrill whistle of falling bombs. Bobby turned to stare into the dim half light in which Duke Dell's huge form was still faintly visible, for he had gone slowly and heavily. To Bobby this baffling half light, in which so much could be glimpsed and guessed at and yet nothing seen with clarity, was like the half knowledge and dim guesswork in which his own mind laboured. He said to Kayes:

"Mr. Langley Long knows Miss Foote. He has been seen with her."

"There was a tall, thin bloke with her this morning," Kayes remarked. "I didn't notice him much. I've never seen him before that I know of. What did you mean, telling Dell he could be run in as an accessory?"

"He told me he knew who murdered Brown," Bobby answered. "He said he saw something—heard something."

"Did he though?" Kayes muttered, and now it was impossible to mistake the note of dismay, of terror even, that was so clearly evident in his voice.

CHAPTER XX

FOUR OAKS DINING-ROOM

ON THE MORROW, Bobby had a busy morning. Various information had come in. Many different rumours had to be traced and checked. It was all lost labour, all of it leading only to dead ends, and so need not be put on record. In every such investigation three quarters, sometimes even nine tenths, of the work done turns out to be either superfluous or irrelevant and so in the end not even worth mentioning. All the same it has to be done, because, by one of the ceaseless contradictions of life, it is not only futile, it is necessary too. As Bobby himself sometimes remarked, when sending one of his men on some errand only too likely to turn out a wild goose chase: 'It might lead anywhere.'

All this kept Bobby busy till late in the afternoon. Then he decided that things were sufficiently in order for him to be able to return to Midwych. But when he rang up headquarters to ask that a car should be sent for him, he learned to his dismay that every single police car was out on duty. Of course, as deputy chief, he was accustomed to that. If a junior is ordered by a senior to carry out some duty, he has to be provided with the necessary tools. Otherwise the excuse for failure is too easy. So often enough juniors must ride and seniors manage as best they can.

The way Bobby managed was to borrow, firmly, the bicycle belonging to the reluctant but sedentary Sergeant Hicks, and to set off thereon. The day was fine and warm; and Bobby would thoroughly have enjoyed the ride, itself so pleasant a contrast to a seat before a table piled high with documents, had not his mind been so ill at ease.

True, there was at last a hint or semblance of some things falling into place, but also there were many that still remained recalcitrant. Moreover much of what he knew, or thought he knew, was merely a logical construction deduced from facts that might turn out to bear an entirely different interpretation. Not till this possibility was eliminated, not till there had been reached a harmony of all to make a complete and perfect whole, could action be taken. Precipitate action in a wrong direction might bring about a complete fiasco.

Bobby, as he cycled on, was turning all this over in his mind, in the forefront of it the huge enigmatic figure of Duke Dell and the troubled fear Denis Kayes had shown when he learned that Dell claimed to know the murderer's name because of what that night he 'saw and heard.' His way took him through Chipping Up, drowsing so peacefully in the sun that it seemed impossible that there angry passions should ever rise. From Chipping Up, a secondary road led presently to the main Midwych highway. But by going a little way round he could pass Four Oaks, the residence of Mr. Goodman, and he decided to do this and to call there for a brief talk. A useful pretext would be Mr. Spencer's injury and Mr. Goodman's half promise to consult Spencer over the disposition of the store of sovereigns found in Brown's possession. The real reason was that Bobby wanted to see Miss Foote again. Did she, he wondered, play a part, even a leading part, in the secret drama now, he felt, being played out to an end he could not foresee, a secret drama in which the murder of Brown had been merely the opening scene? Another talk with her might help him to make up his mind about her, to form a better estimate of her character—flirtatious or murderous. He wondered if he, too, would see a 'killer' look in those wide innocent blue eyes, in that soft round baby face? Difficult to believe. Yet he remembered well enough that strangely derisive swing of the shoulders he had seen mirror-reflected in a shop window as the girl left him the day before, and the still stranger, more disturbing hint of menace she had somehow managed to put into the gesture with which she had lifted her handbag. Her back had been towards him though, so he had not been able to see whether there was a 'killer' or any other look in eyes he chiefly remembered as extremely 'forthcoming.'

At Four Oaks Bobby dismounted and wheeled his cycle up the short, gravelled drive. There seemed to be no one about. It all looked as drowsy as Chipping Up itself—or as Sergeant Hicks after a good dinner of rabbit pie. The door hung open. Bobby leaned his cycle against the wall and was about to knock when he heard quite plainly a woman's voice that said:

"Drop that. Don't move. Don't dare."

There was menace in that voice, a deadly threat, or so it seemed to Bobby. The voice came through the partly open door of a room on his right, just across the entrance hall. Swiftly and silently—he was a big man but he knew how to move softly enough when need was—Bobby crossed the passage and pushed back the door. It was the dining-room he saw and in it were

Mr. Goodman and Theresa Foote, facing each other across the mahogany table, above a great vase of freshly gathered flowers. And in Theresa's hand showed a small shining automatic, and before Mr. Goodman, on the table, as though he had just put it down, lay a heavy ebony ruler, a formidable enough weapon at need.

Softly as Bobby had moved, both Goodman and Theresa had heard the door swing back or perhaps were conscious of the vibrations his movements had set up either in the air or on the boarding of the floors of passage and room. Goodman gave a low cry—was it of fear or relief or both? Theresa turned and for that instant Bobby saw what he supposed Denis Kayes called the 'killer' look. For just that one fraction of a moment he felt as it were a whisper of death, so balefully glared those wide blue eyes, so deadly a snarl twisted those raddled lips. Then the change. Once again the wide blue eyes were soft and inviting, the lips a pouting smile, the small white jewelled hand where before death had seemed to wait outstretched now in gladsome welcome.

"It's that nice policeman again," she exclaimed in dulcet tones where no threat or menace lingered; and when Bobby looked past her he saw that Mr. Goodman was trembling violently and that drops of sweat showed upon his forehead.

Remembering this incident, Bobby was inclined later on to count it one of his failures. He ought to have rushed into the room and seized, before she had had time to dispose of it, what he had seen gleam in Theresa's hand, that hand now empty and outstretched in welcome. But in that moment when he had his first glimpse of the scene the opening door revealed he had hesitated for the fraction of a second as he took in its full significance, as Mr. Goodman cried out and Theresa turned and looked. Also between him and her had been chairs that would have hindered a direct rush and most certainly she possessed a gift of an incredible certitude and speed in action. As swiftly and as certainly as she could change her expression and her mood, so swiftly could she act. However quickly he had moved, she might have been quicker still and the automatic been safely disposed of before he could reach her side.

Bobby himself, at this moment, could have believed he had dreamed. For now there was nothing but a pleasant room gay with flowers on a table at which were seated an elderly gentleman apparently about to sneeze or blow his nose since his face was hidden in his handkerchief and, opposite him, a smiling pretty baby-faced girl, her eyes, her pouting lips all laughing invitation, her gay, dulcet voice saying:

"Oh, but I mustn't call you a policeman, must I? Aren't you ever so awfully too important?"

Bobby was at her side now. Her small upturned face still smiled gay invitation, smiled admiring wonder at this great big man towering over her little, little self. No trace now visible of that wicked little automatic he had seen, or dreamed he had seen, just the moment before. He picked up her handbag and emptied it on the table.

"Oh, how rude," said Theresa, quite shocked.

No automatic there of course. Just the usual clutter of feminine belongings that accumulate in a woman's handbag as naturally as things of another nature accumulate in a school boy's pockets.

Bobby said:

"What had you in your hand just now?"

"I don't know—was it this? I think I was holding it," Theresa said, and picked up from the small pile of her possessions on the table a flat metal lighter.

She pointed it at him much as he had seen her the moment before level the automatic at Goodman; and Bobby saw clearly in her eyes that she mocked him. He turned to Goodman.

"Well," he asked roughly, "have you anything to say?"

Goodman put his handkerchief away. His face was still pale, his hands were still shaking, but his voice was steady as he answered:

"No. Why? What about?"

No help to be expected from him evidently. Bobby turned back to Theresa. Her eyes still mocked him but in her red and smiling lips was an evil invitation. Neither of them spoke, but between their eyes challenge and defiance tossed to and fro. All the same Bobby knew that he was beaten—for the time. Very likely the girl had that small flat deadly automatic hidden on her person and therefore safe from him. He could not search her. He could take her with him of course for the matron at headquarters to search. Useless. She would have innumerable opportunities for disposing of it before he got her there. Again it might not be anywhere on her person. So swift, silent, secret, were her movements when she wished them so, that quite possibly she had got rid of it in some other manner. She might even have passed it to Goodman who seemed to be now her accomplice as before he had seemed likely to be her victim. Bobby picked up the great ebony ruler from where it lay on the table. He said:

"You could kill a man with this or even a woman."

Theresa gave her pretty little scream.

"Oh, what a horrid thing to say," she protested. "I shall just simply be ever so awfully frightened now every time I see Mr. Goodman pick it up."

Her silvery, girlish laughter trilled out in the quiet room. Neither of the other two responded. Bobby told himself gloomily that there was nothing he could do. Plain enough that between these two, the little smiling girl with the deadly eyes, the elderly, retired solicitor, there lay something hidden, deadly and menacing; but plain enough also that whatever it might be and whatever its nature, they meant to ask no help from him, but instead, to deal with it in their own way.

Apparent then, that not only did there lie in the past the unsolved mystery of the death of Alfred Brown but also that the future was heavy with the threat of murder still to come. Nor did he see how he was to deal with or avert a threat of which he knew only that it existed, but knew neither its cause nor its object; neither its provenance nor its imminence.

"I'll go now," he said, and stood and looked at them, and neither of them showed by any sign or movement that they had so much as heard him speak.

He went towards the door. There he paused and looked round. He said:

"Well, if you want me, either of you, you know where to find me, day or night." There was no answer. He said very softly: "I think it might be safer for one of you and perhaps for both."

They remained unresponsive. He might have been addressing the dead, so still and silent were they. The ugly thought came into his mind that perhaps he was—the living dead, the as-good-as-dead, those for whom life was as near to ending as for the condemned who hear approaching the footsteps of the executioner. He wondered which was executioner and which was victim.

"Well, now then, it's up to you," he said and went away, and left them there, facing each other across the shining mahogany table, above the vase of newly-gathered flowers.

CHAPTER XXI
PLAIN FACTS

"AND WHAT," asked Olive, looking very bewildered, when Bobby had finished telling her of the events of the afternoon, "what does all that mean? Do you think the girl really was going to shoot Mr. Goodman? Why should she?"

"I don't much think she wanted to shoot," Bobby answered reflectively. "My own idea is that she was defending herself, self defence. Don't forget the ebony ruler. I rather imagine the last thing she wants at present is Goodman's death. And I don't know that I would give an awful lot for Goodman's chances if she did want to get rid of him."

"Oh," said Olive, and added, with a touch of unease in her voice: "Well, if she's like that, I hope there's no one else she wants to get rid of."

"Shouldn't wonder," said Bobby, thoughtfully sipping his coffee, and pausing for a moment to thank heaven for having provided him, all unworthy, with a wife who really knew how to make it. "Me, for instance."

"Bobby, don't," snapped Olive.

"Quite all right," Bobby informed her. "I only said I shouldn't wonder and I don't suppose for a moment she wants it badly enough to have a try. Too risky, too difficult. All the same, I wouldn't take her on as cook, or sit with my back to the door if I knew she was in the next room."

"What did you mean about the ebony ruler? Why had she got to defend herself against Mr. Goodman?"

Bobby put down his coffee cup, ran both hands through his hair in a sort of gesture of despair new to him, and said:

"If only I knew that ... I've been trying to work it out till I feel like resigning and getting a job selling ice-cream or something I could feel I could get really on top of."

"You surely haven't begun to think it's Miss Foote who did it?"

"Killed Brown? No. Good alibi and not even suspiciously good. I've been on the phone to Mr. Childs and one of the Oldfordham men knows the Four Oaks cook, Mrs. Fuller—he's some sort of cousin or something. Mrs. Fuller says Miss Foote had a bad cold coming on that night and went to bed early, and that she—Mrs. Fuller—took her up some sort of private, patent concoction of her own just as Childs was going; gave Miss Foote the stuff and tucked her up in bed; remembers distinctly hearing the car go off with Mr. Childs, and then went to bed herself; and in the morning the cold had vanished without trace. Mr. Childs confirms. Miss Foote was sniffling at dinner; she went to bed early; he remembers seeing Mrs. Fuller taking her concoction up to her as he was waiting in the hall for the car to come round, and he remembers hearing them talking upstairs. Mrs. Fuller may be lying. The Foote girl may have slipped out instead of going to bed and got to Oldfordham somehow—perhaps she hung on to the back of the car that took Childs there. But it would take rather a lot to persuade counsel to put any theory like that before a jury. No, I think we must count Theresa clearly out—out—out." He repeated the last word three times, staring blankly in front of him. "All the same, there's an idea there," he said.

"Where?" asked Olive. "All that's just fantastic."

"Yes, I know," agreed Bobby, but he was looking intent and even excited. "What was Childs' story?—accepting him as a witness of truth. He says Goodman's small car was out of action, so Goodman told the chauffeur, who said he couldn't make out what was wrong, to bring the big Rolls Royce round—and never mind the petrol. Goodman gets his ration, of course, like every other country dweller, for shopping and so on, but not for sending visitors home, not even when the visitor happens to be an elderly parson, nervous about cycling in the dark. There could have been a prosecution and a fine. When the chauffeur brought the car round, Goodman helped to put Childs's cycle in the back seat and then there was a phone call and Goodman ran back into the house. He closed the door with a bang, and the night was dark, so it couldn't possibly have been opened again to let Miss Foote out. The light from the hall would have shown. Nor, even if you let your imagination run wild, could she have been lurking outside, since Childs says he heard her and Mrs. Fuller talking as he was waiting in the hall. If the stories told by Mr. Childs and Mrs. Fuller are true, and there's no reason to doubt them, it seems pretty conclusive, doesn't it?"

"Well, then," said Olive, but she was looking puzzled, "what's your idea?"

"Also, though a woman could smash in a man's head with a poker if she really put her mind to it, it's not, so to say, what you expect."

"Well, then," said Olive again.

"Seems to wash out Theresa all right," Bobby said. "All the same, she comes in somewhere, somehow. Only how? So does Goodman. He is in it. But where? Nothing I can put up to the public prosecutor crowd. They would probably remind me I was supposed to be investigating Brown's death, and all of that was entirely irrelevant, so hadn't I better stick to my job?"

"Well," said Olive somewhat impatiently, "if there is something going on, what's it all about?"

"Exactly," said Bobby. "What is it all about? Religion? Religion comes into it somehow and so does money, and religion and money can make people do queer things."

"Very queer things," agreed Olive. "Only—"

"Excessively queer things," confirmed Bobby, ignoring the 'only.' "In fact, the very queerest things people do are generally mixed up with one or other. More so even than with girls."

"I don't know about that," protested Olive, always ready to stand up for her sex. "Boys and girls are so very odd about each other. Why, look at me," said Olive, wide-eyed with reminiscence; "look at me about you."

"Lunacy, of course," agreed Bobby, "but temporary lunacy only. Religion and money—permanent. And the older you are, the more they count. High explosive if you don't handle 'em right. I'm working on the idea that what happened to Brown is a part of what's going on now. Generally, murder is a climax and an end. This murder, if not a beginning to the play—perhaps there never is a true and real beginning, everything is always so tied up with everything else—was, at any rate the opening of a new act. Take the religious motive. Brown seemed indifferent for years and then suddenly shows an active interest. Why? Because, apparently, of Duke Dell's preaching. That brings Duke Dell in. Dell claims to have had what he calls a Vision. Brown said he had had one, too, and then thought most likely he had only been drunk. And you are apt to see things when you are drunk. Rats and pink elephants generally, but why not a Vision instead? Brown also had a lot of gold sovereigns hidden. There's your money motive. Why hidden? Miser instinct? Some people think it safer in these uncertain days to keep their money or valuables by them. You often hear of it. Old people with large sums they carry about with them. Some people stock up with razor-blades and postage stamps all ready for the Nazi invasion or a revolution, or any other old thing that comes along. Just as others provided themselves with poison. It may have been like that with Brown. Something solid in a changing world, and what could be more solid than gold? Can you think of any other reason?"

"Yes, of course," said Olive.

"Good," said Bobby, without asking what it was. "Next point. Why did he make a will leaving the whole lot to Goodman, his old employer? Affection and respect? Gratitude? It doesn't seem likely. Goodman suggests embezzlement and restitution, and says he discharged Brown, because he suspected Brown's honesty. Bit difficult to accept that a managing clerk could do down the solicitors employing him for such a large sum and the loss not be spotted for so long. But if Goodman is lying or keeping something back—well, why?"

"It's always 'why'?" complained Olive. "What's the good of 'why'?"

"None," agreed Bobby, "so let's take the bare facts and see what they add up to—if anything. About Brown we have the facts of hidden gold, revived religious emotion, general secrecy; a former employer living fairly close whom he makes his heir, though there's no trace of any intercourse or connection between them. Any deductions?"

"Only that it's time to go to bed if you mean to be fit for anything in the morning."

"Two more things we know about Brown. He was a secret drinker, he had a passion for music, and you re-member he was listening in to New York when he was killed."

"Does that help?"

"Well, does it? Go on to Duke Dell. It was Duke Dell's preaching that seems to have stirred up Brown. Brown becomes a bit of a disciple, but shows signs of relapsing, so Dell expresses the opinion that Brown would be better dead. So did he? Dell has no alibi but he says now he is troubled in his mind and goes prowling about at night. Also he says he knows who the murderer is but he won't tell. Can you deduce, argue from that, that he has the best possible reason both for knowing and for not telling?"

"He's an awfully big man," Olive said thoughtfully. "I suppose he could smash in anyone's head as easily as anything."

"Oh yes," agreed Bobby. "Next, our young airman, Denis Kayes, coming to Oldfordham on a not very clearly explained errand. He visits Goodman to ask for details about the distribution of an uncle's estate and a claim to some house property under that uncle's will. Goodman tells me the claim is probably good but would be difficult and expensive to establish and, anyhow, the property is of small value. Also it is leasehold and the lease hasn't long to run. In any case, he wouldn't want to handle it himself as he's retired. He advised Kayes to consult someone still in practice. If we weren't sticking to facts and facts alone, I should be wondering if there wasn't something behind that story —I mean the story of a claim under a will proved nine years ago. Come back to bare facts. Denis Kayes denies all knowledge of Langley Long, but it is a fact that between them there is a distinct personal resemblance I'm not very willing to put down to chance. Kayes says he didn't know Brown or even where Brown lived, but his card was in Brown's cottage. Another fact is that Kayes was at Chipping Up the day of the disturbance there. More mere chance? And what did he mean when he said something about something being washed out? When I asked him, he said 'nothing'. If that's true and it was nothing, why did he say anything? Again, when I found Spencer after the attack on him, he said something that sounded very like Kayes's name, and another night I found Kayes prowling about Brown's cottage. What does all that add up to?"

"Nothing much," said Olive. "All misty. All somethings and nothings, and whats and whys. Nothing you can take hold of."

"No," agreed Bobby. "Nothing, is there? Nothing solid. Next, there's Langley Long who backs up Denis Kayes in declaring their complete and mutual ignorance of each other, seems unaware of their odd personal resemblance, is pals with Theresa Foote, possesses a heavy walking-stick that shows traces of careful cleaning and that came from Australia—like Kayes—and who also has recently turned up in Oldfordham on some not very clearly defined errand. I've seen his identity card. Seems genuine and gives no help. Doesn't all that add up to something you can take hold of?"

"It might," agreed Olive, "and it might not. It could just as well add up to zero. Do you think the two of them are only pretending to be strangers and are really working in together?"

"I'm trying to stick to facts, to what we actually know," Bobby reminded her. "No evidence to show it's like that and even their personal resemblance, if you tried to point it out, other people might fail to see. It depends on a basic bone structure and on one or two other small points that mightn't carry conviction to people who had never thought much about such things. Counsel wouldn't be very keen on putting it before a jury."

"Is a thing a fact if you can't make other people see it?" Olive asked.

"No," said Bobby. "Go on to Mr. Childs. Two facts. Brown had been making a nuisance of himself and Childs admits to a scuffle. Take Duke Dell next, we know he talks about a Vision, feared Brown was becoming a backslider, and now he says he is much troubled in his mind. Which, for both Childs and Dell, may mean nothing or a lot."

"If you are really religious you don't go about killing people," protested Olive.

"More people," Bobby told her severely, "have gone about killing other people because of religion than for any other cause—more even than because of gold and that's here, too. Finally, the two girls—Miss Jebb and Miss Foote, about whom we know practically nothing."

"You know a lot about Miss Foote, don't you? For one thing, you know she is Mr. Goodman's secretary."

"No, all we know is she says she is, but is she?" retorted Bobby. "We know she gives you the glad eye, but does she? Or is it something very different? We know she says she saw Miss Jebb trying to get into the cottage by the back way, but did she? I don't even know if what I saw her holding this afternoon was really an automatic. I'm sure it was but I don't know."

"Well, if you're sure ... well, you know, don't you?" protested Olive.

"There's all the difference in the world between being sure and knowing—especially in the witness box. What the soldier said isn't evidence and what you're sure of isn't, either."

"I call that silly," said Olive with decision.

"So do I," agreed Bobby. "Most things are, if you notice."

He began to walk up and down the room, his mind in a ferment. Olive watched him. He said presently:

"It's all there. I'm sure of it. All of it. If only I could put it together. The whole story's there. All that's necessary is to pick out what matters."

"Do you mean enough to tell who committed the murder?"

"Oh, I think that's fairly plain," Bobby answered. "One or two things we know show that all right. But it has to be put together before I can do anything. No good if there are gaps. It's got to hang together to satisfy counsel and I don't quite see ... I don't see ... it comes and goes. I get it plain for a moment and then there's always something else that doesn't quite fit in as it should. And no chance of getting it through till it does. Prosecuting counsel's one idea is to find holes, and if he does you know all about it. Why, I've known a poor, unlucky, harmless, innocent detective-constable at Scotland Yard, only just posted, packed off on Christmas Eve to the north of Scotland to verify some little bit of information counsel thought he might possibly want and never did." Bobby paused and looked sadly into the depths of a melancholy past. "It was me," he said simply.

A sympathetic Olive said "Oh." The phone bell rang. This time she said "Oh dear." She always said "Oh dear," when the phone rang, and generally with good reason. Bobby went to answer it. Presently he came back and said:

"That was our Chipping Up man. He says Duke Dell is at Four Oaks and won't budge. What do you make of that?"

"How do you mean? Won't budge?"

"Just that. As far as I can make out, Duke Dell has planted himself there and refuses to go. Miss Foote rang up for a policeman to come and throw him out. Our man went and had a look and decided reinforcements were needed. I don't wonder. They would be. A lot of reinforcement. I rang up Four Oaks to ask for more detail. Goodman answered himself. He said it was all right and not to bother. Dell was quite amiable and peaceful. So we left it at that, but I'll go over first thing in the morning."

CHAPTER XXII

FOUR OAKS ASSEMBLY

NEXT DAY, accordingly, Bobby started for Four Oaks as soon as his other duties permitted. He was driving his own small Bayard Seven and as he neared his destination he saw, turning in at the Four Oaks gate, a cyclist he thought he recognized. He followed; he saw the cyclist look round to see who was coming and then hurriedly dismount, a little as if intending to seek refuge somewhere. But for that there was not much time or opportunity, nor any obvious refuge at hand, and Bobby, who now had been able to see it was Langley Long, drew up by his side.

"Good day," he said cheerfully. "Nice bright morning, isn't it?"

Langley Long did not respond with equal amiability. He looked indeed sulky and resentful as he muttered: "Oh, it's you. What do you want now?"

"Well, really, Mr. Long," Bobby protested, "it wasn't you, you know, I expected to find here. I'm just making a friendly call on Mr. Goodman."

"Fat lot of friendly calls you make," retorted Long angrily.

"Friendly to all law-abiding folk," Bobby answered. "Are you calling on Mr. Goodman, too? Quite a coincidence, isn't it? Shall we go on together? Oh, by the way, did you know Mr. Duke Dell has turned up here?"

"What about it if I did? What's it to do with you?"

"Now, now," Bobby rebuked him gently. "I'm a policeman—Police Constable X, so to speak, and Constable X has a certain right to ask questions and even to expect answers. If an answer is refused, he often finds that quite useful, too. But others haven't got quite the same right to ask questions, though they can draw their own conclusions in the same way, if they don't get any answer."

"You've been asking questions enough about me," Langley Long grumbled and looked now not so much sulky as vicious. "Mason told me."

"Not about you, about that rather unusual walking-stick of yours," Bobby corrected him. "Talkative gentleman, Mr. Mason. Australian wood, wasn't it—with native carving? Quite took my fancy."

But if this was an attempt to smooth over Langley Long's doubts and fears, it was not a success.

"If you want to know," he said, "I tripped over the thing last night and it broke in half." He paused, staring at Bobby as if challenging him to make the most of that he could. "They are short of wood for making fires at the hotel, so I gave them the bits to use up like that."

"Now, isn't that just too bad?" Bobby asked sympathetically. A proof of a guilty conscience, he felt, a proof that the one or two remarks he had made had had an effect they certainly would not have had upon anyone entirely innocent. A stupid thing to have done on Langley Long's part, for the stick had been far too carefully cleaned to have been of any value as evidence. But the action showed very clearly an uneasiness for which there was probably good cause. No more reason now, though, for not making clear suspicions Langley Long evidently anticipated. Bobby said: "Did you get it in Australia? Ever been there?"

"I bought it in London years ago. What about it?"

"Oh, nothing. I was only wondering what you would use next time you want to knock anyone out. Because, it's pretty clear, isn't it, that it was you who attacked Mr. Spencer?"

"I didn't. Nonsense. Nothing of the sort. That's what you've been getting at all this time, is it? Well, I didn't and you can't prove I did."

"If I could," Bobby agreed, "I should have had you under arrest by this time. Plain enough, though. What were you doing there at that time of night?"

"I wasn't. I told you so before. Anyhow, there's nothing wrong in looking round an empty cottage."

"Something wrong, though, in violently assaulting other people," Bobby suggested. "Mr. Spencer isn't out of danger yet. If he dies—rather serious, don't you think?"

"Nothing to do with me," growled Langley Long. "All the same, if some fool makes a sudden rush at you in the dark without saying a word, you can't expect a fellow not to hit out, can you?"

"A good line of defence," Bobby approved. "It might get a murder charge reduced to manslaughter. Another thing a judge would take into consideration would be what help the accused had given or whether he tried to bluff it out to the end. Mr. Long, we both know it was you who attacked Mr. Spencer. I can't prove it at the moment but very likely Mr. Spencer may be able to tell us something when he is fit to talk. Don't you think you would be wise to reconsider your position? My job at present is to get the murderer of Alfred Brown. I've tested your alibi. It seems all right, so that clears you of the actual murder—unless there's a flaw in the alibi. Alibis are always a bit tricky. I've known some funny ones. In any case, it doesn't prove you weren't an accessory before the fact, and that's pretty nearly as serious. Because it's plain you are mixed up somehow in what's going on."

Langley Long made no answer. Bobby had hoped that his carefully thought out words might produce some sign of weakening, but no such result was apparent. Still, it might come. Nothing like, in his experience, letting doubts and fears do their own work on a troubled conscience. No result as yet though. Langley Long merely continued to look sulky and vicious. Bobby went on:

"Well, you must make your own choice. I know a good deal already. I may be able to take action at almost any moment. But I've got to have my case complete. Fatal to make an, arrest and then find a smart lawyer persuading the magistrates there's no case to answer. Police persecution, if a man is arrested twice on the same charge. Hopeless then to expect a conviction. I thought you might help if you were willing to and felt uneasy in any way."

"I know nothing about it. I don't even know what you're trying to get at," Langley Long answered, as sulkily as before.

"Well, think it over," Bobby repeated. "I've a strong idea there may be more trouble soon. I even think it possible it may be yours."

"More likely yours," the other snarled, and quite evidently that was his ardent hope.

"Oh, it's always my trouble," Bobby told him. "It's my job. Trouble. Lots of it. That's why I'm paid a wholly inadequate salary. Do you know Miss Theresa Foote?"

Langley Long looked startled now, as though he found this sudden question disturbing. He hesitated a little before replying. Then he said, with evident caution:

"Goodman's secretary? I've met her. Why? What about her? What are you trying to get at now?"

"A friendly, pleasant little lady," Bobby remarked. "But dangerous perhaps. Pretty girls are sometimes. The female of the species—You know. That sort of thing. Don't you think so?"

Again Langley Long made no answer. Yet there was an odd look now in his eyes that Bobby thought might be a hidden terror, and a quivering momentary trembling at the corners of his mouth that Bobby noted, too. He thought to himself: 'The man's scared—and scared of that girl.' Then he thought: 'So am I, but what can I do?' For a moment or less the two of them stayed so, and there was fear between them like a strange, invisible bond. Finally, Bobby said:

"I've got to see it through, for that's my duty, but need you?"

Langley Long was still silent, but the fear in his eyes was plainer still, and still was it there when he began to laugh—a high, affected laugh.

"You're simply making a fool of yourself," he said shrilly.

"Oh, well; nothing new about that," Bobby agreed. "I daresay I do as often as most people. I wonder if you've heard about the joke she played on me? I thought I saw an automatic in her hand. It turned out to be a lighter. Funny, wasn't it? We had a good laugh." Langley Long showed no disposition to share in this suggested mirth. He muttered suspiciously:

"What are you telling me all this for?"

"To warn you," Bobby answered, his previously light and pleasant tone changing to a sudden sternness. "I think Miss Foote is dangerous and I don't mean dangerous in the way in which any pretty girl is dangerous to any man's peace of mind. Think it over, Mr. Long. Carefully. You can always come to me for a talk any time you like. Shall we go on to the house now? Quite an assembly here to-day, and, you know, I don't much like that, either."

"Go on if you want to," Langley Long growled. "I'll wait."

"As you like," Bobby said, and drove on the short remaining distance to the house where, as he alighted from the car, the front door opened and there appeared the huge form of Duke Dell. In a voice a little more subdued, a little less like thunder than usual, he said:

"I saw you talking. I've been watching. Why have you come?"

"Well, if it comes to that," Bobby said, "why have you?"

"I have a work to do."

"Same here," said Bobby cheerfully.

"My work is the Lord's."

"And mine is the law's," retorted Bobby, "and my warrant is clear. I'm not so sure of yours. I have only your word for it and I'm not too fond of accepting unsupported statements. Doesn't do."

Duke Dell seemed puzzled by this. He stood still with his hands clasped before him and was silent at first. Then he said:

"It is hard to convince the sons of Belial."

"Now, now, Mr. Dell," Bobby protested, "you mustn't call police that. Hurt our feelings. Hurt them very much. Almost actionable. Once again, Mr. Dell, why are you here?"

"I was sent," Dell answered. "Word came to me. For evil things have been done and I think there is evil still to come. I am here to warn and to prevent if that may be."

Bobby was beginning to notice something else. The big man seemed, he thought, less vigorous in manner and speech than usual, nor was his eye so bright and clear, his stance so steady, his complexion so ruddy as hitherto. Now, too, he put his hand to his forehead and Bobby said:

"Feeling all right, Mr. Dell? You don't look quite up to the mark."

"Thank you, it is nothing," Dell answered. "After my breakfast here this morning, I was in some discomfort," and, apparently, this fact greatly surprised him.

"I thought you never took breakfast, except for a slice of dry bread and a cup of tea," Bobby remarked, remembering what Mrs. Soames had told with such wonder.

"It is all I need, it is enough," Dell said. "This morning I drank two cups of tea," he said, and went away abruptly.

"Will you tell Mr. Goodman I am here?" Bobby called after him.

"He knows. I told him it was your car," Dell said over his shoulder, and was gone.

In fact Goodman now appeared from his room he called his study at the back of the house. Bobby thought he, too, was looking pale and strained, with restless eyes and nervous, twitching lips; and his voice boomed out with less confidence and volume than usual as he said:

"I wasn't expecting you. You shouldn't have troubled. I phoned you not to."

"That's why I'm here," Bobby answered.

Goodman did not seem to appreciate the relevance of this remark and looked merely puzzled. He muttered something about there having been no need to bother and Bobby said:

"Dell looks a bit seedy this morning."

Goodman took no notice of this remark which evidently failed to interest him. He went back into his room and Bobby followed. He had apparently forgotten Bobby was there or else was deliberately trying to ignore him. Bobby drew up a chair for himself. Goodman was trying to light a cigarette, but he fumbled awkwardly with the 'book' matches he was using and gave up the attempt. Bobby offered his lighter. Goodman took it but did not use it. He said:

"That was Langley Long you were talking to. What's he want?"

"I asked him but he didn't say," Bobby answered.

"Has Dell told you why he's here? You didn't ask him, did you?"

"Some idea of converting me," Goodman said, and laughed harshly. "A little late in the day," he commented. "All humbug, anyway."

"You never know with these chaps," Bobby remarked. "Sometimes they are clearly humbugs on the make. We meet lots of that sort in our job. But sometimes they make you think they may be what we call 'witnesses of truth.' What do you think of Dell?"

"Oh, he seems harmless enough," Goodman said. "He doesn't seem to want anything. I don't know."

"Have you told him he can stay here?" Bobby asked. Goodman shook his head. "Or told him to go?" Again Goodman shook his head. Slightly puzzled, Bobby asked next: "What does Miss Foote think of him?"

"Miss Foote thinks he ought to be under restraint," said a voice from the door that had just been quietly opened. Theresa was standing there, wearing her sweetest smile, her most languishing look, as harmless and empty a little bit of sex consciousness as this world has ever seen. "I know you'll think I'm a silly but I'm simply ever so awfully frightened, the way he stares." She was looking pathetic and appealing now; and then, when Bobby looked back steadily, she began to fumble in her handbag where Bobby felt as sure no automatic was as he felt sure that it was not far away. She produced a handkerchief, small and dainty and lace-trimmed, and put it to her eye, though the thing was hardly big enough to mop up a single tear. Not that there was any sign of any tear in the hard, bright eye, bead-like and sharp, Bobby could see peering at him through the lace edging of the handkerchief. Then she repeated: "I know you'll think it's awfully silly, but he does frighten me. Can't you do something? I'm sure he might turn violent any moment."

CHAPTER XXIII
UNINVITED GUEST

THERE WAS THAT in the girl's soft voice as these words dropped from her raddled lips that sent through Bobby the oddest, strangest thrill of horror and dismay. Nor was that impression altered when now, as she watched him, she quite deliberately began to touch up her lips, her complexion, just like any young, feminine thing, simply thinking of making herself attractive. Bobby had known, often enough, threats and menaces of danger and violence, but never in such a guise as this. The very incongruity of the thing affected him in a way he had never known before, even with a feeling of helplessness as though here were something as new as dreadful; something he did not know how to meet.

He jumped to his feet, an odd, instinctive gesture as though to ward off an immediate and instant threat with which he must be prepared to grapple on the spot. But in that same moment, before he could make another movement or even speak, Theresa, like an evil flame, vanished from the room; swift, direct and certain she went, as the downward stab of a dagger. He did not attempt to follow. It would have been useless. He turned to Goodman. Goodman was shrinking back in his chair with unsteady hands and lips that trembled. He managed to stammer:

"That girl ... that girl." Then he said again and more loudly: "That girl."

"Yes," agreed Bobby.

"Why don't you do something?" Goodman demanded abruptly.

Bobby did not answer this. He knew no reply that he could make. He was telling himself that now he was faced with an entirely new position, a new problem to solve, a position, too, of which he knew nothing and a problem of whose terms he was ignorant. Till now his business had been to piece together, laboriously, undramatically, patiently, the evidence needed to convict of murder a culprit of whose guilt he had long since been certain in his mind; even though, he remembered with caution, that in almost every certainty there may still lurk an element of doubt. It had always been his contention that the work of the detective is as unspectacular, as undramatic, as tedious and dull, as that of the scientist in his laboratory, weighing and measuring in endless detail; and more often than not finding at long last that he had followed a wrong trail and reached a dead end. But now into this investigation that he had believed was nearing its end, had flashed a new element; and the question now, he had begun to feel, was no longer how to avenge an old murder but how to prevent a new one. Yet how? When there was nothing to show who was threatened or why. Nor was there any possibility of taking action to ward off the danger at the source. Who was going to believe that any danger threatened from a blue-eyed, round-faced, little girl, whose one interest and purpose seemed to be to enhance what to-day is called her sex appeal? He had no tangible evidence to show; and until he had, and his own uneasy feeling was that she would take good care to provide none, he was helpless.

He felt it all most strangely resembled one of those nightmares in which the dreamer is conscious only of unseen, unknown, slowly suffocating, all surrounding pressure. He had the impression that events were escaping his control, that he was becoming no more than a spectator. Fiercely he told himself that he must bend them, mould them, see that the guiding will was his and not another's.

But still when now he turned to Goodman it was a little hopelessly that he said:

"Don't you think it would be wise for you to try to help a little?"

"It's your job," Goodman muttered.

"What do you know about her?" Bobby asked, no need to mention any name.

"She's my secretary," Goodman answered. "Very efficient. I advertised and she came along and I engaged her."

"Did she bring any references?"

"Oh yes. Not that I bothered. In these days you are only too glad to get anyone."

"Has she registered for National Service, do you know? She is within the age limits."

"She told me she was born in the Argentine. Her parents were British and she came here when she was a child. But she says she is an Argentine citizen and so she's exempt. I didn't check up. It's what she said." The story might be true, Bobby supposed. In any case it would take a very long time to prove or disprove; and though he did not know what the danger was he feared, he was sure that it was imminent. He could ask to see her passport, but she could easily answer that she had never thought of getting one and never thought of herself as non-British, until registration was ordered and she was told that her birth abroad made her an alien. No doubt he would be able to get proof in the end that she had broken various regulations, but there was neither time for, nor object in, troubling about such technicalities. Her youth and sex, and that air of girlish innocence she was able to make such effective use of, whatever dark depths they might hide, would certainly be her sure shield and protection in any court in the land. No time to play that card now, he decided, though as well to keep it in reserve and to remember it was there. Abruptly he demanded of Goodman:

"What was behind it all that time when you were grabbing an ebony ruler and she had her automatic out?"

Goodman did not answer for a moment or two. He was plainly hesitating, and at first Bobby hoped he was going to explain. Instead he said, and with some sort of an effort to return to his previous manner of a kind of cheerful bluster:

"Automatic? A pistol, you mean? Nonsense. It was her lighter. She showed it you. What do you mean about my ebony ruler? I suppose I had picked it up. I don't remember. Why?"

"You mean you don't intend to help," Bobby said. "Well, it's your decision. But not very prudent. For I rather think you may be in some danger yourself."

There was a look in Goodman's eyes that suggested he knew that well enough, better indeed than Bobby knew it. His voice, too, had lost again, as quickly as it had been re-assumed, its tone of busy, cheerful bluster. It had become thin and uncertain in its pitch as presently, in a kind of squeaky rush, the words came out: "Why don't you arrest her or something?"

Bobby did not trouble to answer this. As a lawyer, Goodman must know well enough that the first move is the privilege and advantage of the lawbreaker. Until intention is translated into fact nothing can be done, since, so long as intention remains intention and no more, nothing need be done. Instead Bobby said:

"I suppose the Brown gold is at the bottom of all this. Don't you?"

"I wish to God," Goodman answered with a sort of groan, "you had never found the beastly stuff. I didn't want it. I don't want it. You know yourself I promised it Spencer for charity. It's nothing to me."

He spoke not only with sincerity but with a kind of fear, as if in some way that legacy of the gold seemed to him a disastrous and fatal gift. Bobby said:

"Is she trying blackmail?" Goodman did not answer and Bobby did not press the point. Often as he had thought of blackmail the explanation seemed inadequate. Blackmail may produce violence but does not use it as an instrument. Nor was it conceivable that Brown had been blackmailing Goodman and met the fate that does sometimes overtake the blackmailer. Not reasonable to suppose that a blackmailer would make a will in favour of his victim or indeed that that victim would have paid in gold. Blackmail, Bobby had long felt, was no explanation here. Presently, he continued: "If it is the Brown gold she's after, I don't quite see where she comes in, what claim she can make—that is for herself. Does she intend to make it for someone else? But that suggests she knew about the gold beforehand; and if there's the motive for the murder, why wasn't it touched? The whole thing seems such a jumble of contradictions, doesn't it?"

"I don't believe anyone had the faintest knowledge of Brown's gold," Goodman said. "Stands to reason. He knew no one knew, or else he would never have gone off and left it in the house where anyone who had any suspicion of its existence could easily have got at it. Anyone with a little common sense can see that."

"What was the motive for Brown's murder, then?" Bobby asked. "If it wasn't blackmail or greed, what was it? There seems to have been no woman in his life. Some very ancient grudge? From all accounts he was an inoffensive little man, not at all likely to have given anybody such desperate offence as all that. What was the motive?"

"I suppose you haven't heard there's been a lot of trouble at St. Barnabas?" Goodman asked with a faint sneer. "Outside any police line of investigation, I expect. Religion, that is. Well, if you choose to make a few inquiries, you'll find there have been violent scenes there. Violence breeds violence. Suppose one of the St. Barnabas congregation went to have it out with him? Eh? That's always been my idea."

"No evidence," Bobby said. "No actual violence reported at St. Barnabas, either. I'm told Brown always walked out at once as soon as he had made what he called his protest. Brawling perhaps, but not violent."

"Where there's religion, there's always trouble," Goodman said dogmatically. "Religion breeds it. Bound to. Well, haven't you any ideas of your own?"

"Ideas aren't evidence," Bobby answered, somewhat ruefully. "You can't sell a judge and jury ideas. Perfect Gradgrinds for facts, all of them. The whole thing cluttered up with alibis, too. Mr. Childs says you and Miss Foote were both here when he left. If that's so, neither of you could have got to Oldfordham in time. Mr. Langley Long—"

"Who is he?" asked Goodman quickly, as if the name were new to him.

"Don't you know him?" Bobby asked, surprised. "I think he's here. I was talking to him in the drive."

"Oh, the fellow Miss Foote talked about," Goodman said. "She said something about his being here to lunch and did I mind? Someone she's met before. What about him?"

"I checked up on him," Bobby explained. "On general principles. Because he was a stranger who had just arrived in the place. He has an alibi if I had been really suspicious. He was playing cards at his hotel till quite late. An alibi is a perfect defence—if it's perfect itself with no flaw in it."

"Has Childs an alibi?"

"No. Your car got him there just in nice time. But you would want a good case against a clergyman of Mr. Childs's standing."

"What about this Duke Dell fellow? What's he hanging about for? Remember what happened at Chipping Up? Has he an alibi?"

"Not a good one anyhow. Nor has Mr. Denis Kayes. No proof one way or the other. Alibis don't mean much and lack of one means just nothing at all."

The door opened and Miss Foote appeared again. She had a dainty little lace apron tied round her waist now and looked as meek and demure as the heroine of a mid-Victorian novel come to life. She said shyly:

"Oh, please, Mrs. Fuller says lunch is ready and she's as cross as two sticks because she didn't know there was going to be anyone else, and there's Mr. Dell and Mr. Long, too, so she says there's not enough to go round with everything so short, but she's done her best, only it's rather lucky, isn't it, that Mr. Owen isn't stopping?"

"Oh, I am," Bobby declared promptly, accepting this strong hint to go as a warning that it might be as well for him to stay.

"You never told me you had asked Mr. Owen," Theresa said, opening surprised eyes to their widest and turning them in an innocently bewildered way on Mr. Goodman.

"I didn't, he asked himself," answered Goodman, and had very much the air of leaving Bobby and Theresa to fight it out together—with the odds on Theresa.

"We should be most awfully delighted any other time," she was telling Bobby now, "but there just simply isn't enough to go round. I know it sounds dreadful and Mrs. Fuller's simply terribly upset, but if there isn't enough, well, there isn't, is there?"

"No, indeed," agreed Bobby, "but don't you worry about me. Not the first time I've found the path of duty leading to lost lunches. I'll come along and watch you others feed."

"It would be most awkward, most embarrassing," Theresa asserted, shaking a grave and troubled head. "I'm so sorry, Mr. Owen, but I'm sure you understand it would make us all most uncomfortable. We really can't ask you to stay."

"Me as the uninvited, unwanted guest," Bobby murmured. "Too bad, but there it is, or rather here I am."

Theresa was to all appearance as meek, gentle, and demure, as she had been all through this brief talk, but Bobby sensed now, though how and why he hardly knew, that there was rising in her that kind of fierce and utterly reckless heat of passion which was at once so strangely inconsistent with her general appearance and which also made her so strangely formidable—an untamed, elemental force from dark and hidden depths that here somehow seized possession of and became incarnate in a human form in manner and appearance, incredibly remote and different.

"You'll be going then," she said, and her voice was low and soft as before and yet now with an undertone like the snarl of a hidden panther.

Bobby, and he did not take his eyes from her as he spoke, answered:

"No, I'll stay."

"You've no right," she said, but this time with that note of a fierce and angry undertone less marked, as though before opposition it tended to die away, possessing full force only when unchecked. "This isn't your house. Police have no right to force themselves into private houses. Please go away."

"Oh, well, if it comes to that," Bobby said, "every policeman has a right to ask to see identity cards. I think I had better ask to see all your cards in turn and then I'll have to copy out full details. A long job because I'm such a slow worker—slow and sure, you know. But the job will give me a 'locus standi.' Is that the right phrase?" he asked Goodman.

"Better let him alone," Goodman said to Theresa.

"Police. They've always got something up their sleeve."

"Needs a good big sleeve, too," Bobby said cheerfully, "to hold it all."

"I'm getting my lunch, anyhow," Godman said and walked out of the room.

Theresa gave Bobby one of her sweetest, most girlish smiles.

"I do think it's such a shame," she said. "It's horrid to have people when there's practically nothing to give them. So awkward, so embarrassing. Mrs. Fuller will be giving Mr. Goodman notice most likely unless I can manage to smooth her over."

"Such a lot of things need smoothing over, don't they?" Bobby remarked, as he followed her across the passage to the dining-room; and as he did so he heard Mr. Goodman say querulously:

"My soup's cold. I didn't know it had been put out, I didn't know you had started."

And Bobby was aware, but again without knowing how it was he knew, for her back was to him as he followed her, that Theresa was smiling to herself with a quiet and horrid triumph, as though in some way this meant that in something she had attempted she had succeeded.

CHAPTER XXIV
BOWL OF SOUP

IT WAS WITH anxiety, for there was a fear in his mind of what might soon be happening, that Bobby looked about him to see if he could tell what had called that dark smile of triumph to Theresa's eyes. The luncheon table seemed well supplied, he thought, a better table indeed than was often to be seen in war-time homes. At one end there was fish with some sort of white sauce. At the other end was a veal and ham pie. No doubt a veal and ham pie that pre-war veal and ham pies would have scorned to acknowledge, even as a poor relation. But eatable and giving a rich appearance of plenty to the board. The soup had been served in small bowls and Langley Long was saying in answer to their host's complaint:

"So awfully sorry. I thought we weren't to wait, I thought Mrs. Fuller said so. Jolly good soup," he added with appreciation.

On the other side of the table, opposite him, his back to Bobby at the door, Duke Dell was sitting. There was something rigid in his attitude, as if he were making an effort to hold himself upright.

When Bobby moved so as to see his face clearly, he thought it looked more unnaturally pale even than before. Dell seemed in pain, too, for his hands he held before him were being pressed against his body. Bobby said to him:

"Why, Mr. Dell, I thought you never lunched."

"I did to-day," Dell answered. "To-day I did."

"You don't look well," Bobby said. "Are you all right?"

"Oh dear, is anything the matter?" said Theresa, all anxiety. "It isn't the soup, is it?"

"Did you serve it?" Bobby asked.

"Oh yes, but I didn't make it, if that's what you mean," Theresa answered brightly. "And I'm not such a frightfully bad cook as all that," she added, pouting.

"Did it taste all right?" Bobby asked Dell.

He took a step towards Dell as he spoke, meaning to take possession of the empty soup bowl. Quickly Dell took a piece of bread and began solicitously to mop up what few drops still remained, till he had the bowl so clean and polished one could hardly tell it had been used.

"Why are you doing that?" Bobby asked.

"I'll go and rest a while," Duke Dell said. He got to his feet, not too steadily. He looked much worse now as he moved towards the door. "It is nothing," he said. "Nothing at all. I shall be all right again in a moment."

"Oh dear, I am sorry," Theresa exclaimed. "I'll get you—oh, I'm sorry," she repeated, but this time speaking to Bobby, in whose way she managed to be as he hurried towards the door, after Dell. "Don't trouble," she said as she still hovered before him, "I'll call Mrs. Fuller and we'll—"

But Bobby had got by now and was out of the room and running up the stairs. He was just in time to see Duke Dell enter the bathroom. Bobby would have followed but Dell turned the key. Sounds from within told what was happening and Bobby heard them with some relief. He stood there waiting. Theresa was coming up the stairs. He said to her:

"I take it this is why you didn't want me to stay to lunch. You know, I think it helps."

"What a horrid thing to say," Theresa protested, all wide-eyed surprise. "How can poor Mr. Dell being ill help anything?"

"I expect he'll be all right," Bobby said, listening. "I'll smash the door in if I have to. I think it helps because I think it may help to show the connection."

"What connection?" she asked.

"The one," Bobby answered slowly, "between what happened at Oldfordham when a man was killed and what is happening here—or going to."

She gave him a hard stare and went away without speaking. From within the bathroom came sounds of running water. The door opened and Duke Dell came out. He looked very ill and badly shaken. Gone was his earlier manner of superb physical well-being. His voice had become a mere faint echo of its former trumpet note.

"Been putting your finger down your throat?" Bobby asked him. "Got rid of it all, I hope. Good thing, too, but why did you wash it down the waste pipe? I meant to have it analysed."

"That was why," Dell said.

"I guessed as much," Bobby agreed. "Just as a matter of curiosity, I wanted to know what poison was used. Probably the same you had in your tea this morning."

"I have nothing to say to you," Dell answered. "I must rest."

"There are some questions I must ask you first," Bobby said.

"I'll answer none," declared Dell. He was holding the bathroom doorpost, as if for support. He said again: "I must rest. Let me pass or I must deal with you as I may be guided."

"Now, now, Mr. Dell," Bobby said reproachfully, "you're in no condition to talk like that. You might have been earlier on, though I can do a bit of dealing with people myself if I'm put to it. There—you see," he added, for Dell, moving forward as if to push past, had very nearly fallen. "Steady on. Feel a bit dizzy, eh? Lean on me."

Dell had perforce to accept the aid offered. He nodded towards the half-open door of a room near. "In there," he muttered. Bobby helped him to the indicated room, got him lying down on the bed, loosened his clothing, felt his pulse and his heart, and then went to the head of the stairs.

"Hullo, Mr. Goodman, somebody," he shouted. "A hot-water bottle, please. Quick." Theresa came to the foot of the stairs and looked up. "A hot-water bottle, and quick, too," Bobby repeated. He went back into the bathroom, found a glass, rinsed it carefully, drew a little water from the tap—it might come, for all he knew, from a storage tank but at least could not have been tampered with—added brandy from the flask he always carried, and returned to Dell, still lying on the bed and still looking very ill.

"Drink this," he said.

Dell drank obediently, almost automatically. A little colour came back into his cheeks. He sat upright.

"That was brandy," he said, aghast. "You've given me brandy. Brandy!"

"No, I haven't," Bobby told him. "It was medicine. You can't call brandy, brandy, when it's medicine. It's done you good already." He was feeling Dell's pulse and heart. "Much stronger," he announced.

"I swore that I would never taste the evil stuff again," Dell exclaimed with what seemed real distress. "You've made me break my oath."

"Don't be childish," Bobby snapped, losing patience. "You can plead force majeure if you want to. I take it you know you've been poisoned?"

"I have nothing to say to you," Dell repeated.

"I have to you," retorted Bobby. "There's more to all this than your own safety. If you want to be poisoned, that's O.K. by me. I don't care. But there's been a murder—"

"There's no room in all this for the clumsy and brutal methods of the law," Dell said. "The law murders the spirit. That's worse still. There's another way."

"Isn't there something in the Bible about the duty of obeying lawful authority?" Bobby asked.

Dell gave Bobby a disapproving look.

"The devil can quote Scripture for his own purposes," Dell said. "Get thee behind me."

"Well." Bobby said, drawing a deep breath and then another before he felt he could trust himself to reply. "Of all the conceited, thick-headed, self-willed fools—"

He paused, not for lack of things he wanted to say, but because he felt he had better take another good long breath or two before continuing. Duke Dell took advantage of the respite to murmur with closed eyes: "When thou art reviled, revile not again."

"Look here," Bobby said, but with something like despair, "someone is trying to kill you. Isn't that because you know something, saw something the night the man you called your friend was killed?"

"You understand nothing," Dell told him. "Leave me in peace. Because you understand nothing, know nothing, you would do well to meddle no more. There is no room here for clumsy and brutal police methods. The law is very evil and full of deceit and how can it be otherwise, when it comes from the heart of man that is most desperately wicked?"

Bobby nearly gave up then. He felt quite baffled. Then he thought of another argument.

"Do you mean then," he said, "that it is right to stand by and let a human soul take on itself the guilt of murder?"

"If murder is intended," Dell answered, "then the guilt is already there. Guilt is in intention, act or no act."

To Bobby's mind, constrained to some extent by his official and legal position, the exact contrary was the case. So far as he was concerned, anyone might wish murder, plan murder, contemplate murder day and night; but until there was some kind of overt act, there was no offense.

"Well, you can argue that way if you like," he said, "argue about it till the cows come home for that matter. But I think there may be more than your life to consider. I think there may be danger to others. I think even that in your case, possibly murder wasn't intended. It may be all that was wanted was to get you out of the way for the time, while someone else was got out of the way for good."

Dell opened his eyes now and looked very surprised.

"You've found that out?" he said. "I thought you were much too stupid. Plain enough, of course, but I never expected you to understand it."

"Oh, didn't you?" snorted Bobby. "Well, never mind that. The thing is, will you help me to save the life that's threatened?"

"We have nothing to say to each other," Dell repeated once again. "You think only of the body, of safety for it, of hurting it by what you call punishment, of its well-being or ill-being. I am concerned only with the spirit. Trouble me no more. Those to whom the Vision has come are free of those who know it not."

The door opened and Theresa bustled in, all gushing sympathy and eager helpfulness.

"I'm here at last," she said. "The first hot-water bottle leaked and we had to find another and do it all over again. Oh, and I've brought a cup of tea, too."

Bobby was in a vile temper—a state of extreme frustration is the current phrase, and very nice, too, because it so clearly and firmly puts the blame on the frustrator and not on you. He took the hot-water bottle without a word of thanks. He took the cup of tea and threw the contents out of the window. Not that he supposed for a moment there was poison in it this time, but he wanted to relieve his feelings and he felt there was no reason now for any pulling of the punches between himself and Theresa. On her side though, she put on an air of great surprise and said in her most innocent tones:

"Well, I never."

"Get out," Bobby said and meant it.

She gave a little girlish squeal and scuttled away. She shut the door behind her and then opened it again and peeped in.

"You great rude horrid man," she said, and was gone, and well Bobby knew that once again she mocked him.

Duke Dell had tried to get to his feet to interfere, but had collapsed on a chair. Bobby helped him back to bed again.

"You had better keep still," Bobby told him. "You're only doing yourself harm. Keep quiet and I expect you'll be all right soon."

"I thank you," Dell said feebly. "You mean well, I know, though so blind and dull of spirit."

"Blind and dull all right," Bobby said bitterly, for that was how he felt. "Mr. Dell, you refuse me your help, though I think you could give me much. You must answer for that—perhaps to your Vision you talk about. Tell me, does this Vision you say you have, ever tell you anything about the possibility of demoniacal possession?"

"It is told of in Scripture," Dell reminded him. "You can read about it there. Why do you ask? Have you seen any signs of it?"

"I'm beginning to wonder," Bobby said.

"No need," Dell told him. "It is plain for those with eyes to see. You are less blind than I had thought. Then you must be beginning to see that the work to be done here is mine, not yours. For these are matters you do not understand, deep and very strange and dreadful. Let them be and go your way. Leave me to mine. And be not over-concerned for her safety. She is threatened but she is under protection."

"Who do you mean by she?" Bobby asked.

"Who else but the young girl, our sister, Theresa Foote, whom evil forces threaten, but who knows well where she must place her trust, though not in you. Be not over-concerned for that dear child."

"Oh, Lord," said Bobby helplessly.

CHAPTER XXV

DIFFICULT TASK

BOBBY DECIDED GLUMLY that it was no good trying to get any help at present from Dell. Events might bring about a change in his attitude; though what those events might prove to be, Bobby did not care too much to guess at. But for the present it was plain Duke Dell's mind was closed, his belief absolute in the guidance he seemed to be so sure he had received from what he called his 'Vision,' but that Bobby was inclined for his part to think was no more than the complacent working of Dell's sub-consciousness, obeying the directives received from his own uncontrolled instincts. Then, too, he had not yet fully recovered from the effect of whatever drug had been given him, and he was very clearly in great need of rest and quiet.

"I'll leave you now," Bobby said to him. "Better try to get a sleep."

With that he left the room but he did not go downstairs. He had forgotten he had had no lunch, his mind was too full of troubled and uneasy thoughts for him to be conscious of hunger or fatigue. He sat down on the topmost tread, and tried to get into proper perspective the trend of recent events, so far as he knew them, and to deduce from them the probable shape of things to come. For now he was faced with something he had never known before in all his experience. Normally a detective's task is to discover the truth from the study of the past. Now what he had to do, he reflected moodily, was to discover from the present what was likely to happen in the future.

A difficult task. Even an impossible task. He told himself angrily that he had never pretended to be a fortune teller.

Once, when he was still in uniform, patrolling a city beat, starting a career that had brought him to the position he now occupied, a senior officer had told him that the only thing a detective could do in a difficult case was to sit and wait for people to come and tell him what it was all about.

Sound advice if undramatic. Bobby had proved its worth on many occasions. But in this case no one would tell him anything. A wall of silence met him on every side; and behind that wall worked and planned the most formidable adversary, he believed, that he had ever met—ten times more formidable by reason of concealment behind a camouflage of incredible effectiveness.

There were three separate aspects of these recent happenings he had to reconcile, three angles to be resolved before this triangle of a problem could be set up four square and firm for reasonable solution. All were related, he felt sure, in action and reaction—the death of Alfred Brown, his store of hidden gold, the dark and hidden activities of little smiling baby-faced Theresa Foote.

From this confusion of speculation and of doubts, wherefrom he was still struggling to extract some guiding principle, he was roused by the appearance of Theresa herself, coming tripping lightly up the stairs.

"Don't you want any lunch?" she asked solicitously. "Mrs. Fuller wants to clear away but I told her poor you hadn't had a bite yet."

"I believe I do feel a bit hungry, now you mention it," Bobby said, rising to let her pass, very conscious of the irony of this polite small talk between two who knew so well each other and each other's purpose.

"Only whatever you do," Theresa warned him earnestly, "don't let Mrs. Fuller think you think it was her soup upset poor Mr. Dell. She's most awfully touchy about her cooking. She might walk straight out of the house if anyone said that. And whatever should we do then?" asked Theresa, opening her china-blue eyes to their widest.

"I shouldn't dream of saying anything of the sort," Bobby declared with equal earnestness. "Most unfair to do so, when it wasn't the soup but only what you put in it."

Theresa put on an even more innocent air. She pouted. She looked exactly like a spoiled child receiving an unexpected rebuke. One thing though Bobby had noticed in all her airs she could assume with such speed and skill—she could never manage tears. Her clear, wide-opening eyes of such bright china blue remained always hard, undimmed, watchful. Bobby felt he ought to recommend her to carry a slice of onion in her handkerchief. Crude perhaps but effective. She said now with a pretty little sigh:

"I can't think what makes you so horrid to me."

A real artist in her way, Bobby thought. He remembered being told that the born actor would act even at his mother's death bed. He thought Theresa was like that. Though she knew well that he knew well what she was, yet she enjoyed presenting to him this facade of guileless youth, enjoyed imposing herself as what her age and sex and looks seemed to proclaim so emphatically she must be. Or did it all go deeper? Was the mystery more profound? Did she truly revert at times to a more normal, natural self? Were there moments when the strange dark influences whereto her will seemed to yield itself, relaxed for a time their power? A useless question and one to whose implications it might be fatal to yield. In that queer uncanny way of hers she seemed to be aware that certain hesitations were present in his mind, even though she evidently did not fully understand their nature. With a confiding, tender gesture she put out a small hand towards him.

"I do so wish we could be real friends," she said pathetically. "It's lovely to be friends."

Bobby took her proffered hand and pressed it softly. She seemed a little surprised and even just a little hopeful, as if wondering if just possibly it wasn't beginning to work at last. Very gently she returned the pressure of his hand. He said in his softest voice:

"It is, isn't it? Lovely, and it'll be lovelier still the day I see you in the dock well on your way to the gallows."

"You never will," she assured him, looking up with a confiding smile. "Not you. And even if you got me there, it wouldn't do you any good. No one would ever be so cruel as to keep poor little me in such a nasty place. Now, would they?"

Bobby was inclined to agree with her. He could see even the judge himself basking in the freshness of her innocence and youth, the jury practically in tears at their first glimpse of her, he himself in imminent danger of being lynched on the spot.

"One has one's hopes," he told her. "I play with bits of string sometimes, making a noose I feel would look awfully well on that round white neck of yours."

He went on down the stairs then. He did not suppose that what he had said would have any effect or shake her nerve in any way. She moved as it were invulnerable, in magic armour, triumphantly safe. From this conviction, Bobby felt, she had acquired that odd and reckless irresponsibility her actions so often showed, as though she knew that she was secure in her certainty that all doubt or suspicion would vanish automatically before her pretty face, her trustful upturned eyes, her pouting lips.

"The little devil," Bobby said to himself and felt a chill, for indeed there were moments when he almost believed those words had a truth beyond that of mere metaphor.

He went into the small room at the back used by Mr. Goodman as a study. There was a telephone there. He called up his headquarters and gave instructions for two constables to report to him as soon as possible. He had a feeling that presently he might be glad of help. He wished his chief assistant, Inspector Payne, was available, but he knew Payne was laid up with a bad cold. Then he rang up Oldfordham police and told Sergeant Hicks to get in touch with Mr. Denis Kayes and ask him to ring up Bobby at Four Oaks, or, if Bobby wasn't there at the time, then to ring up county police headquarters in Midwych. Also Sergeant Hicks was to impress upon Mr. Kayes that until he heard from Bobby, or from Midwych headquarters, he was on no account to venture out, or take any notice of any message he might receive. This, Hicks was to impress upon Mr. Kayes was of the utmost importance. Hicks, though sounding very puzzled, undertook to carry out these orders at once, and Bobby had only just hung up when Mr. Goodman came in. He was in the middle of a tremendous yawn, but when he saw Bobby the yawn changed to a snarl.

"Don't mind me," he said sourly. "It's only my house and my phone. May I ask how much longer you mean to favour us with your company? Perhaps you want a room got ready for to-night?" and quite suddenly, as if the word 'to-night' had associations too strong to resist, he indulged in another tremendous yawn.

"I know I'm not exactly welcome," Bobby said sadly, "but then that's part of the policeman's job—to be always precisely where he isn't wanted." Again Mr. Goodman turned his yawn into a scowl. He didn't seem to like the implications of this remark. Bobby went on: "I have a feeling we are likely to see a good deal of each other for some time yet." Mr. Goodman looked as if he liked this remark still less. "But don't bother about a room," Bobby added consolingly. "Very nice of you to think of it, though. If I have to stay around to-night, I'll sleep in my car. I've told my people to send the biggest they've got. I don't know yet."

Goodman was not scowling now. Nor yawning. He had a frightened air instead. He went towards the door. Over his shoulder as he was going out, he said:

"I don't know what it's all about. It's getting me down. I think I'll get a rest. Lie down. If I can get a sleep, it'll clear my head a bit perhaps. I'll talk to you later."

He departed then, leaving Bobby puzzled. Was this sudden drowsiness genuine or was it put on for the occasion? If so, why? Bobby decided that if he did stay the night in the vicinity, possibly it might be prudent to choose another sleeping place than that he had now mentioned. He left the study and went into the dining-room. Lunch was still on the table but Bobby did not attempt to help himself. He was hungry enough but in that house he had no wish to eat. Mrs. Fuller appeared and when he said he wanted nothing, began to clear away. Bobby had a feeling that Theresa was watching outside the room, but he took no notice. He lighted a cigarette, the next best thing to food when a man's appetite begins to draw attention to itself, and sat down by the window.

The table had been cleared. Bobby was alone, his second cigarette well under way. Even the brooding presence that was Theresa seemed to have withdrawn itself. From the window presently Bobby had a glimpse of an approaching cyclist. He wondered if it could be Denis Kayes, come in person instead of using the phone. Disconcerting if it were, but there had hardly been time. Then he saw that it was Mr. Childs, the Oldfordham vicar.

"Now, what's that mean?" Bobby asked himself. "What's up now? Quite a gathering of the clans."

He got up and strolled out into the drive. Mr. Childs, turning in at the gate, saw him, seemed surprised, and alighted from his cycle.

"I didn't expect you would be here," he said. "I hope there's nothing wrong?"

"I suppose I am rather a bird of ill omen," Bobby admitted ruefully. "Where are the police, there is trouble gathered together. I didn't expect you either. Any special reason? I am asking in my capacity as policeman, of course, not out of mere curiosity."

"No, no, just a friendly call," Mr. Childs answered, but with such evident embarrassment that Bobby said: "Is that really all? Are you sure? You see, I feel there's a crisis coming. I feel the cards are on the table but I don't know what cards—or what table. Any trifle, any smallest hint may be a help."

"No, no," Mr. Childs insisted, "nothing whatever to do with all these most unfortunate, most distressing events. At least, I mean. In a sense of course. I thought I would like a chat with Mr. Goodman. A most admirable man. A most generous man. We, at St. Barnabas, have every reason to know that. Characteristic of him to refuse to accept for himself the Brown legacy. Is it a fact by the way that the itinerant, self-appointed preacher—I think his name is Dell, Duke Dell—is he staying here now?"

There was an unmistakable gleam in Mr. Childs' eyes as he spoke—a kind of vicarious greed so to speak. Very plainly there was a clear vision before him of new schools for St. Barnabas, a new church hall perhaps, a new mission chapel, all provided out of the legacy the excellent and generous Mr. Goodman had announced his intention of devoting to public purposes—and what better, more public, more desirable than those connected with St. Barnabas? For himself, even had he been starving, Mr. Childs would have scorned to ask a penny, but for St. Barnabas now was the light of battle in his eyes, his nostrils twitched, his mouth was set and grim, no hound following strong scent could have been more eager and intent. Clearly he meant that the claims of St. Barnabas on Mr. Goodman's generosity should not be overlooked; clearly, too, he had scented a rival on hearing of Duke Dell's presence at Four Oaks and so had come full speed to the battle. Had there been any question of the money going to, say, the cottage hospital, Mr. Childs would have sighed as a vicar and submitted as a citizen. Utterly intolerable, though, to think of such a sum going to a hedgerow preacher, a blind leader of the blind, a ranter on the roads, a fomenter of heresy and schism; for so Mr. Childs, forgetting charity for the time, was thinking now of Duke Dell. His mouth was set in grim determination that nothing of the sort must be permitted, too much loose thinking and careless talk already; and Bobby, watching his air and manner of the very militant churchman indeed, could not help wondering again how far the strength of such passionate conviction might not carry him.

"Mr. Dell is here," Bobby said, "but he doesn't seem very well. At the moment he is resting in his room."

"Oh, I'm sorry," Mr. Childs said, promptly forgetting everything else. "Anything I can do? Not too bad for me to see, is he?"

"I shouldn't think so," Bobby answered; and if he had not been so used to the inconsistencies of human nature he might have wondered at this sudden change from bitter rivalry to eager sympathy. But it is a commonplace that men can easily keep their feelings in watertight compartments. This war has shown how the same man may willingly offer his life and the lives of those nearest and dearest to him in the service of the country, and at the same time be secretly planning to hold back for his private use and enjoyment the money and resources his country needs as much. Human nature, Bobby reflected sagely, is the damnedest, queerest, most tangled thing that is or can be. He said abruptly: "May I ask you something?"

"Certainly, certainly," Mr. Childs answered at once, quickly and gravely. "I shall be delighted to do my best to answer."

"Do you believe in demoniac possession?" Bobby asked.

"Demoniac possession?" Mr. Childs answered and was plainly rather taken aback. "Demoniac possession?" he said again, as if not quite sure he had heard aright. "You mean actual possession of a human being by an evil spirit? As a possibility, yes, most certainly. There is the authority of Holy Scripture. One hears, too, of strange cases from time to time. But they can only be accepted with considerable hesitation. A very difficult question. Some recent writers, certainly to be regarded with great respect, are evidently inclined to think that cases still occur. A recent work by an Oxford scholar, for instance. There are spiritualistic phenomena, too, which are most disturbing. One hesitates to make a definite pronouncement. I must admit some such idea had crossed my mind in connection with recent events."

"Oh, yes," Bobby exclaimed, startled and impressed. "I put it out of my mind," said Mr. Childs firmly. "I would not consider it. But I did see clearly that much of what was happening was so harmful to the Church, much of his conduct—"

"'His'," repeated Bobby, even more startled now.

But Mr. Childs did not hear what he said. Theresa had just come into the dining-room, clearly visible through the window, and Mr. Childs beamed.

"Ah, there is that dear child," he said. "I have counted much upon her aid in this household. One wonders if her sweet young innocence—if there is such a possibility as you mentioned, one wonders if she has felt instinctively ... " He paused. He went on: "One might try to ask her—discreetly, very discreetly. About Mr. Duke Dell, I mean. The innocence of a young girl like Miss Foote is a very wonderful and sacred thing."

"Oh, Lord," said Bobby helplessly.

CHAPTER XXVI

BELLE DAME SANS MERCI

THERESA HAD COME skipping to the door, all happy smiles and shy, bright-eyed welcome, to greet Mr. Childs. Bobby could hear her prattling prettily as she led the way into the house. Plainly came to him her dulcet tones of sympathy and concern as she spoke of poor Mr. Dell and how bad he had seemed just before lunch—no details neglected, Bobby reflected grimly. What an artist the woman was, already the idea was being firmly implanted in Mr. Child's mind that Dell's illness could have nothing to do with what he had eaten at lunch since his attack had come on before the meal. Only a small unimportant trifle in a way. Yet, as has been said in a very different connection, by trifles perfection is attained and perfection is not a trifle. Now, too, Theresa was telling the sympathetic and approving Mr. Childs how dreadful it was to hear Mr. Dell saying such funny, awful things, even about Bishops sometimes. It made her quite uncomfortable and she simply didn't know how people could listen to him.

Her voice died away and Bobby felt gloomier than ever as once again he recognized the odds against him. She had them all bemused, as thoroughly bewitched as ever was knight of legend by fairy glamour. 'A belle dame sans merci,' he told himself; and he was the pale knight wanly wandering, no victim indeed himself to her sorcery, but lost in the magic maze she wove, unable to protect others from her spells, unable even to be sure at what end her evil magic aimed.

He found himself wondering once again how old she was. Eighteen or nineteen apparently, by what she had told Goodman; a young, inexperienced eighteen or nineteen by dress and manner, as indeed was clearly the impression she wished to give.

"'The dewy bloom of innocence, fresh on girlhood's cheeks'," he quoted to himself. "That's her line."

He was inclined to put her real age as getting on for thirty. He would have liked to put it at forty, but that he felt was only bad temper. Thirty or less, he decided; even though in these days of short skirts and make-up, it is not always easy to distinguish the grandmother from the schoolgirl. Except, perhaps, that the schoolgirl often knows more. Any jury would have adopted for Theresa the schoolgirl theory instantly and firmly; and Bobby smiled wryly as he pictured to himself the tender paternal care, the fatherly protective benevolence with which counsel would question her—the poisonous little viper.

He felt too uneasy even to light another cigarette, and he had quite forgotten he was hungry. He wondered if he dared make an arrest. It would delay and disturb any plans being made, but only delay, only disturb, not frustrate. It would be a gamble. Doubtful if he could justify it, doubtful if the magistrate would commit. And it would be a gamble with the lives of others at stake, for any delay and disturbance caused might only result in the provision of firmer ground for the next leap forward, for the perfecting of plans of whose purpose and intention he had so little proof or even evidence, of which he could only be sure that they were deadly in their aim.

In such troubling thoughts he was still deeply immersed when he saw another cyclist approaching. Denis Kayes he hoped this time, and then he saw it was a woman and recognized Janet Jebb.

"What's brought her here?" he asked himself and hurried down the drive to meet her, for he had the thought that it might be better if no one at Four Oaks knew of her arrival.

Probably, though, Theresa knew. Probably she was already watching from one of the windows of the house. Perhaps even it was Theresa who had brought it about that Janet should be there. Not very likely he knew, but better to suspect Theresa everywhere than to overlook her anywhere.

Janet alighted as she saw him coming. She said:

"Oh, I'm so glad you're here still. Mr. Kayes had gone before the sergeant came to say he mustn't."

"Gone where? What for?" Bobby asked quickly.

"I don't know, he didn't say," Janet answered. "Is. anything wrong?"

"I don't know," Bobby answered in his turn. "I wanted to get in touch with him. Didn't he say anything at all before he went?"

"There was a phone call," Janet said. "Mr. Kayes seemed rather puzzled. He said he didn't know what on earth it meant, but he supposed he had better go and see. He said he thought it was a woman's voice, and he thought anyhow he had enough petrol."

"He went on his motor cycle?"

"Yes. He said there wasn't much time and he would have to hurry if he was to be there when it said."

"But he didn't say where?"

"Only something about a café in Wychwood Forest—the Hiker's Arms. I remember the name because I thought it was rather silly. I thought it was legs with hikers, not arms. He was to turn right when he got there and then go straight on. He said it didn't seem very clear but he might as well see what it was all about."

"The Hiker's Arms," Bobby repeated, searching his mind. "Closed I think." He remembered some argument about an allocation of food in which a cafe of that name had been mentioned, until the discovery was made that it had been shut down at the beginning of the war. This fact, its proprietors who were also owners of other places of refreshment, had forgotten to mention when applying for their share of the food supplies available. "It's a rather out of way place, I think," he said. "Did Mr. Kayes know where it was?"

"I think they told him on the phone," Janet said, "and we looked at the map, too. I mean, how to get there."

Bobby was rubbing the end of his nose as hard as ever he had done in the days before, under wifely injunction he had tried to abandon a habit that, she told him, was fast becoming a rather silly mannerism. But now he rubbed and rubbed; and, as he rubbed, memory began to grow clearer. The Hiker's Arms was in a lonely part, deep in Wychwood Forest, but close he thought to a well-known beauty spot; and close to one of the favourite walks for less ambitious hikers, those who looked forward to a good tea and a comfortable rest and were not of that stalwart breed content with a packet of sandwiches, a pocket flask, and thirty miles twixt dawn and dusk. But now that hikers were mostly doing their hiking in different conditions, in far-off lands, the place had become as solitary as it had been before people discovered nature by force of living only in towns. Less and less did Bobby like the idea of this rendezvous given to Denis in so lonely a spot. Janet was speaking again. She said:

"The sergeant told us it was you said Mr. Kayes wasn't to go anywhere. So I rang up to ask why and they said they didn't know, but it was your orders, and you were here, and so I thought I had better come and tell you."

"I'm very glad you did," Bobby exclaimed fervently. "I don't know what it all means but I think I had better go along to this cafe place and try to find out."

"Oh, thank you," Janet breathed. "Oh, I hoped you could help."

"What we are for," Bobby told her. "To help—or to hinder," and he wondered grimly enough if there was much chance of his arriving in time to do either.

He asked quickly one or two more questions. Janet answered briefly and sensibly. A big car came round the corner of the road and drew up. It was one belonging to the county police that had been laid up almost since the beginning of the war because it used so much petrol —not to mention its own special and remarkable gift for breaking down at critical moments. Two of his men got out and

Bobby was glad to see them. One of them he knew had at one time been stationed in the district near the Hiker's Arms. He said:

"Oh, Morgan, lucky it's you. You know a cafe, the Hiker's Arms? Somewhere in Wychwood Forest, isn't it?"

"Oh, yes, sir," Morgan answered. "It's shut down now, but it used to do a big summer trade."

"What's the best way to get there from here?"

"Well, sir," Morgan said, considering the point, "it's not such an awful distance in a straight line, but you would have to go a long way round by car. Quickest way would be to cycle. There are good paths. Not for cars, but all right for cycling. It's downhill most of the way and you can't go wrong because there's the tower on the top of Quarry Hill for a landmark. You can see it everywhere."

"Quarry Hill?" repeated Bobby, startled. "Isn't that where there were so many accidents before the war? I remember someone writing to the papers to say it ought to be called Quick Death Hill."

"Yes, sir, that's the place," agreed Morgan. "People used to say they put the cafe there so as to get the custom of what weren't killed but only smashed up. Not much traffic now but a very nasty tricky bit of road—corkscrew turns and if you don't mind you go bang off and into the quarry. There were danger signs put up but people don't always notice. Regular death trap if you don't; and now the roads are so neglected and no repairs done, it'll be worse than ever."

Bobby wondered if possibly someone had been busy there, removing those danger notices, or perhaps changing them—putting a sign 'Turn right' for example, where before there had been a notice 'Turn Left.' Or, perhaps, tacking, say, a previously prepared 'Trespassers will be Prosecuted' notice over a danger sign. Or any similar trick. As, for example, placing an obstruction on the road in some strategic position, round a sharp bend very likely. Then a motorist coming round the corner at speed, hurrying, speeding a little, as Denis Kayes might well be, since he had remarked that there was not much time to get to the given rendezvous, would, seeing it, be sure to swerve, swerve instinctively, swerve so as to make it certain he would go over the quarry edge. All that would take hardly an hour to arrange, if a few preparations had been made beforehand, and less than half an hour to remove, leaving no trace. Nothing would remain except a dead man and a wrecked motor cycle at the foot of the quarry. Merely one more road accident and not so much as a breath of suspicion aroused—or if suspicions did stir in the mind of a nosey deputy chief constable, nothing he could do about it.

Impracticable in normal peace-time conditions, with other traffic on the road, but now that by-roads, side roads, were almost deserted, feasible enough.

"The quarry's pretty deep, isn't it?" Bobby asked, almost mechanically; his mind busy planning what to do, what precautions to take, how best to achieve the swift, decisive action called for.

"Oh yes, sir, thirty or forty feet," Morgan assented. "And ten foot of water at the bottom now. The military had it flooded for one of their battle-training stunts and it's never been drained."

That would be fairly conclusive, Bobby told himself. A man might survive a fall. In some way a fall may be broken, extraordinary what the human frame can survive with just a modicum of good luck. But a fall into ten foot of water would be very sure. No room there for lucky escape. A 'dead cert,' as the racing men say—a very dead cert indeed. He said:

"Drive on to Chipping Up—full speed. Morgan, get a cycle there somehow. Beg, borrow, buy, steal if you must. But get it. It's life and death, I think. When you get it, follow on to Quarry Hill. If you get there first or without seeing me, do what you can. I expect there's been an arranged accident to a motor cyclist. Watch out for it if you get there first. Don't ask at the house here for a cycle. Better they shouldn't know. White," he added to the second constable, a man much older than Morgan, "while Morgan's getting busy, ring up H.Q. and tell them to send help to Quarry Hill. Say there may have been an accident and to bring a doctor. Then bring your car back here. Keep out of the way but wait. You may be wanted. Understand?" To Janet he said: "Give me your cycle. It'll stand my weight, won't it? Lucky you're tall."

"Oh, I'm coming," she said. "I must."

"Give it me," he repeated. He took it from her without waiting for her consent, and though her foot was on the pedal, ready to mount. For there was a drumming in his brain, a clamour in his mind, like a warning bell to urge him on. "Every moment counts,"

he said; and on her machine he flashed off down the road, bending low, riding as he had seldom ridden before.

CHAPTER XXVII
RUNNING EFFORT

THE GOING WAS EASY at first. The tower on Quarry Hill, visible for many miles, showed the direction. The road Bobby followed as he pedalled so desperately on, was still in good condition, not yet much affected by wartime neglect. But when presently it turned sharply north, he had to leave it for what began as a lane and so continued till it reached the farm it served—and here Bobby ran into a flock of sheep. Cows will scatter, pigs will grunt and run, but sheep remain. Nothing much to be done with sheep. A flock of sheep on the road resembles some natural phenomenon on which no effort of man avails. He is as helpless as he is in blinding snow or impenetrable fog. Except perhaps that fog and snowstorm grow at least no worse for all your efforts and your struggles, whereas the more you try to force a way through sheep, the more they mass themselves together defying all things but patience.

Nor was there any help for Bobby from the two or three men in charge. "What's your hurry?" they said indignantly, and Bobby wasted no time in efforts to explain. "Thinks there's no one going anywhere except him," they told each other loudly. "Roads ain't for racing," they said, and Bobby had no leisure to explain that he was racing a rider on a pale horse, an invisible rider whose name was death.

At last though he was free of that difficult, amorphous, bleating barrier, but not until the lane he had been following had begun to degenerate into a track, a track, too, that presently became little more than an indication to show that once upon a time a track had been there. Now it had become much obliterated by a growth of grass and bramble, of intruding undergrowth and of bracken here and there and of fallen branches, relics of winter storms. Swiftly, strongly, silently, does nature resume her empire, once the restraining hand of man falters and withdraws.

Constable Morgan, in saying the way was clear, the paths good, had trusted too much to pre-war memories. Six long years of neglect and absence, six years when nature had been allowed to flood back

like the incoming tide on the seashore, had sufficed for much of this part of the forest to return to almost primeval conditions. No longer did the hiker or the picnic party come all through the long summer days to trample down the uneven ground, to thrust aside intruding growths, to toss away fallen obstacles, to make clear and plain the footpaths and the byways. As he pedalled on, riding his cycle rather like a bucking pony on that uneven ground, its spokes and wheels snatched at by entangling bramble growth; sometimes not sure even whether he were still on a path; twice having to dismount where the overflow of a stream, choked by fallen forest debris, had turned the ground into a morass, Bobby began to feel he was making such slow progress he had small chance of arriving in time. Indeed it might well be too late already.

Though he had an unusually good sense of direction he might easily have lost his way in what was so swiftly becoming again primeval wilderness but for the glimpses he still got at times of the Quarry Hill tower. Then came disaster. He had already had cause to ask himself uneasily how long Janet's bicycle would endure the combination of this rough usage and his own twelve stone or thereabouts of solid flesh and bone. Now as he tried to put on a burst of speed when he came to what seemed a clearer stretch of forest than usual, his front wheel went deep into a hidden cavity in the ground, an old burrow of some sort perhaps, and he himself went head first into a bush that did indeed break his fall but not without inflicting some slight facial damage and damage more serious to trousers that only Olive's expert care had kept still fit to wear. Worse, when he extracted himself from the clinging embrace of a bush reluctant to release him, and dived to recover his cycle, he found the front wheel so badly buckled, the handle-bar so bent and cracked, that plainly it could be no longer of any use.

He flung it down and set himself to run. Arms pressed to side, head back, he ran. He was not dressed for it, his shoes were a light city pair, but he ran as not often athletes have run on smooth cinder tracks, with applauding crowds to cheer them. For he ran for no challenge cup, no silver goblet to display on dining-room sideboard. It was pale death he had to overtake and he knew the hope was small; and so the smaller the hope, the more desperate the need for all he had to give.

He ran. He ran beneath the unregarding skies, and only the trees and the bramble and the bracken, only the unheeding small things of the wood, saw as he flashed by. The ground slipped away under his flying feet, he crashed through obstacles rather than seek a way round, he took no heed of the clutching bramble that tore at his legs, of the overhanging branches that lashed so viciously at his face. Fiercely, more fiercely still, he fled on, with throbbing temples and a singing in his ears, with a daze before his eyes and no thought in his mind save of the need that drove him. Now, to his aid he called all he possessed of that strange reserve that lies somewhere hidden in all men, ready for the time when spirit makes on body its ultimate demand. So he fled, so he ran, all his being merged in the need for such speed as he could make; and it was as though all his world had ceased to be save as an urge to drive his reeling steps, his gasping self, to greater efforts and to effort greater still, and yet not enough, not enough, so that still more must body give to the call of spirit, master and lord of body.

He was still running, still on his feet, though the run had become little more than a blind reeling forward, though his steps were unsure and uneven, though three times he had fallen and hardly known why he had risen again, when at last he burst through the fringe of trees that here lined the road running down from the hill by the quarry edge. And there by the side of the road he fell down and lay.

Gradually consciousness of himself, of his errand, of why he was there, returned to him. Nothing to show whether he had come in time or whether he was too late. The road lay silent and still, it was as though its tranquil indifference mocked all that frantic effort which at last had brought him here. Nothing to show if any had passed all the long day, nothing to show whether or no, if they had done so, they had passed in safety.

His strength was beginning to come back now, his pumping heart to return to normal, return to its accustomed rhythm, his eyes to clear, the drumming in his ears to cease. There was a trickle of blood from a scratch above his eyes he had to keep wiping away and this annoyed him. He felt able to sit up now, but he did not try to stand. His legs were as yet hardly steady enough for that. The road was still deserted; peaceful, calm, in the pleasant afternoon sunshine. He began to wonder if he had been a fool to run and race like that. Very likely, he thought, he had been exciting himself unnecessarily. He tried to light a cigarette. His hands were still shaking from the effects of his exertions during that great run and he gave up the attempt. He lay back and waited. When he tried again after an interval, he succeeded. Cautiously he stood up. He was a trifle dizzy still, not quite sure of himself yet, not altogether sure of his ability to control his legs. They were still distinctly wobbly. But the store of strength he had so utterly expended was now beginning slowly to replenish itself. Leaning against a post stuck in the ground near by, he smoked reflectively. He supposed there was no need for further exertion, for haste, unthinking hurry, speed. If he had got here in time, before Denis Kayes arrived, it was all right. Kayes could be warned as soon as he appeared. If he were too late and Kayes had already gone by, then either he had ridden the hill in safety and the trap had failed, or else he was by now a dead man in ten foot of water at the bottom of the quarry.

Fortunately, so far as Bobby could tell, there was no sign that any such tragedy had happened. As calm, untroubled, peaceful a looking stretch of road as one could wish to see. Still, it would be as well, he supposed, now that he felt stronger, to make further investigation. He flung the butt of his cigarette away and noticed for the first time that the upright post against which he had been leaning bore one of those danger notices of which Morgan had spoken—a bold, conspicuous warning it would be difficult to avoid seeing or heeding.

Bobby gave it another and a closer glance and stiffened to attention. He examined it again, standing on tiptoe to get a nearer view, to bring his eyes on a level with the board. He assured himself that in each of the four corners was a small, fresh mark, as if a tintack had been recently driven in and then extracted. Extracted somewhat hurriedly, too, for two of the holes were slightly splintered as if the nails or tacks had been pulled out with more haste than care.

Very clearly Bobby remembered thinking how easy it would be to fake a 'Trespassers will be prosecuted' or similar notice and then to nail it over a 'danger' warning. Perfectly easy to secure a piece of wood of the required size—plywood could be used as being thin and light—and fasten it in position, then remove it again when its mission had been accomplished. At close quarters, of course, the substitution would be quickly noticed. No one would be deceived. But a motorist driving by at his normal forty miles an hour or more, would have no chance of noticing anything suspicious and would go on unwarned to almost certain death—a death made quite certain if in addition round some convenient turn or corner, a temporary obstacle had been placed at a suitable spot.

Had that, in fact, been done, he asked himself, and he began a hasty search, thinking that possibly any such substituted board might still be lying about in the vicinity. He found instead, close by, behind some bushes, signs in the long grass where apparently someone had been lying, someone who watched and waited in concealment, or so it seemed, and if so, waited and watched for what? Looking more closely Bobby saw that near by were two half-smoked cigarettes and some match stalks. Carefully he picked them up. The cigarettes were of the somewhat rare Balkan brand Mr. Goodman smoked. The match stalks were of the 'book' type, and Bobby remembered how Mr. Goodman had once chanced to remark that the only matches in the house, the only ones they had been able to obtain, were of this 'book' variety.

Too late? Bobby asked himself. Was that what all this meant? And his look was dark and angry as he went back to the roadside again. On the other side of the road, on the quarry side, the fence guarding the quarry edge, though in bad repair and with many broken slats, was still upright, giving no indication of any major break. But further on the road curved sharply, and it seemed likely enough that that curve presently developed into one of those sharp hairpin bends of which Morgan had spoken. Had something happened here, just out of sight from where he stood, and was it because it had happened, whatever it was, that the 'danger' sign had been restored to its former condition? He felt guilty that he had rested so long, though indeed his exhaustion had been complete and utter, leaving him for the time being hardly the strength with which to think, much less to stir or stagger another yard.

He started off to run now and was at once checked by a sharp pain in his side, another in one foot. When he looked he found his foot was naked and bleeding. Both sock and shoe had been torn away at one time or another. He was very surprised. He had had no idea. He had felt no pain. His nerves had been too busy conveying to body the relentless demands of spirit that knows nor bounds nor limit, to have had any time to bring any such smaller matter as hurt or wound to his attention.

Fortunately now he was on a comparatively smooth and level road, very unlike the rough surface of the forest land. He had to give up attempting to run, but he was able to progress well enough by the aid of a sort of hop and skip and jump movement; even though, on each spot where he put that one foot to ground, a red stain showed.

He reached the corner where the road turned and then the sharper bend beyond. There, only a little further on, was a gap in the fence, a fresh break with broken slats lying near. Plain enough to see what had happened. He forgot his injured foot. He began to run again and now once again spirit asserted supreme authority and forbade that pain in his side to make itself felt. When he had thrust aside the smashed and splintered remnants of the broken slats, he was right upon the quarry edge where marks deeply scored in the earth showed what had happened only a brief time before.

He knelt down, for he was still a little dizzy, and peered over. Below a dull expanse of water lapped against the steep quarry sides and extended half-way back across the quarry floor. He saw, too, where twenty or thirty feet or so down that precipitous descent, ten feet or so above the silent, sullen, waiting water lay a man's unconscious form, caught on a projecting spur that was already showing signs of crumbling under the weight resting upon it. Of the motor cycle there was no trace. Deep beneath the surface of the water, no doubt. Even as Bobby was looking he saw a piece of that projecting spur fall off, break away, drop with a dull splash into the water and vanish.

CHAPTER XXVIII
RESCUE

In such a moment as this, Bobby's mind always worked swiftly and clearly. On a public platform, facing an audience, it might suddenly become the complete vacuum, in which he could search vainly for a thought or even for a word. As on that ever to be forgotten occasion when speaking on behalf of a charity, the name of that charity had fled from him, fled entirely away, so that he had had to be reminded of it by the chairman.

But now the one quick glance he threw around enabled him to grasp instantly every phase of the situation; reminded him that if the quarry face had been used in battle training, to climb it must be possible; showed him where faint signs suggested exactly where ascent had been found practicable and where therefore descent must be practicable, too; dismissed as irrelevant the suggestion that the soldiers might have been provided by their battle-training camp with toggle ropes; decided that a naked foot and consequently a prehensile toe would be a help rather than a hindrance; encouraged him with the reflection that, the ten foot of water immediately below—if it were ten foot—would be there to break his fall if he should slip; reminded him that he was a good swimmer so that it didn't matter if it were twenty feet deep; cautioned him that it might not be either ten foot or twenty foot deep and that therefore it would be better not to fall and that certainly he must not try to dive; and presented all these considerations to his mind not so much in swift succession but as it were in such a whole, complete and simultaneous possession of the facts as would have reminded him, if he had ever heard of it, of the celebrated definition of eternity by Boethius.

To an onlooker it would have seemed that Bobby merely gave a casual glance around as he was rising to his feet, that he next walked a few yards, dangerously and impossibly balanced on the quarry edge where no space existed between it and the bordering fence, then in some fit of lunacy lowered himself over the edge at the exact spot where the quarry sides were more precipitous than elsewhere, and finally began to emulate the feat of the fly walking up and down the window pane.

The spectator, however, unless a graduate of the aforesaid battle school, would have failed to notice, as Bobby had noticed, that here, running down the quarry face, was a kind of slanting ridge, or one-sided chimney formation, that would support a pressure of the body held strongly against it. Also here and there in its neighbourhood were tiny knobs of stone or shallow hollowings that would give a measure of aid to clutching fingers or to groping toes—especially to a toe unhampered by shoe or sock. One or two of such outstanding knobs were probably of recent and artificial fabrication, the work of the battle-training school to make the climb possible and to test the candidate's eye for picking out the best line to follow.

By this time Bobby was well over the brink of the quarry, clinging to its face as desperately as ever politician clung to office. With infinite care he made his way downwards, half inch by half inch, holding tightly with the tips of his fingers to any grip, however small and insecure, that they were able to find, groping with his bare toes to find other support, feeling none of the pain the wound in his foot would at other times have made him well aware of, careful never to relax for a moment the pressure of his body against the ridge that hitherto had served him well. But then that flattened out and now he hung precarious on a sheer wall. He had time to wonder how the soldiers under training had managed. He felt himself slipping. Difficult to hold a hundred and seventy pounds of solid weight in position by the aid of two fingers in a hole the size and shape of a walnut and a bare toe on some knob of rock about the shape and size of the end of a cigar.

The path of his descent had brought him nearer to, and almost on a level with, the spot where lay Denis Kayes, caught on a crumbling ledge from which smaller or larger fragments were still breaking away at not infrequent intervals. To Bobby it seemed he must be dead or at least that he would be soon, so still he lay, so quiet. Bobby decided that the only thing for him to do was to let himself fall. Impossible, as far as he could see, to continue the descent. The soldier boys might have been able to ascend, but descent was different. Equally impossible to hold on in his present position. Nor for that matter would it have been any advantage to do so. A good deal depended now on the depth of the water below and on its freedom from obstruction. Bad if it were only a shallow covering over a hard floor. Worse still if by ill fortune it concealed some sharp pointed stake or some jagged end of stone. Deep water would be safer by far. It would preserve him from risk of injury that might effectively put him out of action. And he could not afford to be put out of action. He wasn't going to allow that run of his that had tested him, his strength, his resolution, as seldom they had been tested before, to go for nothing. Janet's bicycle, too. Very likely he would have to pay for that himself, since it would be no easy job to get it through an expense list. 'Destruction of civilian property due to careless usage,' would most likely be the verdict and a surcharge the result. If so, if he had to pay up, he didn't mean it to be for nothing.

The time had come now to let go, to chance what the water below might hide. Best perhaps would be to slither and slide as best he could down the bare face of the rock and so into the water as gently as might be. He still hesitated though, for that would very possibly mean the end of the suit he was wearing, and where he would get another neither he nor his coupons knew.

The issue was suddenly decided. Without warning or apparent cause Denis Kayes's body slid from the ledge on which it had balanced till now, and disappeared into the water that closed again above it with a sullen dull content, as though its evil patience had been satisfied at last.

Bobby followed instantly, sliding down the bare rock, dropping into the water, infinitely relieved to find himself safe in its cool depth that was fortunately really deep, then vigorously rising to the surface, and striking out towards the spot whence the slow ripples were still spreading outwards. He dived, he found Denis, luckily unentangled in the drowned bushes that had grown thickly here before the flooding, luckily unconscious, since so it was the easier to get him by his shoulders, turn him on his back, then, with a good strong kick come to the surface and with only another kick or two reach where the water was shallow enough for him to stand upright.

He took advantage then of the help given by the buoyancy of the water to get Kayes, alive or dead, Bobby did not know which, on his back in the position known as the fireman's lift.

In that manner, the weight well balanced, Kayes's inanimate body poised easily across his shoulders, head hanging down on one side, feet on the other, Bobby waded through the rapidly shallowing water to dry land, towards where he supposed must stand the deserted Hiker's Arms Café, somewhere at the foot of Quarry Hill.

Soon it came in sight. His foot was hurting badly now. The nerves that before had been too pre-occupied to tell him of pain, seemed now to be making up for lost time by positively screaming for attention.

"Put that fellow down off your shoulder and attend to us," they seemed to be shouting. "Foot's bleeding like Old Harry. You're losing pints and pints of blood, you'll lose foot itself if you don't mind. Won't listen, heh? Well, how's that for a twinge to help you think it over."

It was a twinge all right, a twinge 'and then some', as they say to-day, but Bobby knew well that if he let Kayes drop, he would never get him up again. Bobby knew, too, that if he yielded, if he let Kayes fall, then he would probably collapse himself. If that happened, then in this tangled growth of weed and grass and bush through which he was forcing his way, it might well be long hours, perhaps not even till morning, before they were found. He was inclined to suspect that they might not both survive that ordeal.

Luckily the distance to the cafe building was not great. Soon he was in sight of it, shuttered and deserted, its back towards him as he came reeling from out the quarry. On its front, facing the road, it was provided with a deep verandah where, in happier days, teas had been served. There Bobby dropped and there he lay, he and Denis Kayes together, and the last thought he was conscious of was a wonder whether Kayes were alive or dead and what was that faint hooting he seemed to hear? Was it an approaching car or the beginning of an air raid warning? Because, if it were the latter, he ought to be up and doing. But he wasn't going to stir, not he. He would just go on lying there, not budging for air raids or anything else, not even for the last trump for that matter, not now when it was bliss even to lie still; and the next thing he knew he was lying on cushions, in what once had been the café kitchen where someone now had lighted a fire. There was someone else pulling his foot about. Bobby made an effort to sit up. He said:

"Here, what are you doing? You're hurting."

"It's this toe of yours. I'm afraid it'll have to come off," said the someone else.

"No, it won't," said Bobby.

"No good saying that," declared the other. "If it has to, it has to." Bobby said unpleasantly:

"It's my toe and don't you play any tricks. Or there'll be trouble."

"Well, I'm a doctor," came the somewhat indignant retort, but Bobby interrupted.

I don t care if you're the college of physicians and the tower of London rolled into one," he said. "That's my toe, I tell you, and I'm keeping it."

"Patients," said the doctor, growing quite fierce, "are the limit, the absolute limit. Always think they know best. If only," he sighed, "if only we could do without them."

"Well, you do your best to get rid of them, don't you?" Bobby asked, making his voice so amiable this time that it was a moment or two before the doctor got it.

When he did he flounced away indignantly and Bobby beckoned to Morgan of whom he was now aware in the background.

"Morgan," Bobby said. "I want you to make a close search along the side of the road where it runs down Quarry Hill and see if you can find any bits of wood—plywood squares probably—with a notice 'trespassers will be prosecuted' on them. Anything like that. Near the top of the hill most likely. If you find them, handle them carefully. There may be dabs. Get all the help you can. And look out for anything like a hurdle or rope or anything else that could have been used to make an obstruction in the road. Understand?"

"Yes, sir," said Morgan promptly. "Road trap suspected and we're to look for evidence."

"That's it," said Bobby. "Oh, and Morgan, warn my chaps to keep that doctor fellow off my toe, or—or I'll see there's no leave going till next Christmas."

"I'll warn 'em, sir," Morgan promised, turning quite pale at the mere thought of the possibility of so dire a threat materializing into fact. "By the way, sir, the young lady's bicycle. She seemed worried about it. If I could have it, I could put it in the back of the car to take back."

"It broke down," Bobby answered. "I don't know if I could even find the place again. All smashed up anyhow. My weight and the rough going were too much for it. A total loss."

"Bad luck, sir," said Morgan. "I don't know how you managed."

"I had to push along on foot," Bobby explained, and Morgan gave a satisfied nod; and no more was ever said about that great run for another's life, only in Bobby's memory does it still live as a fantastic nightmare of effort and struggle, of endurance and exertion.

CHAPTER XXIX

DUKE DELL TALKS

IT WAS LATER in the day, much later, but still daylight, when Bobby came back to the house, Four Oaks. Previously he had sent a message asking that all there should stay on till his return. To Constable White, still on duty at the entrance, he said:

"Are they all here still?"

"Yes, sir, I think so, sir," White answered. "Some of 'em may have slipped out at the back, but I don't think so. I've kept an eye on the back, well as I could. The clergyman gent said it was most awkward as he had a mothers' meeting, but I put it to him as orders were orders and he couldn't say they wasn't."

"No, he couldn't, could he?" agreed Bobby. "I'm sorry about the mothers' meeting though."

He had arrived in a small car with an inspector and two constables to give help should that be required. Another car followed behind, but this he had instructed to remain out of sight for the present, waiting and watching for a signal he might give presently. His own small car drove on up the short drive to the house. Theresa opened the door and stood there, grave and demure, to admit them.

"We're all terribly frightened," she said. "It's that message we had that we were all to wait. It's upset every-one most awfully. They can't think why."

"That's what I've come to explain," Bobby answered. "Do you think I could have a chat now with you all? Together somewhere. Would it be convenient?"

"Oh yes, I think so," she said, and then with sudden concern, for Bobby was limping badly, supporting himself on a stick or sometimes accepting help from one of his companions: "Oh dear," she said, "you've hurt your foot. Oh, I am sorry."

"That's very kind of you," Bobby said, and beamed on her and she beamed back on him; and little was there to show what lay behind those smiles, given and returned.

Theresa tripped away and opened the door of the dining-room. Mr. Goodman and Mr. Childs were there already, talking together. Mr. Goodman was still looking heavy and sleepy, even curiously so. Theresa said she would tell the others and went off. Janet came in almost at once, pale and anxious-looking, and then appeared

Langley Long, he with a sullen and a watchful air. Bobby noticed that his shoes had been recently cleaned and now were shining and spotless. Theresa returned and said Mr. Dell was still feeling 'queer,' but would be down in a few moments. Then she seated herself near the window, apart from the others, as one naturally but little concerned. She had brought some needlework with her, a table centre she was embroidering, but not very skilfully, for sewing was no great hobby of hers. She spread the table centre over her lap and grew busy. Bobby whispered to his inspector, who looked incredulous, but supposed the deputy chief knew what he was talking about. 'Our Bobby', as his men had begun to call him, had an odd trick of saying things you took to be mere guesses, and just luck if they turned out to be exceedingly good guesses. Only later did it appear that the apparent guess wasn't a guess at all but a matter of careful reasoning, a deduction of probability from observed fact. Sometimes though some people didn't like to acknowledge they might have made the same guess from the same premises, and then they shrugged their shoulders and said they didn't trust luck, it didn't last, and they didn't like lucky detectives. You never knew. But the thought crossed this inspector's mind, as he strolled over to take for himself a seat near the window and near Theresa, that very often 'Our Bobby' did know. All the same, even though the inspector was a recently married man, his heart did give a little jump—oh, only a very small one—when Theresa looked at him so trustfully, so sweetly, as much as to say that now he was sitting there she felt ever so safe.

He felt inclined to lean across and say something reassuring and paternal, only he thought Bobby might notice—Bobby generally did notice, he knew—and then Duke Dell came into the room, very pale still but all the same much recovered.

Bobby said:

"I don't know what you've heard or if you've heard anything at all. There has been a bad accident. Flight Lieutenant Denis Kayes—I think you all know him—was going down Quarry Hill on his motor cycle. I expect you know Quarry Hill, too. There have been several fatal accidents there before. Mr. Kayes seems, somehow, to have lost control of his machine. Going too fast probably, and then he's a stranger here and very likely had no idea what a tricky, dangerous hill it is. There are danger signs but he may not have noticed. All we can say for certain is that he went clean through the fence bordering the road and over the quarry edge. That meant a forty foot fall or thereabouts and about ten foot of water waiting at the bottom. The quarry has been flooded. The cycle went right into it. Please," he added, lifting a hand to check comment, "let me continue. You know Mr. Spencer, in charge of the Oldfordham police, is laid up because of the attack made on him, and so I've had to take over the investigation into the murder of Alfred Brown. In some very curious and complicated way I don't fully understand yet, this accident at Quarry Hill is tied up with that murder. It rather seems as if it might be a direct consequence. And I can't help being afraid that there may be other consequences if I don't take action, even though I'm not yet quite ready, not yet quite sure of my ground. Now I'm a bit inclined to think that some of you could make useful suggestions. Till now you may not have wanted to say anything about suspicions you felt were only suspicions and you didn't want to bring accusations you had no solid grounds for holding. That was all right, quite reasonable. Vague suspicions aren't much good to police. We are always full of vague suspicions ourselves. It's our job to suspect everyone. As we do. But I think the time for that is over now, in view of what happened to Flight Lieutenant Kayes this afternoon. I want to remind you, too, that things have got so far that if I make an arrest, even if I arrest the wrong person, you will probably all be called as witnesses—and witnesses have to talk. But I would much rather, it would be a much greater help, if any of you who doesn't feel quite comfortable about what he knows or suspects will tell me right out, before you all, so that you may all know what you each think, and without my having to ask questions. Questions so often miss the real point. Of course, you understand that you needn't say anything if you don't wish to, or if you feel you really have nothing to say. So there may be no mistake or dispute afterwards, I am going to ask one of my men to take everything down in shorthand. Afterwards his note will be typed out and you will be asked to read it and sign it as correct if you are satisfied. And I do most earnestly ask you to be entirely frank. At present I am still much in the dark and a life may be at stake, as has been shown during these last few hours on Quarry Hill."

There was a silence when Bobby stopped. From the window came a hushed and trembling, long drawn 'Oh', as Theresa let her needlework fall and looked all about her questioningly, from one to the other, in shocked bewilderment. The inspector felt very sorry for her. He felt slightly indignant that the other girl present, Miss Jebb, should be sitting so far away, at the other side of the room, aloof, in a shadowy corner, with shadows all around her. The two girls, he considered, ought to be sitting together, to give each other mutual support, mutual comfort. He felt he wanted to comfort Theresa himself and he wished his wife were here—and then on second thoughts, he didn't. And Bobby wondered how many of them knew, or imagined for one moment, that all this was but the climax and the period of a deadly duel between himself and the child busy with her needle-work by the window. He went to the door and called in one of the newly arrived police, Constable Davies, whom he knew to be a highly competent shorthand writer. He established Davies at a side table with note-book and pencil, and Duke Dell, sitting upright and stiff on a chair that looked much too fragile for his weight, began to speak, holding his hands stiffly clasped before him, his usually booming voice both less steady and much weaker than usual. He said:

"I had meant to be silent, for we should put our trust in guidance from above, not in our own works. Nor is it for us to talk of punishment. Let him that is without sin mete out punishment to others. Sin is its own penalty. That is the teaching of the Vision. Yet human life must not be cut short or opportunities may be lost. I don't know anything about Mr. Kayes's accident. I don't see why there should be any connection. I don't think there is. I didn't know there was any danger to anyone. Except myself. But that didn't matter. I am prepared. Others may not be. That is why life may not be cut short before the ordained time. There are things I know and others I believe. But only believe, for of them the Vision has not spoken. Our brother, who has gone before us, told me two or three weeks ago how angered was the man Alexander Childs, called reverend though none are or can be, by the rebukes publicly administered to his Roman practices and how he had attacked him and they had wrestled together, though then with little hurt to either. He told, too, how the man Childs, called reverend though none are reverend, knew of a store of gold in sovereigns he had by him, and how he feared that there might be an intention to seize it and use it for the very purpose of those Roman and Popish practices our brother had so righteously denounced. On the night when our brother left this world by the way of a sudden and unhallowed violence, I went again to his house where he lived, for when we had parted he had been bitter against me, complaining of an accidental blow I had dealt him, and I wished to bring him to a better and more reasonable frame of mind. But when I drew near where he lived I heard music, not godly music but unhallowed as I thought, for I know little of music, but enough to tell that which is only worldly. And I knew that when our brother listened to music there was little use in speaking to him for he would not heed or hear. He said to me that the Vision come to him in music then he would have known it was true, but it did not and that was why he doubted in blasphemy. For the Vision comes as and when it wills. Therefore guidance came to me to wait till he had ceased listening to what to him was as a drug or strong drink. I waited and as I waited I saw the man, Alexander Childs, falsely called reverend though none are, come up the hill, and I saw him stand waiting at the door of the cottage. But I did not look longer, for I knew it was useless to speak to our brother while there was music, and I went back to the roadside where I had been sitting, and there I think I fell asleep. When I woke the music was still being played and I thought that surely now there had been enough and I thought I would go in and turn it off so that I might be heard. But when I opened the door he was not there, but only his body he had left behind, and left because it had been violently beaten about the head. So I prayed for guidance; and it seemed to me that the thing had been permitted that no longer might it be possible for our brother to deny what he had seen, deny the Vision that had been granted him. Therefore I held my peace and I went away in silence, though greatly troubled. It may be I was wrong, and that I understood wrongly the guidance I received, if it is true that in consequence another life has been cut short too soon, before its full time. That is all."

He sat back in his chair and Mr. Childs got slowly to his feet.

"I must be permitted to say one thing," he began, his voice not too steady in spite of all his efforts to control it, for indeed his indignation and his anger were extreme. "Our friend has spoken most ignorantly, most presumptuously, of the title 'reverend,' which belongs of course, as you all know, not to the man but to the office and—"

"Please, please," interrupted Bobby, "we mustn't discuss that. It is murder, not words, I am here to deal with. Mr. Dell has told us—"

"Surely—" Mr. Childs interrupted in his turn, "considering that besides the utterly mistaken and very, very foolish remarks I was referring to, a kind of accusation of being concerned in a murder is made, I may at least say, whether I or my office is reverend, and on that point—"

"No," Bobby interposed, as firmly as before, for it seemed clear Mr. Childs was a good deal more concerned and indignant about that than he was over the murder accusation, "no, this is not the place or time for any argument of that sort."

"If I am not to be allowed to speak," declared Mr. Childs with dignity, "though I did indeed believe—erroneously it now seems— that the meanest criminal was allowed to defend himself, I will wait for a more favourable opportunity. I shall probably take the matter as subject for a discourse I trust our sadly mistaken friend here will attend for his instruction. Oh," he added, remembering something he apparently considered of much less importance, "I could add that Mr. Owen already knows all about what Mr. Dell has been telling you. We have talked it over. I could add, if necessary, that Mr. Dell's own story shows he was near the scene of the murder that night, that he had returned there in secret as the result of a quarrel, that he had apparently already once that day nearly killed Brown." Mr. Childs paused and looked very bewildered and surprised, as if only now he had realized the full effect and implication of what he was saying. He said slowly, half to himself: "It does almost look as if Dell were the murderer himself—perhaps he believed, as people do sometimes persuade themselves, that he was 'guided' as he calls it."

CHAPTER XXX

MR. GOODMAN TALKS

WITHOUT RISING, almost indifferently, Duke Dell said: "Had I been so guided, as I call it but others do not for they lack understanding, so I should have acted. But there was no such guidance, none, and therefore no such action by me."

"The thought came to me," Mr. Childs said, looking very troubled. "I would accuse no man."

Mr. Goodman got to his feet. Now he was wide awake and alert. All trace of his earlier odd drowsiness had entirely vanished.

"I think," he said, "these two gentlemen are on the wrong track. I think Mr. Owen is on the right track. I'm told he often is. This terrible accident on Quarry Hill—if it was an accident, I'll come to that later—seems to clear up a good deal that has been greatly troubling me. I may be open to blame for not having spoken before of some things I became aware of and some doubts they gave rise to. Professional training and instinct, I expect. The first thing a lawyer learns is caution, and I'm still a lawyer, even if I've retired from practice. A lawyer does see so many cases where a hasty word, often expressing a merely unformulated passing suspicion or doubt, has done incalculable mischief. That's my excuse. I argued that the case was in the very capable hands of our deputy chief constable. I think now I took a mistaken view but I do want to explain why I shirked action till now, till this new dreadful tragedy. A sort of catalysis. It changes, it clears up, one begins to understand. When Miss Foote—"

"Me?" said Theresa, looking up from her busy needlework, astonished, as her whole manner proclaimed, that her name should be mentioned. "Me?"

"When Miss Foote," repeated Mr. Goodman firmly, "called to see me on the pretext—I am sure now it was a pretext—that she had heard I wanted a secretary, I realize very fully that I should have questioned her more closely. But at the moment I could only think how lucky I was to have a smart, competent girl applying for the job when I had long since given up hope. I knew very well there was hardly an office in Midwych wouldn't have jumped at her. I didn't ask a single question, I didn't take up her references. And when she dropped a hint about being willing to help in the housekeeping—well, that settled it if it had needed settling. Not that it did."

"I love housework," Theresa interposed, still all sweet innocence. "Of course I wanted to help. And Mrs. Fuller's so nice."

"I remember thinking it was almost too good to be true," Mr. Goodman went on. "That's just what it was. I ought to have known. I admit that. At the time I thought of it as almost like winning a first prize in a sweepstake you didn't know you had a ticket for."

"Me?" said Theresa, gently puzzled, appealingly puzzled; and Mr. Childs had an air of wishing to comfort and reassure her; and Duke Dell edged his chair a little nearer still; and Bobby sent his inspector a warning glance that was acknowledged by a faint bend of the inspectorial head but that the inspectorial mind dismissed as superfluous and unnecessary. Mr. Goodman, speaking with obvious care in choosing his words, continued:

"Such doubts as did persist in my mind, I would not listen to. I had a secretary, a very efficient secretary, a secretary who not only helped Mrs. Fuller but was on excellent terms with her, and I considered that I was exceedingly fortunate. Then I became aware that there was a young man occasionally visible in the vicinity. I thought that explained Miss Foote's presence. I suspected that the young man was the attraction. Very natural. All I hoped was that the young man wouldn't carry her off too soon. It did just occur to me as strange that the young man seemed also to be a newcomer here. But I hardly gave it a second thought. Any number of possible explanations. Then one day Miss Foote told me that a Mr. Brown had called while I was out and wanted his will made. I was surprised because I told her when I engaged her that I was retired from practice and yet she had apparently told this Mr. Brown that she would ask me for an appointment. I reminded her I wasn't in practice and forgot all about it. Even when she said she would call on Mr. Brown and explain next time she was in Oldfordham, I didn't pay attention. Brown is an exceedingly common name and it never once occurred to me that he was the Brown who had been my managing clerk. Indeed, in the light of later events I am inclined to believe the whole tale was an invention and that Brown never called at all."

"Oh, he did," exclaimed Theresa, quite shocked evidently by such a doubt; and Mr. Childs looked more sympathetic than ever; and Duke Dell edged his chair yet another inch or two nearer; and the inspector felt so sorry for the poor young lady, he never even noticed another warning glance that Bobby gave him. Mr. Goodman, disregarding the interruption, continued: "Why should Brown have suddenly wanted to see me when apparently he had been living in Oldfordham for years and all that time had kept very carefully out of my way? But it seems to me probable in view of recent developments that Miss Foote knew well who he was, knew he had been in my employ, and knew also that in addition to embezzlements committed in my office, he had managed to get hold of a large part of the estate left by one of my clients, a Mr. Kayes, an uncle of Denis Kayes, of whose death we have just heard. How did Miss Foote become possessed of this knowledge? I think from the third of the Kayes brothers. These were the eldest, my client; the second brother, the father of the unfortunate Denis Kayes; and the younger brother, the father of—of Mr. Langley Long, whose real name I think is Kayes."

"Nonsense," said Mr. Langley Long from where he sat, a little in the background. "It's Langley Long. I don't know what in thunder you think you're talking about. I've my identity card here and you can look up my birth certificate if you want to. All rot."

"Well, I never," said Theresa; and if a lost little girl ever looked like a lost little girl, she did.

"There is a distinct likeness," Mr. Goodman said. "It may be accidental. I don't know. I merely remark on it. I do not think our very capable deputy chief constable is likely to have overlooked it. I think it almost certain there was knowledge—it may have been only strong belief—that the portion of my late client's estate Brown had managed to lay hands on was in gold, and I suggest as a probability that this knowledge was arrived at through some hint or communication of some sort from my client during his life to his two brothers. Put in a rather vague form perhaps, but enough to rouse interest and speculation. More particularly when on my client's death, I, as executor, reported an estate almost negligible. It consisted only of a small sum in the bank and personal belongings. Not that I was very surprised. I knew that, contrary to my urgent advice, old Mr. Kayes had been speculating on the Stock Exchange. A bottomless well. My managing clerk, Mr. Brown, had been doing the same thing. The reason for his downfall. I hadn't the least suspicion of that at the time. I had no reason whatever to distrust Brown. As I was under great pressure of other work I allowed Brown to carry out the routine work of winding up the Kayes estate. He had, of course, no authority to dispose of any portion of the estate and it all seemed duly accounted for. Everything in perfect order. Nor was there any reason to suppose that the small apparent estate presented any unusual feature or any special temptation or opportunity for dishonest practices. But Brown evidently discovered in the deceased's papers or elsewhere, indications that though there had been speculation and heavy losses, there was also a large sum in gold Mr. Kayes had accumulated and kept concealed in his house, or nearby. I imagine as a precaution against the possibilities of invasion, of inflation, even of revolution, of all the other dangers of our unsettled times. I have known similar cases, in which securities have been sold and the proceeds used to purchase gold, sovereigns if possible, if not, then wedding rings, or any other gold object. Sometimes other things. Postage stamps, for example. Pictures, too. Anything tangible, as opposed to paper money that may depreciate or to shares in concerns that might be confiscated. Gold is always gold, and there will always be a market for postage stamps. Very interesting things, postage stamps. Take up very little room. I know all this is largely theory. I'm just trying to put things together to help Mr. Owen."

"Very kind of you and it's all most interesting," interposed Bobby, and thus encouraged, Mr. Goodman went on:

"Mr. Owen has told us to keep nothing back. I'm trying not to, though a lawyer's instinct is never to speak till he is sure. But there are one or two facts I can speak of from personal knowledge. Recently Denis Kayes called to see me. Ostensibly over a question of a small interest in some house property originally belonging to his uncle, my client. Quite plainly an excuse. The amount involved was small and the claim doubtful. There was some evidence to suggest that it had in fact been acquitted. I was puzzled but I answered the questions put me to the best of my ability and I referred him for further information to the very well known, leading Midwych firm who took over my practice when I retired. I feel I left him fully convinced that I, at least, knew nothing about any possible, hypothetical hidden assets whether taking the form of gold or in any other shape. Evidently the conclusion was arrived at that since I knew nothing, it must be Brown who had obtained unlawful possession. So he was visited in an attempt to make him disgorge. Persuasion at first. The attempt failed. It would. Brown wasn't likely to give up tamely what he had held so long. He couldn't, without, incriminating himself. From persuasion to threats, from threats to violence, are easy steps.

I think that's what happened. There is something else I am inclined to suggest. That the actual murder was committed by Mr. Langley Long."

Mr. Langley Long laughed.

"While I was playing solo at Mason's?" he asked. "With three other chaps?"

"I'll come to that," said Mr. Goodman equably. "I do not speak without a full sense of responsibility. I suggest that Denis Kayes, on arriving in this country from Australia, was determined to secure the hidden assets, in whose value and existence he believed. Possibly—this is only a guess—something fresh had come to light, some letter or note of some sort, previously overlooked. Probably the first thing he did was to get in touch with Langley Long, either because Mr. Long is in fact a relative or because of an accidental resemblance, which I don't think of any high degree of likelihood. But after the murder, very probably an unpremeditated murder, they failed to find the hidden store of sovereigns. Panic may have overtaken them. I can believe that." Mr. Goodman paused, his voice failing him as, for the first time, he showed some emotion. But he controlled it and went on in the same careful, slightly pedantic tone, a little like that of a professor expounding a thesis: "I am coming to the facts of which I was an eyewitness and that have led me to my conclusion that the actual crime was committed by Mr. Langley Long, and that Denis Kayes knew this and so had to be disposed of—on Quarry Hill!"

"Me playing solo all the time," interposed Langley Long. "You ask Mason, ask the others."

"On the night the murder occurred," Mr. Goodman continued, again ignoring the interruption, "I was wakened by the sound of voices. I got up to see who it was. It was dark but I could distinguish a man and a woman. Then one of them flashed a torch and I saw it was Miss Foote in company with the young man I had previously noticed dawdling about near the house. I suppose I'm still old-fashioned enough to be slightly shocked. But I don't pretend to be a judge of other people's morals and I went back to bed. Besides, there was nothing to show there had been actual misconduct of any kind. But when I heard a murder had been committed that same night I was, I confess, worried. I tried not to think of it. But I was unable to prevent myself from remembering an earlier incident. I had come accidentally on Miss Foote with a box of what I believe are called 'grease paints.' I understand they are used by actors. I hardly noticed at the time. If I thought about it at all, I expect it was merely to reflect that amateur theatricals are highly popular. After the nocturnal incident I have just mentioned, I did remember. And I was worried, distinctly worried. I found myself wondering whether those grease paints had been used for purposes of disguise. If so, to disguise whom—and why? A lawyer does, in the course of his professional experience, gain knowledge of very strange expedients occasionally adopted and I could not wholly exclude from my mind the possibility that Langley Long had come straight from the killing and that Denis Kayes had taken his place at the solo game—remember, all the players were strangers to each other—in order to provide an apparently unshakable alibi."

CHAPTER XXXI
THERESA TALKS

ALL THIS TIME while Mr. Goodman was expounding his ideas of how and why recent events had been as they had been, Theresa was looking more and more innocently astonished. Theresa in wonderland indeed, listening to such things as she had never dreamed could be.

"Well, I never," she said now. "I never did," she repeated with even greater emphasis. She sat still, her embroidery spread out on her lap. Very slowly she said: "It's all so funny, isn't it?" She paused to contemplate the 'funniness' of everything and the others waited in silence. She continued: "It's quite true what he said. I mean about asking him. About killing poor Mr. Brown, I mean, but he said he didn't, and I didn't think he was telling a lie," and evidently in her girlish innocence a lie to her seemed almost as inconceivable as murder.

"You mean you had become so far suspicious of Mr. Goodman that you asked him plainly if he were guilty of the murder?" Bobby said; and with an imperative gesture silenced the beginnings of an angry protest from Mr. Goodman. Bobby turned to the shorthand writer, one of the newly arrived police. "Davies," he said, "call in Morgan to relieve you. He's waiting just outside. You can start typing out your notes. You remember," he added to the others, "I'm going to ask you all to read them when they are written out and sign them as correct, if you are satisfied they are. It'll be a verbatim report." Davies had left the room by now and the second constable had taken his place, armed equally with note-book and pencil. Bobby continued: "Miss Foote, what reason had you for asking Mr. Goodman if he were guilty?"

"It's what I saw," she answered. "I mean that night, very late. It isn't a bit true about me and Mr. Langley Long, though we are friends and I think he wants us to get married some day, but not yet, and I wouldn't let him give me a ring, and I wouldn't even think of meeting him late at night, and then I was so awfully ill and most likely looking a perfect sight. I was simply feeling awful and I couldn't sleep and I hadn't even closed my eyes when ever so late I heard someone on the stairs. At first I thought it must be Mrs. Fuller—she's ever so nice—coming to see if I was all right. She had before. Only it was someone coming up the stairs and Mrs. Fuller's room is next mine and besides I could hear her—she does snore just a weeny bit, though she gets so cross if you say so. So then I was frightened. I thought it might be a burglar and he might kill us all, and I jumped out of bed to put a chair against the door so he couldn't get in. Only first I peeped out and it wasn't a burglar at all, it was Mr. Goodman carrying a candle and he hadn't his clothes on. At least I mean, only his underthings, so I didn't look any more. I was most awfully glad he wasn't a burglar and I got back in bed. I thought very likely he had been downstairs to get a drink of water or something, only it was funny he hadn't put on his dressing-gown and he wasn't in his pyjamas, only underthings. I thought perhaps he hadn't liked to go downstairs just in pyjamas—I shouldn't—and so he changed to his day things and then he couldn't find his dressing-gown. Men are like that, aren't they? I mean, about not being able ever to find things. But it did worry me because I remembered when Mr. Childs was going Mr. Goodman called out suddenly that he heard the phone and he must answer it, and he said 'good night' and Mr. Childs answered, and then the front door banged as if Mr. Goodman had shut it to hurry off to the phone. But I hadn't heard the phone ring, and after the door closed, it was all quiet and still. I mean you couldn't hear Mr. Goodman moving about or opening the study door where the phone is or anything. I did just wonder if the door had banged to and left Mr. Goodman locked out. But I knew he had his key so it wouldn't really matter very much and I was feeling much too wretched and ill to bother. But afterwards I did think it was just like his not having come inside at all, only pretended. I tried not to think about it because it was so funny and worrying and I know I'm not very good at thinking. Then Mrs. Fuller told me Mr. Goodman had sent one of his suits away to the 'Clothes for Occupied Europe' fund, and she was cross because she would have liked it herself for someone she knew. It was the blue serge he had been wearing the night Mr. Childs was here and it did seem funny he hadn't asked me to do it up and send it off, because I'm his secretary, and why did he do it himself? Besides, there was what Mrs. Cox told me. She lives in the thatched cottage down the lane. The poor old dear has rheumatism so badly she hardly ever sleeps and she told me she had seen a light in the trees at the end of the field behind the house. She was dreadfully frightened because she said it was her death light. But I told her it was most likely boys playing at being Red Indians or pirates or something, and I went to look, and I found a hole where a lot of burnt rags had been buried. It was just as if petrol had been poured on clothing to make it burn and then what was left had been buried. But I didn't tell anyone, not even Mrs. Cox when I went to see her next time. I go sometimes, when there's anything nice Mrs. Fuller can spare, or some of my sweet ration sometimes. She's so grateful, poor old thing, if I give her some of mine. I just said someone had made a fire there but I didn't know why. I was awfully frightened all the time, because it did all seem so funny and it made me quite ill and I saw Mr. Goodman noticed and one day he asked me what was the matter. So I said it was the murder at Oldfordham had got on my nerves and he hadn't done it, had he? O-oo, he looked awful and he snatched up a great big ebony ruler of his and I was—petrified. I wasn't exactly frightened, I just thought I was going to die of fright. Only before I had time even to scream, Mr. Owen walked in. Oh, it was such a relief I think I would have fainted or something, only it didn't seem real, not really real, I mean. I didn't say anything. I didn't know what to say and Langley had told me not to, and Denis had as well. He said it might cost him his life and I didn't think he meant it, but perhaps he did and perhaps it has."

"You had better let me go on," Langley Long interrupted. "Miss Foote's had a bad time and if I had known it was going to turn out anything like this I wouldn't have asked her to help. I should have taken jolly good care to keep her out of it. Goodman's saying that I'm the murderer is just plain silly nonsense.

That yarn about Denis getting himself up to look like me and taking my place playing solo and none of the other chaps noticing— well, I ask you. Laughable. And my proper legal name is Langley Long. There's my birth certificate, anyone can see for themselves if they want to, and it says my father was Langley Long, master baker. He had three shops till he drank himself out of them. He was a swine. You needn't take my word for it. They all know where he lived and he was run in more than once. Drunk and disorderly. He died before I was born and he wasn't really my father, either. Thank God. Mother had an awful time with him and Mr. Stephen Kayes—he was the youngest of the three Kayes brothers—was sorry for her and tried to help her and one thing led to another and that was me. I'm not ashamed of it. I would rather my mother had me outside marriage than inside marriage by such a drunken brute as the man the law chooses to call my father, though he isn't. Everyone knew. Father—my real father, Mr. Kayes, tried to have me made legitimate when the drunken swine they called my father died. The lawyers wouldn't. Some dirty trick they worked. But he did leave me everything in his will. Not that it was much. A bit of money and the house and furniture with a mortgage on it. Denis and his father knew all about it, too, and when Denis came to England, the first thing he did was to look me up and tell me he thought there had been crooked work in the way the estate of his uncle, Mr. Alfred Kayes, had been dealt with. I thought so, too, but I couldn't say anything. In law, I was a perfect stranger and had no standing. Denis said there were letters. He said his uncle had been worrying a lot about invasion and all that and about the Fascists and what they might do if they got control and so on and there were hints about his investing in what would always be valuable and how if England had gone off the gold standard, he hadn't. Denis seemed to think there was something in it. His idea was even if there hadn't been any funny work, gold or something might still be hidden somewhere. He asked me to help and of course I said I would."

"In what way, help?" Bobby asked.

"Help to make them cough up if they had been pinching the best part of the old man's estate, which is what I told Denis was most likely," Langley Long answered. "We knew Goodman had retired on a fortune soon after. You couldn't help putting two and two together when you knew that."

"I shall know how to deal with that slander," Goodman interposed; and again Bobby made him a stem gesture to keep silence.

Langley Long went on unheeding:

"Denis promised I should have a share of anything we recovered. A good scout, Denis. I think he had a sort of presentiment. He told me once he might be giving up flying, though he wasn't sure it would be because of Jerry. I didn't catch on at first to what he meant. He meant he might have to give up flying because of being done in, but he wasn't sure it would be enemy action. It is a bit dangerous sometimes, if you try to rake up things and get your own back. I told poor old Denis he might get done in. I told him no one like Goodman was going to give up his loot so easily as all that, not if he knew it, not after having had a good time with it so long. I said he had better watch his step all the time and all the way, and he said he would; and he said if I liked to come in and help he would go shares, only to think about it because it might be a bit risky for me, too. And he said if anything happened to him and I pulled through, then I was to have all he owned in Australia, because we had rather palled up and I was the only one left he knew of with Kayes blood in him, even if it hadn't all come the way it should. I don't know whether he ever put anything in writing. I don't expect so. That's O.K. by me. I don't think what's in Australia amounts to more than a few pounds anyhow."

"Could that be the paper he asked Mr. Goodman and me to witness that first time he was here?" interposed Theresa; and the fierce denial Goodman began, was once more checked by Bobby's stern and swift gesture.

"Later, you'll have your chance later," Bobby told him. "Just now I want to listen to Mr. Langley Long. I find it most interesting and enlightening."

Langley Long looked relieved. The last word—enlightening— was the very one he would have wished to hear. Theresa still wore that air of innocent inquiry and surprise with which she had made her suggestion the moment before. But Bobby knew that behind that air of innocent inquiry lay challenge and defiance and despair, for plainly she perceived, as Langley Long did not, that 'enlightening' might imply enlightenment in many ways. Now, he thought, the long duel between himself and her had reached its term and climax and he watched her warily, for he did not know, nor could he guess, what her next move might be. Yet until matters were further advanced and made more clear and certain—not so much to himself but to those to whom he was responsible—there were no overt steps he could take without risk of leaving loopholes for escape.

Langley Long went on:

"Poor old Denis told me about his visit to Goodman. He didn't say anything about getting anything signed, though. He seemed to think Goodman was all right. He said Goodman put things in a new light. All the same, if you ask me, it must have been a shock to Goodman. Like one rising from the dead."

"That would be a shock to anyone," agreed Bobby. "Yes, a great shock," he repeated.

"Wouldn't it?" agreed Langley Long, pleased again to find Bobby still so acquiescent. "Goodman stuck it out all right. Swore he knew nothing about his old managing clerk, being in Oldfordham. He said if there had been any funny work over old Mr. Kayes's estate, then it was Brown who had worked it, but he didn't see how it was possible. Executors have to account for everything. If you ask me, Brown only came into it, because he tumbled to there being crooked work going on, and Goodman paid him to keep quiet. But Denis didn't see it that way. He went to talk to Brown and what he told me was that he thought Brown's conscience was troubling him. He talked in a religious sort of way but Denis said you weren't sure he meant it. He stalled all the time. If you ask me, my guess is Goodman wasn't paying him enough and he was beginning to think it might be better to stand in with Denis."

"No," Duke Dell interrupted suddenly, speaking for the first time. "His spirit was greatly troubled. When he spoke so, he meant it. How could he help, or anyone help, meaning what alone has meaning? But though he knew his sin, and feared his sin and endured much because of it, yet he clung still to its fruit. Nor could he bear to part from it, though it was terrible to him. The sinner's folly is the greatest folly of them all."

"I don't know anything about all that," Langley Long said, a faint sneer in his voice. "I daresay it's possible Brown didn't worry so much about a spot of swindling in the abstract, if you see what I mean, but didn't like it so much when the chap who had been done down came along—brought it home to him perhaps. That's the way Theresa put it once when I was telling her about Denis. But Denis wouldn't have it when I told him."

"It's all so difficult and muddling, isn't it?" Theresa said with a little sigh, and still she constantly watched Bobby and he saw her hands were moving now beneath the embroidery lying on her knees.

"There was a large sum in gold found in Brown's possession after his murder," Bobby said. "Mr. Long, how does that square with your idea that Mr. Goodman was paying Brown blackmail to hold his tongue?"

"Oh, very likely Goodman thought it was safer stored there than in his own house," Langley Long suggested. "Brown was living alone. Goodman had servants and servants get to know a lot. I expect Brown was allowed to help himself in reason. Goodman could check up when he wanted to make sure Brown wasn't taking too much."

"Rather a trustful spirit on Mr. Goodman's part if it was like that," Bobby said, and Goodman snorted contempt to such an idea. "I must say," Bobby continued, "that both Mr. Spencer and I felt quite satisfied that Mr. Goodman was utterly and completely surprised when we told him."

"I certainly was," agreed Goodman, and now it was his turn to look complacent and relieved. "I couldn't believe my own ears. I hope that disposes of the absurd suggestion that I killed Brown for the sake of getting hold of something I had no idea even existed."

"It wasn't that at all," Theresa said very quietly, as if she were asking someone if they took sugar in their tea. "The gold was what old Mr. Kayes had been getting together because he thought there wasn't anything else you could trust, what with invasions and revolutions and all that. But poor Brown got hold of it after his death without your knowing; and then Mr. Duke Dell got hold of him, and so you were afraid of his telling and telling about you, too, and so you killed him."

"Sit down," Bobby ordered Mr. Goodman who had jumped angrily to his feet but who obeyed Bobby's sharp command. "All very interesting," Bobby continued. "We've heard what Mr. Goodman and Mr. Langley Long and Miss Foote have to say and it's all been most—enlightening. Now we'll hear what Mr. Denis Kayes can tell us and that may be more enlightening still."

As he spoke he crossed to the door and opened it and Denis Kayes came in; still pale from his recent experiences, availing himself of the support of a walking-stick to help legs still a trifle unsteady, but otherwise little the worse for what he had gone through.

CHAPTER XXXII
AN ARREST

FOR A MOMENT following Denis Kayes's abrupt appearance, there was in that room a strange and utter silence, such as is seldom known, a silence in which it was as though all things hung in a void where nothing moved or happened or ever could. It was broken by Theresa who said softly:

"All dodged up to get us talking. You dirty trickster."

"Meaning me?" asked Bobby amiably; and his inspector he had stationed by Theresa's side stooped suddenly and snatched away the embroidery on her lap and with the same movement seized what that embroidery had hidden.

"You were quite right, sir," he said to Bobby. "It's a point three-two automatic the young lady had." Then as he looked at it he added in a slightly disappointed tone: "It's not loaded." With even more evident surprise and disappointment, he went on: "It couldn't be. It's a dud." He took it across to Bobby to show him, and said: "Looks to me as if the magazine chamber had been filled up with melted lead or something."

"That was me," Langley Long said. "So as not to have to bother about a licence. Nothing illegal about having a dud in your pocket, is there?"

Bobby, without answering this, said to Denis:

"You heard it all. You might give us your side of it now. The side you were never meant to tell."

"What they've been saying is all rot," Denis said. "All mixed up. I don't really know what happened on Quarry Hill. All I remember is taking a header through the air and feeling awfully surprised, and awfully curious and excited about what was going to happen when I came down, and that's all. I had a message on the phone that morning. It didn't say who it was but to cycle over by Quarry Hill and there would be someone waiting who would tell me a lot of things about Brown and Mr. Goodman and what they had been up to together, and who really killed Brown. Only I wasn't to tell anyone and I was to come alone or there would be nothing doing. I thought I might as well see if there was anything in it, though I didn't much expect there was, only you never know, and as I was starting off Miss Foote came with a letter she said to give to the man I was going to meet, because then I could check up, only I wasn't to open it before. So I didn't. I have now. It makes out to be my will, only it isn't. It's faked. A forgery. I suppose the idea was to have it found in my pocket, so as to make it seem all right. It leaves everything to this chap Langley Long, I never knew a thing about till now. I might have guessed though if I had seen that walking-stick. It must be the one father sent Uncle Stephen. Father thought it was about time they made it up after their row, so he sent Uncle Stephen some curios, including a walking-stick that must be the one Mr. Owen told me about. We never even got any acknowledgment, so father never tried again. We took it Uncle Stephen didn't feel the same way. If it's true that Uncle Stephen left all he had to this Langley Long chap, then

I take it that'll be how he got hold of the stick. After father's death, when I knew there was a good chance I might get posted to a home job, I wrote again to Uncle Stephen. I said father always thought there was something crooked about Uncle Alfred's estate being so small and there was an old letter of uncle's with a sort of hint about having taken his precautions—he didn't say what they were—and how he wouldn't quit the gold standard, whatever anyone else did. Gold was always gold, he said, and so it is. I said if I did get home, I would try to do something. I never got any reply to that either. Very likely my letter got into this Langley chap's hands, too, and that's what started him off, trying to get in ahead, and if there was anything in the idea he would see if he couldn't land it for himself. He may have thought he had as good a right to it as anyone."

"Well, I had, hadn't I?" Langley Long asked sullenly. "I'm a nephew just the same as you."

"Please go on with your story," Bobby said to Denis, checking the heated retort Denis was about to make.

Denis continued:

"The phone message this morning said I would be shown a letter to prove good faith. I asked what letter but the phone went dead. Hung up at the other end. I thought it might be this letter. It all seemed rummy, but I thought I might as well try to get to the bottom of it. I nearly got to the bottom of the quarry instead, only luckily for me Mr. Owen turned up on time. Rather a bit of a habit of his. Turning up in time, I mean."

"Then there hasn't been any accident at all?" Mr. Childs asked with a very surprised and somewhat bewildered air.

"No," agreed Bobby, "only an attempted murder."

"Murder?" exclaimed Theresa. "Mr. Goodman again? Trying to hide one murder by another? Is that it?"

"Well, we have found some Balkan cigarette ends of the kind Mr. Goodman smokes," Bobby agreed, "and some book match-stalks. We may find his dabs on them. I don't know yet."

"That's a lie," Mr. Goodman shouted. "You didn't. You couldn't." He was on his feet, shouting, gesticulating violently. "If you did you put them there, planted them, it's a fake."

"Sit down," Bobby said; and when Goodman showed no disposition to comply, enforced obedience by a vigorous thrust that sent the shouting, excited, gesticulating man back into his chair. "We found what I told you," Bobby said, "but there's no proof of identity there. We also found a faked notice-board put up to cover a danger sign, so Mr. Kayes should not see it. There are finger-prints on it we have been able to identify—"

"Not mine," Mr. Goodman screamed. "They couldn't be."

"Mr. Langley Long's," Bobby said.

Theresa sitting quietly in her chair said in her soft voice:

"You fool, Langley, you've finished us, you blundering fool. You said you saw him go over the quarry edge."

"So I did," Langley muttered sullenly. "Motor bike and all. I made sure he was dead. He ought to be. How could I tell? I didn't dare look. I was sure. It wasn't possible."

"And you left your finger-prints as well? I told you to burn everything. Why didn't you? That's finished it," Theresa said as softly as before, and all her face was one still mask of hate.

"How could I guess he would come snooping round at once?" Langley asked, looking almost reproachfully at Bobby. "I hid it all. Behind bushes. I didn't reckon on anyone looking so soon. Why should they? Just another accident. I didn't want to stop there. I knew he was dead. He had to be. I saw it all just as we planned, I saw him go clean over. I knew he must be dead and he ought to be, but then I thought all the same he might come climbing back, dead and climbing back, and I didn't dare wait to see. So I made off. But I meant to come back and burn it all, same as you said. How was I to know?" and again there was a touch of reproach, of indignation even, in his voice as he went on: "How could I tell that Owen would be snooping round so soon?"

"My job, snooping round," Bobby explained. "Or those who try once and fail might try again and succeed."

"You never will any more," Theresa said; and suddenly there was another pistol in her hand.

But Bobby had been watching and was ready. On the table near him, conveniently near, for he had shifted his position that it might be so, was a vase of flowers. With a sweep of his arm, he sent it flying through the air, well aimed, to strike Theresa's pistol hand. At the same moment the inspector dived. Everyone was shouting now, on their feet, jostling each other. On the hearthrug before the fireplace was a kind of heap, composed of the inspector, Theresa, a chair, the flowers and the broken vase, all wrapped in the velvet cover dragged from the table. From it protruded Theresa's hand, her fingers pulling the trigger of her pistol, the bullets flying at random here and there.

"Not so fast," Bobby said, and grabbed by the collar Langley Long who had seized the opportunity to make a dash for the door.

"Ai-e-e," said the inspector, "she's bitten me."

But he had managed to wrest the pistol from her grasp and now he released her and held up his hand indignantly.

"Bleeding," he said. "Look. Calls herself a lady I suppose. Tried to scratch as well. Might have been my eyes."

"I tried," Theresa said, "I tried."

The confusion began to subside. Langley Long was in the secure grip of Constable Morgan who had taken him over from Bobby. Theresa, flushed, fierce, dishevelled, but harmless now it had been made sure she had no other weapon—no other than her teeth and nails, that is, to her good use of both of which the unlucky inspector was able to show convincing testimony—was trying to tidy her hair and straighten her clothing. Duke Dell was standing by the door with his hands held hard and tight before him, for this scene of sudden violence had roused in him old memories and old instincts, so that it was all he could do not to plunge into the scrimmage. Mr. Childs had not stirred. He was still sitting in the chair he had occupied throughout, only now he was examining with puzzled interest a little round hole that had suddenly appeared in the wall close to his head—a few more inches to one side and the hole would have been not near, but through, his head. He said:

"I don't think I understand very well—all most unusual and disturbing," and as he spoke he lifted a cautious finger to touch again that small round hole in the wall, as if to make sure it did really exist.

Mr. Goodman came forward and held out a gravely congratulatory hand to Bobby.

"Now you have brought this case to a successful conclusion," he said, "and shown so clearly who did indeed murder Brown, may I say how much I admire your wonderfully expert handling of this most difficult and complicated case, so full of all kinds of contradictory cross currents?"

"Thank you very much," said Bobby. "Now I have to ask you to come with me to headquarters, where you will be charged with the murder of Brown."

"What? What do you mean?" demanded Goodman, for the moment more puzzled and surprised than uneasy.

"It's them." He swung a hand at Theresa, still mechanically straightening her hair, at Langley Long in the grip of Constable Davies. "Them," he repeated. "You've just said so."

"They will be charged with the attempted murder of Denis Kayes," Bobby explained. "There was a conspiracy to make you seem guilty there, too, but no charge will be made against you in that connection."

"You can't, you're raving," Mr. Goodman almost shouted. "You've no evidence, not a scrap. I've an alibi —an absolute alibi."

"You had better say no more at present," Bobby told him quietly. "You can make later on any further statement you wish to. You had better wait till you know what the actual evidence is. If I did not believe it was sufficient, there would be no charge made. There may be more evidence if Mr. Langley Long and Miss Foote decide to tell it all."

"You'll get nothing from me, you and your tricks," Theresa said, suddenly and viciously.

"For you to decide," Bobby answered. "Just as you wish. Mr. Langley Long may not feel the same way. That's for him to say. In any case you'll both be charged with the attempted murder of Mr. Denis Kayes. I think there's no doubt the case will go for trial. If so, it might make a difference if we could say you had done your best to help. I don't know, of course. Entirely a matter for the judge."

"I'll tell you all I know, everything," Langley Long exclaimed eagerly. "It was all through her, all her from the start. I never wanted to myself. I never should but for her."

"You cur, you coward," Theresa said. "You pretended it was all to get money, so we could marry," and suddenly she began to cry, for now at last tears had become possible to her.

CHAPTER XXXIII

CONCLUSION

LATER ON, talking it over with Olive, Bobby said reflectively:

"What made the whole case so different—and because of that, so difficult—was the way in which it developed from a clear cut, straight-forward, almost routine murder investigation, into a kind of duel between the Theresa girl and myself. At first, it didn't seem she counted for much. Just a little flirtatious, inquisitive, empty-headed bit of skirt in the background, and then gradually you became aware of her as the dark force behind all that happened. Yet she wasn't the murderer. That was plain from the start. It wasn't a woman's crime for one thing. Too violent. Her alibi was sound as well. Mrs. Fuller confirmed and she was clearly a witness of truth. Oddly enough, it was while I was trying to see if I could find a flaw in it, that I spotted how Goodman had worked his dodge. I asked myself if Theresa could have played the stowaway in the car that took Mr. Childs back home. Only she couldn't have known the big Rolls-Royce was going to be used. But Goodman might have fixed it that way. The small runabout had developed a defect. Of Goodman's own making? Then there was the ostentatious banging of the front door. Mr. Childs heard it and took it to mean Goodman had gone indoors. Actually what happened was that Goodman showed himself for a moment against the lighted hall within, and then stepped back and slammed the door, leaving himself outside. Then in the dark he ran back to the Rolls-Royce where Mr. Childs was still busy settling himself in the front seat, and he dodged into the back where he had put the bicycle so as to make sure Childs would sit in front beside the chauffeur. Easy enough to slip away unseen when Mr. Childs stopped the car at the foot of the hill. It all fitted in once you saw the idea, but it worried me, because 'could be' doesn't prove it actually 'was' that way. With the additional evidence we have now, it's good enough. Of course, I was always sure from the start it must be Goodman. He managed to provide me very soon with three clear indications of his guilt. One might not have meant much. But three all pointing the same way simply had to."

"I know there was the one about the music," Olive agreed. "There didn't seem any way Mr. Goodman could have known it was a New York concert, playing Sibelius music, if he hadn't been there. But you never told me there were three things like that."

"Oh yes, I did," Bobby asserted. "I didn't emphasize them, but I did mention them. The very first time I saw Goodman he talked about 'killing.' Why? Village rows don't usually lead to people being killed. I wondered if that meant the idea of killing was already in Goodman's mind. As in fact it was. And he mentioned Brown by name. But I was told in the village no name had been given. But it did suggest that 'Brown' and 'killing' were two ideas linked in his mind—in his subconscious they say nowadays. Three plain hints, but you can't go into court on 'hints,' however plain. Any clever counsel would have thoroughly enjoyed himself making hay of them."

"I suppose," reflected Olive, but with some regret in her tone, "I suppose there have to be clever counsel."

"I don't know about 'have,'" answered Bobby, reflectively, too, "but there jolly well are. Anyhow, those hints kept me on the right track, though no good for a jury. Too much like mere psychological stuff, and no jury would hang a cat on psychology. Then there was the religious element. That helped to make the case unusual and therefore difficult. Religion, I mean. You never know where you are with religion. Dangerous stuff. The strongest motive of all, once it gets you. And it gets every one, though often people don't know it, and often it's the wrong religion. Stock Exchange even. I couldn't rule out the possibility that Duke Dell or even Mr. Childs—"

"Oh, Bobby," interrupted Olive, "not Mr. Childs—how could you?"

"I had to go into it," Bobby answered. "You can take nothing for granted in a murder case. He admitted a violent scene, you remember. But the main theme was always the sort of duel going on between Theresa and me. She was in it somehow, that was plain, but why? I considered blackmail. But a blackmail game is a silent, secret game. All the blackmailer does is to sit still and suck the victim's life blood. Theresa was clearly aiming at something, had some plan in hand. Only what? And why? Goodman was certainly in a bad funk the first time we called—and not of us. There seemed no one else but Theresa for him to be scared of. That looked like blackmail but had she proof? Or had she just been dropping hints because she saw him coming back late at night? But hints aren't enough for blackmail. It would only have been her word against his. In the same way, though, I was at once convinced he must be the murderer or how did he know about Sibelius? It wasn't anything like enough for action. So I ruled out blackmail on Theresa's part just as I ruled it out as explaining: the connection between Brown and Goodman. The connection between Brown and young Kayes was hard to understand, too, though that there was one was pretty plain. Kayes's presence at the Chipping Up disturbance might have been pure accident, but why did he say that if Brown had been killed, something would be 'washed out'? Of course, we know now he meant all hope of getting any information about his uncle's estate. But when I asked him he said 'nothing,' and so I knew there was something. In addition, there was the sort of family likeness I noticed between him and Langley Long. That made me think at first they were working together, but I soon gave up that idea. Nothing to show it and plenty against."

"You mean," Olive asked, "working together to get hold of all those sovereigns Brown had hidden?"

"That was another thing it was hard to fit into any rational explanation," Bobby answered. "It seemed certain the motive for the murder must be there, and yet no one seemed to have had any idea of its existence. No attempt to touch it and Goodman completely bowled over when he heard about it and that it had been left to him. Clear enough of course that something was going on, something pretty sinister, with one murder already committed and a distinct threat of more to come. I was certain both Kayes and Langley Long were concerned and if not as allies, then as rivals. Goodman's story about embezzlement by Brown and the inquiries Kayes was making about his uncle's estate gave a pointer, only it didn't seem to explain Langley Long. If Kayes had been a little more open, he would have saved both himself and me a lot of trouble—and a narrow escape of being murdered. Apparently he had been solemnly warned by his Sydney solicitors about the risk of being let in for a libel action, if he got making accusations he couldn't prove about the winding up of his uncle's estate. He says he wasn't sure enough to dare risk saying much. When the murder happened he was scared stiff. No doubt it doesn't do a young officer just posted to headquarters much good if he promptly gets himself mixed up in a murder case.

It seems now that that evening, after the Chipping Up row, he tried to get something out of Brown. But Brown wouldn't talk, still in a funk probably, wouldn't let him in, and Kayes lost his temper and told him he would have to talk or else he, Kayes, would knock his head off. What made it worse was that I told Kayes we found his card in the cottage. Kayes didn't believe me. He knew he hadn't left one there. He got the wind up badly, thought I was hot on his trail, and what I said about his card was a trap to catch him out. The discovery of the hidden sovereigns made it worse. He was afraid everyone would think he was the murderer and that was why."

"How did his card get there if he really didn't leave it himself?" Olive asked.

"Oh, that was Goodman. Kayes left his card at Four Oaks when he went to see Goodman, and Goodman took it along to show Brown and warn him Kayes was beginning to make inquiries and they must be careful. When Goodman found Brown so much under Duke Dell's influence as to be likely to make a clean breast of it, Goodman had either to face the consequences, which would have been for him certain ruin and probable prison, or else to make confession impossible. Which he did. And there was Denis Kayes's card left on the scene. I don't think Goodman planned that. Probably accidental. But when Kayes knew Duke Dell was saying he knew who was the murderer because he had 'seen and heard,' he was more scared than ever. He took it as referring to his attempt to get Brown to talk and his threat to knock Brown's head off. I didn't know anything about that little affair and when I saw how troubled and upset he was by what Dell said, I wasn't so sure of his innocence as I had been. Seemed too much like a bad conscience. What Dell really meant was that he had seen Mr. Childs outside the cottage about the time of the murder and that he had heard from Brown about the scuffle with Mr. Childs. Apparently Brown had given rather a lurid version. And possibly there was just a trifle of unconscious 'odium theologicum' in Duke Dell's being quite so ready to suspect a clergyman—a wolf in sheep's clothing is his general description of any of the clergy, I believe."

"Well, that was silly," declared Olive with emphasis. "But you could have made out quite a strong case against poor Mr. Kayes, couldn't you?"

"Oh, yes," Bobby agreed. "The only thing was that I was fairly certain he was innocent and Goodman was guilty. Another thing that bothered me a good deal though was my being so sure it was Kayes's name I had heard Spencer muttering before he lost consciousness again the time I found him after he had been knocked out in Brown's cottage. Then, too, one night I did find Kayes prowling about in a suspicious sort of way. Luckily I came across other evidence to show it was Langley Long who had attacked Spencer, and now Spencer— he is well on the way to recovery—says he thinks what he said must have been that it was the man who looked like Kayes, because the last thing he remembers is thinking that. Of course, it was clear then Langley Long was up to something, especially when he was careful to explain he had a good alibi. Why should he have thought of an alibi at all, unless he knew he was in it? I guessed then that Langley Long was probably the young man Duke Dell said he found once in Brown's cottage when Brown wasn't there. But whoever it was said he was an Air Force man and that brought me back to Denis Kayes again. Every fresh start I made always seemed at that time to bring me back to where I had been before."

"That's what made you keep on saying that it might lead anywhere," Olive remarked.

"It's what I felt," Bobby agreed. "Only at the back of it all, the crux of the problem was always Theresa, smiling and flirting on the surface, and yet allowing glimpses of something very different behind all her girlishness. I soon felt sure she was working with Langley Long. But why? What was the idea? On the face of it, they were both complete outsiders. Was it the Brown gold? Originally they might have hoped to get hold of it somehow. But then how could they have known of it? Apart from the fact that apparently no one did know. And once the gold was in our hands, in the bank, no one could possibly get it without proof of rightful ownership. Obviously Denis Kayes might have such a claim—but no one else. Not while he was alive. That's what made me so uneasy. If there was a plot to secure the gold, it had to aim first at Denis Kayes's life. That was plain—and didn't help me to sleep at night."

"Oh," said Olive, who had never known Bobby stay awake much longer than the time necessary to get his head on the pillow. He had that possibly happiest of gifts—that of being able to clear his mind at will of every doubt and fear in order to give it the repose it needed before dealing with them afresh. "Go on," she said. "I knew you were bothered but not like that."

"I had seen Langley Long's identity card," Bobby continued, "and it gave no hint of any kinship for him to found a claim on. Yet there was the personal likeness to suggest some sort of relationship. Unknowingly Denis gave the explanation when he said his father had quarrelled with his younger brother over some scandal about a woman. That did suggest that though he was never married he might have left illegitimate issue. Langley Long possibly. Which might have given Langley Long—and Theresa if she were backing him—a notion that they had a sort of right to the money. Every criminal always likes to be able to justify himself, even if only to himself. The tribute of crime to honesty, I suppose, like that hypocrisy pays to virtue. Then, too, Denis told us he had written to this uncle—Stephen Kayes—suggesting there might have been crooked work over the administration of Alfred Kayes's estate. But Stephen Kayes had died and the letter got to Langley Long, Stephen Kayes's heir. Incidentally, it is probably from that letter that he and Theresa got Denis Kayes's signature to copy, traced I expect. We know now from examining Goodman's papers that Mr. Alfred Kayes had been busy on a big Stock Exchange gamble. He covered his operations by using Goodman's name. The gamble came off in a big way. But Mr. Alfred Kayes died suddenly, very largely from the sheer excitement and strain of bringing it off. So then it was easy for Goodman, who had been what is called a 'nominee,' to turn himself into the actual beneficiary. He seems to have persuaded himself that as he had taken part in the gamble and helped in a way, he had a better right to the fruits than mere relatives on the other side of the world who had never known a thing of what was going on and would never miss what they had never known. Always the criminal's eternal need to justify himself. It began like that with Goodman and it ended in murder. 'Facilis decenus &c.'"

"What's that mean?" asked Olive.

"'Slipping's easy,'" Bobby translated. "I'm only showing off my Latin because I don't know any. But though I felt Theresa meant to get her claws on the money, I still didn't see how. All I was sure of, was that she had a plan and that it was deadly. There was always something rather terrifying about her. As if, in her, her sex had turned full circle, and she, the woman, the giver of life, had become instead the bestower of death."

"Ugh," said Olive, shivering. "Ugh. Don't."

"Janet Jebb saved us," Bobby went on, "by coming to tell us about the phone message Denis had. Plain enough what was meant as soon as Quarry Hill was mentioned. So I bunked off and luckily was in time.

I saw then that if Theresa believed she had brought it off, she would start showing her hand, and I should have both her and Langley Long. I knew where he had been as soon as I saw he had cleaned his shoes. One of Theresa's careful precautions to make sure there was no dirt on them to tell of Quarry Hill. In the same way she gave Goodman some stuff to make him sleep so that he would be in his bedroom all afternoon, out of everyone's way and no proof he hadn't really been to Quarry Hill, leaving cigarette ends and book matches there. All very ingenious, taken with the forged will she had persuaded young Kayes to put in his pocket so it could be found on his dead body as proof that he and Langley Long had been working together and to establish their claim on Brown's sovereigns—and anything else, quite a lot probably—Goodman might disgorge. Their calculation was that if Goodman could be proved guilty of Brown's murder—Theresa expected her testimony would be enough for that—then it would be natural to assume he was also the murderer of young Kayes. Once a murderer, twice a murderer, was the idea. There was the obvious motive Goodman had to remove a troublesome and dangerous claimant. It might have come off. My idea as against hers was to use Denis Kayes's supposed death to make her think she had brought it off, in the hope that that would start her talking. And if she talked, then Goodman would have to talk, too, and between them, the truth would come out. Between rival liars, the truth appears, you know. But I still don't know even now if I could have proved my case if Denis Kayes's supposed death hadn't acted as a kind of catalyst to precipitate all these complicated and doubtful elements into a coherent whole."

"Will Mr. Denis ever get the money, do you think?" Olive asked, somewhat doubtfully.

"I should think there's a sporting chance," Bobby answered doubtfully, too. "If Goodman is convicted, and that's as certain as anything can be that depends on a jury, his property passes to the Crown. If Kayes can prove that Goodman obtained possession by fraud, the Crown may cough up. But it'll take a lot to satisfy the officials and most likely most of it will go to the lawyers. I dare say Kayes stands a fair chance of getting what the lawyers leave—if any."

"Oh, what a shame," Olive said.

"Well," Bobby pointed out, "lawyers have got to live like the rest of us."

"Why?" asked Olive, but Bobby dodged this searching question and said instead:

"Kayes and Miss Jebb are fixing it up to get married. Rather on the quiet, but they want us to go. I don't know why. I told them I had a job to do, was paid to do it, and so I did it. They began talking a lot of rot so I had to shoo them off. Had my work to get on with. All in arrears. Discipline goes to pot if you aren't there to keep 'em to it. I don't see how I can possibly find time for weddings."

"Bobby, you must," declared Olive indignantly. "Of course, we must go." She added in a reflective tone: "Weddings are rather nice, they do make you cry so, don't they?"

"Do they?" asked Bobby. "Why?" and this time it was his question that went unanswered.

THE END

Lightning Source UK Ltd.
Milton Keynes UK
UKOW05f1235220916

283557UK00001B/20/P